ALL THE
RUINED MEN

ALSO BY BILL GLOSE

POETRY BOOKS

Postscript to War

Virginia Walkabout

Personal Geography

Half a Man

The Human Touch

FICTION ANTHOLOGIES (as editor)

Ten Twisted Tales

ALL THE
RUINED MEN

Stories

Bill Glose

ST. MARTIN'S PRESS
NEW YORK

First published in the United States by St. Martin's Press, an imprint of St. Martin's Publishing Group

www.stmartins.com

Designed by Kelly S. Too

Library of Congress Cataloging-in-Publication Data

Names: Glose, Bill, author.
Title: All the ruined men : stories / Bill Glose.
Description: First edition. | New York : St. Martin's Press, 2022.
Identifiers: LCCN 2022005285 | ISBN 9781250279880 (hardcover) |
    ISBN 9781250279897 (ebook)
Subjects: LCGFT: Short stories.
Classification: LCC PS3607.L664 L78 2022 | DDC 813/.6—dc23/eng/20220203
LC record available at https://lccn.loc.gov/2022005285

First Edition: 2022

10 9 8 7 6 5 4 3 2 1

For Billy Walsh, for encouraging me
to share what scared me most

CONTENTS

ALL THE
RUINED MEN

In the Early,
Cocksure Days

Fastened to the dash of the jingle bus with a double loop of soft wire, a transistor radio plays reedy, atonal music. The wailing reminds Staff Sergeant Berkholtz of a kazoo, but he can't say that to the Iraqi driver. That's one of the cultural insensitivities S2 briefings had warned him to avoid. Along with touching a woman, drawing Mohammed, drinking alcohol—prohibition stacked upon prohibition like sandstone blocks of a pyramid.

Once a competitive bodybuilder, Berkholtz is the only one in the squad with bulk. While his thick torso tapers to a perfect V, the others are lean and knotted with muscle, perfect builds for soldiers required to hump forty-to-fifty pounds of gear into battle on their backs. Sitting sideways in the front seat, Berkholtz eyes his squad spread through the bus. *His boys.* That's what he calls them when jawing with other squad leaders. Partly because that's what they are, young boys, none more than a few years removed from high school. But mostly because of the way they look up to him as a father figure, one responsible for preparing them for life-threatening danger. And then, when danger comes, for sending them charging straight into the face of it.

He's not much older, just twenty-seven, but Berkholtz feels fifty-seven, the weight of his rank aging his mind and body and twisting his gut into knots. The Velcro patch on his shoulder with three chevrons and one rocker gives him absolute authority over his squad; he just never realized how heavy it could be. The two team leaders, Corporals Faust and Parker, command four-men teams, but out of the field they're just one of the guys. Not so for Berkholtz. His is a strange and lonely position. Part of the squad, yet separate. Surrounded by men he would die for, but none he can treat as a true friend.

Some of the soldiers doze, their energy sapped from the 120-degree heat. Unlike the drenching humidity of Fort Bragg's forests, the desert kiln leeches moisture until cracked lips bleed and grit-scoured eyeballs scrape their sockets. No matter how much water they suck from the three-liter CamelBaks strapped to their shoulders, the parched feeling never goes away. The only one who seems immune to the withering heat is Private Mueller, a loudmouth filled with frenetic energy. In combat, he's a perfect soldier, a berserker who never flinches when bullets snap the air around him. But when things calm down, he becomes a troublemaker determined to drag others down with him. As Mueller hops up from his seat and slides in behind Bradshaw, Berkholtz knows he's going to start some shit. He could order Mueller back, tell him to leave Bradshaw alone, but anything that takes his mind off the wailing music is a welcome distraction.

BRADSHAW

PFC Bradshaw stares out his window at a landscape of endless, undulating dunes. Below a cloudless sky pale as a blister, the desert's hills and valleys stretch as far as the eye can see. He seems mesmerized by the endless brown, but his mind is back home in the lush green of Virginia.

That morning, he'd chatted online with his sister, Darla, but it had brought him more aggravation than relief. Each time she said how she was praying for his safe return, he was reminded how his faith had died out here in the brown. He'd carried a travel-sized Bible in his breast pocket all through basic training. Now, he has no idea where it is. Bradshaw vaguely recalls praying what feels like a million years ago. A choir boy, he believed every promise the priest uttered—that God was benevolent, that all faithful souls go to Heaven, that good always conquers evil. Each night Bradshaw would curl on his side, arm slung round the neck of his stuffed giraffe as he stared into its eyes, imagining the beaded blackness stretching to infinity. So easy when you're young to believe a soul is fabricated from starlight and clouds, tucked between heart and lungs, stitched within your skin. Harder once you watch those sacred vessels spill their contents in the sand, animated bodies becoming lifeless corpses. The desert taught him what happens when bullets tear a torso's seams, plunge in like needles without a threaded eye. He knows how few places bodies offer souls to hide.

Bradshaw notices movement in his peripheral vision and comes back to the present moment. It's Mueller getting up from his seat. He hears the pestering squadmate plop down behind him and lean over the tall, row seat.

Mueller taps the window beside Bradshaw's head and says, *Know what these remind me of?* On the other side of the glass, red tassels dangle from the roof's edge, some with tiny bells affixed to their ends. Mueller drops his hand from the window and taps Bradshaw's shoulder instead. *Hey, know what the tassels remind me of? C'mon, you must know.*

Bradshaw still doesn't turn. As the newest member of the unit, Bradshaw is the continual target of Mueller's taunts. Berkholtz had transferred in about the same time four months ago, but as their squad leader he is beyond Mueller's harassment. Shit flows downhill, not up.

Mueller continues tapping until Bradshaw turns from the glass, irritated. *What?*

They remind me of the pasties on your sister's tits, that's what! He puts his hands up in a mock defensive posture as if Bradshaw might punch him. But Bradshaw just shakes his head and turns back to the window and the ocean of brown.

Mueller spins to see if his squadmates heard the exchange, looking for anyone to give him props. But they're ignoring him, too. *Aw, c'mon,* he says. *That shit was funny.*

BERKHOLTZ

This is what it's come to, Berkholtz thinks. *Picking fights among ourselves.* With the war on hold, it's not just Mueller. They were *all* feeling the tension.

A month ago, when the statue of Saddam toppled in Firdos Square and jubilant Iraqis slapped his face with their sandals, Berkholtz had figured the war was all but over. But the next day they attacked and captured Kirkuk. The following week, they rumbled into Tikrit to battle the last pockets of the Republican Guard. Their battalion fought ferocious battles, all successes with few casualties and no deaths in the company. They were conquering heroes, liberators of the subjugated. Each sandstone city they entered, skinny men and children in ankle-length thawbs raced, cheering, beside their vehicles. When President Bush stood on an aircraft carrier in front of a banner reading, MISSION ACCOMPLISHED, what more was there to say? It was time to pack up and go home to the ticker tape parade.

Except they didn't go home. A provisional government was set up and they stayed on in a peacekeeper role, stuck in the desert, six thousand miles from loved ones. *So here we are,* Berkholtz thinks, *riding out to a makeshift range in a jingle bus, the hour-long ride feeling more like three.*

Looking back at Mueller and Bradshaw, Berkholtz stifles the smile trying to rise to his mouth. Not because he thinks Mueller's comment was funny, but because he knows one of these days Bradshaw is going to knock Mueller down on his ass. Quiet and contemplative, Bradshaw is a former linebacker who still carries a hitter's mentality. Something Mueller will discover soon enough. Now is not the time for a fight, though, so he orders Mueller back to his seat with a flick of his hand.

Berkholtz runs his hand across the fuzzy stubble on his head and feels the pulpy texture of his scalp. Yesterday had been the squad's first shower in a month. The sensation of being clean is still foreign to his desiccated skin. The uniforms are fresh, too, unpacked from their follow-on duffels, their skunky, salt-rimed clothes collected and shipped off to be laundered. Though no one would have cared if they were burned instead.

MUELLER

Now seated beside his team leader, Corporal Faust, Mueller sits with his feet tapping, his knees jerking up and down. He'd also had an online chat this morning, the scared face of his pregnant wife filling his mind as they made small talk about babyproofing the outlets and what type of crib was best. Mueller was just as scared as his wife. Not that he might come home in pieces or not at all; no, he was scared of becoming a father. He wasn't ready for that kind of responsibility, and he's pretty sure Sophia senses that about him as well. He's probably the only one in the unit who's dreading going home. In battle, everything makes sense. Kill or be killed is a mantra he can embrace.

Mueller's hand drifts up to his eyebrow and fingers a scar bisecting the hair, a remnant from a high school brawl. Rubbing the old scar is something he does whenever he's deep in thought. Anytime someone asks about the white strip of skin, he brags how the guy who hit him broke two of his fingers. Part of the reason why he's nicknamed Blockhead, but not the only one.

Looking down, Mueller notices his tapping feet and makes a conscious effort to stop. Part of the ADHD generation, he can't sit still without his skin itching as if ants were burrowing beneath. He needs action. If nothing's happening, he's got to make something happen. Stretching a hand out in front of his team leader's face, he points outside the window. *Hey, Faust, know what those things remind me of?*

Say my sister and I'll have you doing push-ups in the aisle till we get to the range.

So you were *listening. Thought so. No, man, I'm being serious now. They remind me of those Christmas specials on TV, the sound of bells off-screen just as Santa flies up in his sleigh.*

Faust glances out the window. *You on acid? Ain't nothing like Christmas out there.*

Just the sound, man, that's what I'm saying. Mueller leans back in his seat and fingers the scar again, his head slowly rocking side to side. Soon he's whistling the tune of "Up on the Housetop." After a few minutes, he snaps his fingers, then starts singing. *Out in the desert on a jingle bus, where's Hajji taking all of us? Out to the range to blow shit up, fire off some rockets and some other stuff. Ho, ho, ho, who wouldn't go? Ho, ho, ho, who wouldn't go? Oh, up on the rooftop, click, click, click. There's Saddam, let's shoot the prick.*

HEAVY WEAPONS

The bus pulls up behind three Humvees spread across a dune's hard-packed crest and halts, air brakes hissing. Third squad barely pays attention to the new arrivals. The sun hangs low in the sky like a ripe mango, throwing long shadows from the men, who crowd around a circle of ammo cans, howling and cheering. A couple of them give a cursory glance at the jingle bus, then return their attention to the circle.

Shit, man, says Mueller, *I want in on this action.* He races out of the bus, and everyone but Berkholtz follows quickly behind.

In the center of the ammo-can circle are two scorpions, a thick, black one, with sharply defined segmented sections, and one about half its size, colored a light butterscotch that appears translucent in the sand.

From the bottom step of the bus, Berkholtz leans against the accordion door, giving his boys a little space for the moment. They're like a pack of wild mongrels, and he is the alpha dog who needs to manage their fury. All amped up with no enemy to take it out on, they've been instigating fights with each other, wrestling in the sand, and dry-humping the losers in shows of dominance. He's glad the war is over. How much further they could descend into their animal selves, he hates to think. If this little sideshow can bleed off some tension of their testosterone, Berkholtz won't stand in its way.

Shouldering his way into the circle of men, Mueller shouts, *I want to put fifty bucks on the big fucker.*

Sure, says Corporal Rambali, *I'll take that action.*

The scorpions have already begun dueling, the small one snagged in one of the black pincers. They're scuttling in a clockwise circle, the black scorpion's head and thorax pressed low, scraping a furrow as they spin. The smaller one keeps tugging to get out of the black pincer's grip while avoiding the large, lancing tail. At the same time, the smaller one's tail keeps stabbing its venom into the scabrous sides of its larger foe, until finally the black scorpion's pincer opens up as its body jerks and falls, then sits still. A loud cheer goes up from half the men, a volley of curses from the others.

Rambali steps into the ring and uses a piece of cardboard to scoop the small scorpion into a Tupperware container. After sealing the lid, he pulls a small notepad from his breast pocket and marks down the fifty dollars he's owed. Then he hands the pad to Mueller, who signs it at the bottom. Around the circle, other losers mark similar IOUs in victors' notepads. They won't see any actual cash until they get back to the States, then everyone will settle tabs that have been running for months.

Hey, Rambo, Berkholtz says, *where's your squad leader?*

Rambali points over to the middle Humvee, and Berkholtz walks over. Staff Sergeant Payne is sprawled in the shade puddled on the side of the vehicle, an olive-drab net draped over his face to ward off flies. Berkholtz lightly kicks one of Payne's heels and says, *C'mon, you lazy turd. Time to go to work.*

Payne pulls the net off his face and gives a sour look. He stands up and makes a show of stretching. *Was wondering when you were going to get here. Any longer, we were going to fire off your shit as well.*

Not a chance. My boys need this.

I hear you.

Both squad leaders are thankful for today's familiarization exercise. All of Alpha Company is rotating through the range one squad at a time, firing the heavy weapons belonging to Delta Company. The WWII-era M2 Browning .50-cal machine gun. The chain-fed MK19 grenade launcher. And the wire-guided TOW missile, which only the top marksman from each squad will get to fire.

Here's the skinny, Payne says. He points east with the blade of his hand. *The range stretches out for three klicks in a fan shape. Delta platoon did the safety checkout to double that before parking their vehicles up here. They also marked the left and right boundaries.*

He indicates a row of posts plunged at fifty-meter intervals into the sand and topped with white flags. Then he swings his rigid arm to the other side and points out that line as well. Centered between those boundaries are two bullet-ridden Toyota trucks. Tendrils of white smoke ribbon up from both of them. Beyond those is a blue-and-white Volkswagen van.

The left truck is about nine hundred meters, Payne says, *and the right is eleven hundred. Both well within effective range of everything we've got here. The van is at twenty-five hundred.*

They fist-bump and Payne gathers up his men and loads them into the jingle bus. As it drives away, Berkholtz lines up his guys and gives them a safety brief. Then he points to the Delta platoon soldiers leaning on their Humvees. *Listen to these guys when they instruct you on the weapon systems. Remember, they're the experts; you're just tourists.*

It takes some of his boys a little while to get used to the butterfly-style triggers on the heavy guns. They have to depress these triggers with both thumbs instead of pulling with a finger. But after the first few shots, they get the hang of it.

Mueller fires long bursts from the .50 cal mounted on the left vehicle. Sand erupts ten meters away from the left Toyota, so Mueller swings the gun's long barrel to correct his aim, the splashing impacts stitching a path toward the target. When he connects, bullets punch through the pickup's skin, the punching thump of metal on metal resounding across the range. *Yeah!* Mueller yells from the turret. *Get some! Get some!*

Atop the right Humvee, Bradshaw fires three-to-five-round bursts from the grenade launcher. Compared to the jackhammering thunder of the M2, the MK19 sounds no louder than knuckles rapping on a tin door. But the results are spectacular. A series of fiery explosions engulfs the right Toyota from the hail of 40mm grenades.

When they finish firing, Bradshaw and Mueller dismount the vehicles and get fist-bumps from everyone in their squad. *Man, I tore that shit up,* says Mueller. Bradshaw just nods.

After everyone has fired, Bradshaw is named the day's champion. Mounting the center vehicle, he leans into the eyepiece of the TOW's thermal sight and reaches beneath the launcher for the controls. When he fires, a column of flame spurts out the back of the tube as the missile launches downrange and unspools nearly two-and-a-half miles of filament from its tail. As the missile streaks toward the VW van, the wire carries signals from the tracking module in Bradshaw's hands to tiny compensating thrusters on the missile.

Just after firing, Bradshaw detects movement over the rim of the dune where the van sits. *Camels!* His instincts are to push away from them, and the minor movement of his hands causes the TOW to splash down in the sand and explode in a geyser of brown.

Mueller nearly doubles over with laughter. He kisses his

fingers and points up at the sky. *Thank you for that, God,* he says.

There are camels out there, Bradshaw calls down from the turret. *And a couple of men.*

Berkholtz grabs his M4 and squints through the optics. Sure enough, a line of camels is plodding over the dune with white-robed men sitting atop the two in the lead. As they get closer, the gray-bearded Bedouin in front waves at the soldiers. This is the era of goodwill. Everyone loves GIs.

Dude doesn't know how close he came to getting killed, Mueller says. *Lucky for them, Bradshaw can't fire for shit.*

The squad stands watching as the camels trudge steadily toward them. When they reach the hard-packed crest, the two Bedouins dismount.

Hey, Faust, Berkholtz says, *give me a few minutes alone here.*

Faust herds the rest of the squad to the middle Humvee, where they hunker in its shade.

Berkholtz turns to the lead Bedouin and says, *As salaam alaykum.*

Wa alaykumu as salaam.

Berkholtz only knows Arabic phrases from flash cards in his cargo pocket, and the Bedouins don't speak English at all, so they resort to pantomime. Berkholtz points up at the missile launcher, then out at the ruined vehicles on the range. *Didn't you see?* he asks, tapping his cheekbone near his eye. *Didn't you hear?* he says, touching an ear.

Inshallah, says the Bedouin, shrugging his shoulders. "As Allah wills it."

Berkholtz motions with two hands patting the air for the Bedouins to stay put. Then he tells the driver in the TOW Humvee to radio command and tell them what's going on.

Already done, says the specialist. *Captain Cuneo's coming out here. We're supposed to cease fire and hang tight.*

Berkholtz stands with his arms crossed near the two Bedouins, who gather their camels into a tight pack and tap their legs with sticks to goad them into sitting. Berkholtz can't stop thinking how close they'd come to a colossal fuckup. A civilian casualty would have drummed both Bradshaw and him out of the service. The one who fired the shot and the one in charge.

The Army had trained him to lead troops in battle, but not how to stopper up their wrath once the fighting was done. In the buildup phase to war, Berkholtz had trained the squad relentlessly, rehearsing combat scenarios in the kill house countless times, chewing ass on anyone committing an error, running the men over and over until responses became second nature. *Once bullets start flying,* he'd told them, *there's no time for second-guessing.*

The training had paid off and everyone made it through in one piece. That's all Berkholtz had ever wanted. Not the power of command or the glory of medals. He only wanted to do his job right and bring his boys home in one piece. Looking over to the Humvees, he sees Mueller is still heckling Bradshaw, his nonstop chatter wafting through the roasting air. Berkholtz should break them up, but he's tired of playing babysitter.

Suddenly a commotion breaks out. Bradshaw jumps on Mueller and puts him in a headlock, driving the top of his head into the sand. *You going to cut the shit about my sister?* he says.

Uh-uh, says Mueller. *Gonna ride that bitch like those ragheads on their camels.*

Berkholtz races over. *Let him go, Private. Both of you, on your feet.*

Bradshaw releases Mueller, and they jump up, glaring at each other.

Stand at attention, Berkholtz says. *This shit has gone on long enough. I expect better out of you. Same for you, Private Bradshaw, I know what you're capable of.*

Berkholtz and Bradshaw had previously served together in the 173rd Brigade Combat Team based out of Vicenza, Italy. They went to Kosovo in a show of force. Even though they never fired a shot, they performed a "combat jump," and everyone else in the squad is jealous of the gold stars on their wings. The only jumps here are off the tailgate of their trucks.

Bradshaw says, *But he—*

Don't interrupt. I heard what he said. Ride her like a camel, huh? He starts to nod his head, thinking of the gladiatorial bouts with scorpions. *If fighting is all you knuckleheads understand, that's how we're going to settle this dustup.*

He grabs the squad's box of MREs and strides over to the Bedouins. After some hand gestures and his bestowal of the box of plastic-wrapped food, the gray-bearded Arab nods and gives a snaggletoothed grin.

We're going to have ourselves a little jousting match, Berkholtz announces, *and afterwards I don't want to hear any more lip from either of you. Got it?*

Hooah, Sergeant, they say in unison.

Faust and Private Pearson grab two of the marking poles and wrap hundred-mile-an-hour tape around their ends until they turn into fist-sized balls. Mueller and Bradshaw take up the makeshift lances and head over to the camels kneeling in the sand. The younger Bedouin holds the reins of a camel for Mueller, who hops onto its hump. Then the Bedouin taps its legs and the camel rises in pistoning fashion, rear legs first, then the front ones. When the ass jerks up in the air, Mueller topples over the neck, and the squad howls with laughter.

The gray-haired Bedouin makes a grabbing motion at the rear of another camel, and Bradshaw follows his instruction, climbing on the backside of the hump, his hands digging into the rough fur, the pole clamped in his armpit. When the camel pistons up, he hangs on and everyone cheers.

All right, all right, Mueller says, pointing at his camel. *Get that fucker back down and let's try this again.*

Copying Bradshaw, he climbs onto the camel's back and manages to hold on when it stands up this time. *There you go, there you go. I got it now.*

The Bedouins lead the camels twenty meters apart, then turn them to face each other. The gray-bearded man counts down in Arabic, and then both men swat the rumps of their camels with sticks. The beasts lurch toward each other in a lumbering gait, turning away at the last moment and coming to a standstill. The two soldiers jab at each other with their lances. Mueller's blow glances off Bradshaw's shoulder, but Bradshaw hits his opponent square in his breastbone, and Mueller falls off his mount for the second time.

This time, even Mueller laughs. He clutches his chest and lies there in the sand. Then he rolls over and makes a spastic display of death throes, gagging with his tongue lolling out the side of his mouth. Bradshaw raises his lance in victory, clinging to the camel's fur as it starts to pick up speed as if it's trying to run away. The gray-haired Bedouin chases it down and grabs the reins, tapping the camel's legs until it lowers to the ground.

Bradshaw walks back to the squad, and Mueller is first to greet him. *Nice shot,* he says. *Doesn't mean I'm going to stop riding you.*

That's fine, Bradshaw says. *Long as you stop riding my sister.* He waits a beat, and then smiles.

Mueller bellows a long, wolfish howl and wraps Bradshaw in a hug. Then the rest of the squad collapses on them in a back-slapping scrum, wrapped in the glee of the moment, each of Berkholtz's boys certain he will live forever.

Dirge

PRIVATE PEARSON

In the sandbagged watchtower overlooking the zigzag entry into FOB Salerno, Bryce Pearson slumps across the buttstock of his M240, its barrel aimed skyward like the opposite end of a seesaw. He should be alert, but he's zoning, his mind ten thousand klicks from desert and guard duty. Easy enough to do in this great wash of brown and gray, everything blending into one monotonous blur like television static. Afghanistan's stony terrain was so different from Iraq's miles of barren desert and the great sight lines it provided. This base sits on a dozed shelf of sand with miles of rock-scrabbled hills spreading out in every direction but east, which is dominated by steep, jagged mountains. Occasional shrubs dot the hills and mountains, but otherwise all Pearson can see is sand and rock.

Mail call this morning brought Pearson a care package from home, and he's dreaming of shift change, of chowing down on Mom's corn fritters, sweet potato pie, and tubs of dirty rice. Imagining he's a million miles from mortar rounds and rocket attacks and callouts to scenes where someone's gotten their shit blown off.

On the sandy road below, Tariq Jackson stands at the boom barrier in a Kevlar-plated vest, his torso as blocky as a Lego figurine. He's supposed to ID and search any Afghans who approach the gate while Pearson provides overwatch, but foot traffic is light. It's Thanksgiving and the rest of Task Force Devil is eating holiday dinner, squirreled away within the tank ditches and HESCO barriers surrounding the compound. After back-to-back tours with barely any time off in between, the battalion is finally rotating back to Fort Bragg at the end of the week, and home is all anyone can talk about.

SSG Berkholtz had already given the required head-shrinking talk about how home wouldn't seem the same. *But it's you who's changed,* he'd said. *You who'll feel itchy amid the fat luxuries of the good ol' US of A.* Pearson hadn't bought into it then and still doesn't now. They've only been deployed six months. Yes, he's changed from when he first arrived in country, quicker to flatten on the sand when a launching mortar round pops off in the surrounding hills; unhesitant in lighting up someone who doesn't drop a weapon when ordered; and no longer queasy when the backs of heads explode to paint black smears on sandstone walls. All those things that had shaken him during his first few weeks are now nothing but a tight knot in his gut. A knot he's sure will unravel once he gets home.

But during Berkholtz's talk, he kept these reservations to himself, mimicking the squad's older members, the ones who'd deployed multiple times, their features blank as stone. Even Mueller, that wiseass, just sat there mindlessly rubbing an old scar on his brow. So Pearson stayed silent, too, nodding in all the right places while dreaming of home.

Now, he raps knuckles on his helmet to refocus on the task

at hand. Jackson notices and blows him an exaggerated air-kiss. Jackson is Pearson's best bud. The two youngest squad members, they'd been through it all together. The shared patrols, humping up mountains, every step littered with scree, past boulders and through stone passes scorched black from previous firefights. The night raids with kicked-down doors, each man covering the other's back as he rushed in with the stock of his M4 wedged into his shoulder, his Aimpoint optics painting a red dot on his target. And the wide-eyed moments after battle rehashing how close one or the other had come to being killed, showing off a ballistic plate that stopped a bullet or using his thumb and forefinger to show how close it had come to his head.

This morning, over powdered eggs in the DFAC, Pearson had asked Jackson what he's going to do with all the combat pay sitting in his bank back home. *Cruise the strip clubs on Yadkin,* he'd said. *Make it rain on the honeys.*

Sucking in his cheeks and rubbing his chin, Pearson said, *Indubitably,* in a posh British accent, and they both cracked up. Just one of a thousand of their inside jokes that made no sense to anyone else.

As Jackson went on to describe the choice things he'd like to do with the strippers, Pearson nodded along and gave the occasional fist bump, pretending like he wanted nothing else. But really, the only girls on his mind were the ones writing him from Meadville, the ones who barely noticed him in high school. Main reason he'd enlisted was the way the girls had gone apeshit over the brawny recruiter in the school lobby. Now these former cheerleaders and prom princesses are sending him lingerie pics from their bedrooms. The photos are stuffed in his helmet lining, a bit of inspiration to leer at whenever he pops off his brain bucket. Soon enough, he'll get to stroll into town in his dress greens, silver jump wings on his chest, and his only problem will be deciding which of them to hook up with first.

Blinking back to the present, Pearson sees a woman limping toward the gate, and he feels a sense of déjà vu. In years to come, reflecting on this moment, he'll wonder if something in the woman's gait reminded Jackson of his mother, the way she hobbled on her cane into his bedroom each night to kiss his forehead. Or if, framed within the woman's purple hijab, her expression, angelic as the Virgin Mary, prompted memories of Baptist sermons, echoes of *Thou shalt not* staying his trigger finger.

Protocols exist for situations like this, rules of engagement outlining the rapid progression of escalating force to use against anyone approaching the gate. *Shout. Show your weapon. Shoot to warn. Shoot to kill.*

But he'll never know for sure why Jackson stands motionless and lets the woman come unchallenged, shuffling toward the boom barrier, hugging a bundle the size of a swaddled baby.

When Pearson's fog finally lifts, he yells *Stop* at the limping woman. The hairs on his arms bristle as he notices a mottled bruise coloring one side of the woman's swollen, frightened face. He fires a warning shot over her head and lowers his aim for the kill shot. Then a fist of sand knocks the air from his lungs and the world goes brown.

SOPHIA

Sophia wants to discuss the explosion with her husband, but Brendan, just home from Afghanistan, won't talk about it. He pretends Tariq's death and Bryce's disfigurement don't bother him. And she pretends to not notice his pretense. Even though she can practically feel anger radiating off him in waves.

Brendan's squad is being quartered for the night in a hotel in Newport News, Tariq's hometown. Eyes closed, Sophia stands swaying in their room, hugging their six-month-old baby, one arm cradled beneath her diaper, one hand at the small of her back. Rubbing small circles, she whispers, *Mommy loves you, Mommy loves you.* Chrissie's fussy protests are winding down, surrendering to exhaustion, chubby fingers of one hand worrying the enameled edges that pierce her gums. Finally, her tiny digits fall away and her breathing becomes slow and regular.

Sophia's face is sleep-creased, greasy hair swept back and knotted behind her head. Being a military wife is harder than she thought. Plucked from her carefree life and friends, plopped down in a scrubby base where she doesn't know anyone, and anchored to a teething infant who demands every second of her waking attention. While her husband was being shot at halfway around the world, she nearly collapsed into tears with every knock on the door, the specter of a notification detail waiting on her stoop. Frightened and alone these past six months, she's wanted to scream half the time but kept herself together for one reason: Chrissie.

Sophia lays the baby on the king-sized bed and surrounds her with a pillow fortress. *Can you turn that down?* she asks, nodding toward the TV. Brendan is sitting in a padded chair tilted back on its rear legs, one foot dangling and the other pressed against the edge of a desk. On the television, turned on its stand to face him, a dour anchorman is speaking in a monotone about tomorrow's funeral.

Brendan mutes it with the remote, and closed-captioned text scrolls across the anchorman's face. In the screen's upper right corner is a headshot of PFC Jackson in his maroon beret. Brendan leans over to the minifridge and pulls out another miniature bottle of Jack Daniel's. He cracks it open and slurps down the whiskey in a quick gulp. Then he drops the bottle into the wastebasket where the glass clinks against the other empties in the bottom.

We can talk about it, you know, Sophia says. *I won't freak out or anything. I'm stronger than you think. Strong enough to handle anything but being shut out.*

Not much to say. I was in the chow hall when it happened.

She looks from the two prints of seascapes to the various lighthouses on the wallpaper. It's the type of décor she and her mom used to appreciate on browsing trips through Bassett, Ethan Allen, and Pier 1, but today it jangles Sophia's nerves. Resting a hand on her daughter's chest, she feels the birdlike beat of her heart. Chrissie's face is serene as virgin snow. It bears the brow and full lips of her father.

Sophia wonders what troubles her own parents went through at this age. Their anniversary is coming up in February. Thirty years they've been together. All the parents of Sophia's friends are still married, too. That fact had always informed her idea of relationships. You meet, you fall in love, you go through rough patches, but you stay together, forever, for better or worse. Especially when you have children.

Brendan opens the fridge and grabs another bottle.

Wanna slow that down? Sophia says.

His face screws up into a knot. *I haven't had a drink in months. Give me a break!*

Sophia can't believe *that* is what pisses him off the most about going to war. Not the mortar attacks and IEDs. Not being separated from his family. Not even Tariq's death. Just the forced sobriety. *She* hasn't had a drink, either; she'd been pregnant when he was in Iraq and nursing while he was in Afghanistan. But she bites back her anger. Like always. *I'm just saying, you haven't had any booze in a while. It's gonna hit you twice as hard.*

Brendan shoots out of the chair so fast, it shocks her. He throws the bottle across the room and it bounces off the wall and skitters across the floor. *What do you want from me?* he screams, fists balled at his sides.

On the bed, Chrissie wakes and starts wailing. Brendan looks down at his daughter, and as he does, his rage diffuses into a confused mask. He fingers the small scar curling through his eyebrow. *I don't need this shit right now,* he says. Then he storms out and slams the door.

Sophia stands for a beat, staring at the door's security latch, considering swinging it shut to lock Brendan out. Then she picks up Chrissie and bounces her in her arms, swaying back and forth as she walks around the room. *It's all right,* she says, knowing it's a lie. *Everything is all right.*

CORPORAL FAUST

Faust arrives early at McFadden's and grabs a seat at the bar. The interior is dim, late-afternoon sun dampened by tinted windows. On a TV behind the bar, two hosts of a local talk show face the screen in overstuffed chairs canted at forty-five-degree angles. On the left is a blond woman in a flamingo-pink suit. She rehashes the story of paratroopers coming to town to bury their fallen squadmate. Her companion, a thin man with sad eyes, nods along and grimaces. A picture of the squad appears with Faust, the alpha team leader, positioned near the middle. The camera pans past him and zooms in on Jackson's face. Then a map of Newport News fills the screen, a bright yellow line detailing the route the motorcade will take to the cemetery. After a few moments, the map cuts away to a sharp-faced major spewing platitudes about the cost of war, his bony blade of a face providing an exclamation point to his message. *So come on out,* the sad-eyed newscaster adds, *and show your support for the troops.*

Faust curses under his breath. The news coverage will turn the private ceremony into a public spectacle. He orders a tumbler of Hennessy and sips the amber liquid, gazing down the long lacquered counter. The pub is nearly empty; but not for long. Soon enough, welders and pipe fitters from the shipyard surge through the doors like high tide crashing a levee. They strut in with chins jutting before them like the prows of ice-breakers, their forearms scarred with glossy dots from lique-fied steel, biceps wreathed with knotted ropes or stamped with blue tridents or anchors. As these flannel-shirted men order beer by the pitcher, Faust listens to their gripes about management, overtime, and rising rates of mesothelioma.

None of them bother with Faust, though he almost wishes they would. He's keen for a fight. He's always been the level-headed sort, but that changed this past deployment. Iraq had been a straight-up slugfest with the Republican Guard, but Afghanistan had been a different monster altogether. Their convoys were ambushed regularly, locals took potshots into the compound, and some roving mortar unit lobbed shells at them and disappeared before the quick reaction force could get them; the nighttime mortar barrages rarely hit anything of consequence, but the random attacks screwed with their sleep. Eventually an Apache shot up the mortar unit and the potshots became infrequent occurrences. Oddly enough, without them it became *more* difficult for Faust to sleep. Before, under the constant threat of attack, adrenaline built up in his blood until a chorus of explosions washed it away in one terrifying thrill. But without an actual attack, there was just ever-mounting anticipation with no release.

His best sleep came after contact with the enemy. After the kill-or-be-killed dance, the quick aim through optics and pull of a trigger, ejected brass cartridges pirouetting beside his head as return fire snapped through the air around him. In the thick of battle, he had no time for conscious thought, just instinct and training. Afterwards, the ecstasy of survival coursed through him in a bigger and better high than he had ever felt on any drug. It was only in the long stretches of quiet, when days passed without an attack, that he cataloged the near misses stacking up against him and felt a nervous apprehension. It's the same keyed-up sensation twitching beneath his skin right now. And the only cure he knows is combat.

At happy hour, girls in shimmering blouses glide in like a V of geese landing on a pond. Young and beautiful, they lean over Faust to order flavored martinis and fistfuls of shooters, their perfume stirring his blood. A handful of girls head to a central, raised section of the floor ringed by arm-rails that serves as a dance area. They step onto the platform and dance on the checkerboard floor with drinks in their hands. Immediately the music turns up and the lights dim.

Soon shaggy-haired townies join the girls and the dance floor fills with jostling bodies. Below the gyrating throng, small groups stand in tight knots on the hardwood floor, yelling to be heard over the music. The only break in the carnival-like atmosphere is a hiccup of stunned stillness when a group that everyone recognizes pushes through the door. It's the other members of Faust's squad. Block-shouldered and confident, they part the crowd like beaded curtains, moving as a single unit, each set of eyes sweeping different sectors, assessing the chaos.

They grab a table in the back near the restrooms and Faust joins them, bringing a pitcher from the bar. He sits beside his squad leader, Berkholtz, a powerlifter with pale, Nordic skin. Mueller, the resident troublemaker, is first to pour himself a glass of beer. *You're all right, Corporal Faust,* he says. *I don't care what anyone says about you.*

Coming back from the ladies' room, two slender girls with tight half shirts showing off pierced navels stop at the paratroopers' table. One of them leans over to touch Mueller's forearm. *I'm so sorry for your loss,* she says.

Mueller wraps an arm around her waist and snugs her up against his chest. *No reason for that,* he says. *Sorry is for tomorrow. We're in a partying mood tonight.*

She laughs and allows herself to be pulled into his lap. Her friend steals a chair from a nearby table and joins the group.

In a nearby booth, one of the thick-necked shipbuilders shakes his head and says something to his friends, who all look over and laugh. Faust gives a backhanded tap to Mueller's shoulder. *You see that shit?*

Huh?

Those fuckers disrespecting you, man.

Mueller glances over at the booth, then back again. *Whatever, man. It's cool.* He squeezes the girl's waist and smiles at her. *Not as cool as you though. You're cute as a ladybug.*

Nah, man. It ain't cool at all. It's go time.

Mueller reacts like a switch has been thrown. His smile disappears and he dumps the girl from his lap like dusting off crumbs. *Let's go then.*

Hey, what gives? the girl says. Hands on hips, she looks down at Mueller, but his face has transformed into a landscape of hard plains. *C'mon, Denise,* she says. Her friend rises and the two of them stomp off.

Around the table, the other faces are as dead as Mueller's. Nothing further is spoken. They stand as one and close on their target.

PRIVATE FIRST CLASS MUELLER

Brendan Mueller jerks awake in the tub. First thing he thinks is, *Where am I?* Second thing, *Where's my rifle?*

Then he sees the seashells on the bathroom wallpaper and it all comes back to him. Mostly. As he scrunches his brow in concentration, scenes from last night flash in disconnected bits and pieces. The dark bar. The loud music. The skinny girl with the bare midriff. A whirlwind of bodies. A chair tipping over. A chin thrust forward. Mueller's fist connecting with an uppercut. Then someone else decking him, and the taste of blood filling his mouth. He flexes his sore right hand, its knuckles skinned and bruised. *Worth it,* he thinks.

As he lifts himself out of the tub, spots swim through his vision and he pauses for a self-assessment. His temples are throbbing and his neck feels as if it's clamped in a vise. Rotating his head in a slow circle, he hears vertebrae pop like Bubble Wrap. He licks his chapped lips, wishing for an aspirin.

What the hell did I drink? he wonders. He vaguely recalls moving on to a shitty dive bar and plowing through a slew of pitchers. At one point, he convinced the bartender to sprawl across the bar so he could drink tequila shots from her navel and suck a lemon wedge from her mouth. *That* brings a smile to his face. But smiling makes his head hurt more, so he stops.

That's when the dragging prongs of memory dredge up other images, scenes from the desert, from the day Jackson died, and an icy rush shoots through his veins and a stench fills his nose.

He'd been one of the first out to the gate after the blast. When he'd arrived, Sergeant Berkholtz was pressing a field dressing on Pearson's face and wrapping its long green tails around his head. *Go check on Jackson,* he'd ordered, and Mueller had rushed down to the crater, knowing what he'd find. Jackson's shredded body. Pieces torn away. And that burning smell.

The smell still comes to mind whenever he sits still, whenever noise recedes, whenever he closes his eyes. It's what he thinks of now, even before his wife and daughter in the other room. When his mind finally comes around to them like a sweeping, cinematic, overhead shot, the film is intercut with quick flashes of the skinny girl from the first bar and the bartender from the second. His skin flushes hot with shame.

Last night when he'd returned to the room, Sophia had asked about his fat lip. The disapproval in her face was all it took to knot his fists with sudden fury. Fearing what he might do, he'd turned to the bed and hammered the pillows, howling all the while. Then he'd retreated to the bathroom and sealed himself inside.

Now, with his hand on the doorknob, he takes personal inventory. All those months in the desert dreaming of home, of his wife, of his baby. *They* are what he should concentrate on. Not the smell of burning bodies.

When he opens the door, he sees Sophia playing peekaboo with their daughter. Chrissie giggles in spurts each time her mother pulls her hands away to reveal her face. Brendan sits on the bed beside them and puts his hand on his wife's back, rubbing it in a circle. *Sorry,* he says. *I'll do better.*

Sophia grabs his wrist and pulls it across her shoulder, settling his hand on her left breast. Through the thin fabric of her worn cotton nightshirt, he feels her heart beating. Squeezing, he pulls her back against his chest.

STAFF SERGEANT BERKHOLTZ

From the second limo behind the hearse, Berkholtz stares out the window at the crowd. Bradshaw sits stone faced beside him. Seated opposite are Mueller, his wife, and their little girl, quiet in her carrier. Sophia is sniffling, flicking nervous glances sideways at her husband, who is still enraged from this morning's encounter with the reporters.

As they were leaving Rollins Funeral Home, television crews had ambushed them on the steps, a phalanx of microphones thrust before them. *You want details?* Mueller had screamed. *I'll give you goddamn details.* Berkholtz and Bradshaw pulled Mueller back, hooking arms and duckwalking him to the limo, Sophia trailing behind like a dog with its tail tucked.

Now throngs of locals bracket their route, huddled in long winter coats, hands pressed over hearts or waving flags. Some hold signs that read, GONE BUT NOT FORGOTTEN, or AMERICA THANKS YOU. Old vets stand at attention and salute, their garrison caps studded with pins. Everyone else applauds as the procession breezes through red lights and stop signs, police motorcycles leapfrogging ahead to hold up traffic at every intersection.

Despite the cold, a fleshy girl wearing nothing but cowboy boots, short shorts, and a red-white-and-blue bra bounces up and down with a sign that reads, WE LOVE YOU!

Get a load of that shit, Mueller says, a crooked smile cracking through his anger.

The signs, the applause, the sirens and flashing lights—it's all a blur to Berkholtz. All he sees is Pearson's flapping cheek, his own hands stuffing a white compress against the red hole, wrapping the tails around his head and knotting it in front.

They'd all seen dead and wounded before, mostly Hajji, but

a few Americans, too. Wornom and Santamaria from Charlie Company, Rago from HHC. But this was the first time it'd been soldiers from his squad. Berkholtz was supposed to be the guard on overwatch that day, not Pearson. But when he'd heard about the turkey dinner, he'd scratched a line through his name and written *PVT Pearson* above it. *Rank has its privileges,* he'd told him with a smirk. His next words to Pearson didn't come until he was kneeling in the sand, trying to stuff what had fallen out of his face back in again. *You'll be all right,* he'd said. *You'll be all right.*

He'd meant to tell Jackson's mother about the switch, admit how everything was his fault. If *he'd* been on the gun, maybe none of this would've happened. But he couldn't look her in the eye, let alone get his mouth to work.

As squad leader, Berkholtz should have escorted Mrs. Jackson to the first limo, but he passed that duty off, too. It was Bradshaw who gave her his elbow, and she'd held onto it fiercely, her cane hooked in her other hand as she shuffled forward.

Over the past six months, Berkholtz must have heard a hundred of Jackson's "Mama stories." How she worked two jobs to put food on the table. How she once stabbed a would-be purse snatcher with a hatpin and then beat him down with the very purse he'd meant to snatch. How, whenever Jackson screwed up, she made him peel a switch from the birch tree out front so she could whoop him with it. This morning, though, she'd been as frail as a desiccated leaf in winter.

Ashes to ashes, Berkholtz thinks. *Dust to dust.*

MRS. JACKSON

Graveside, Jackson's mother is glad the day is miserable, cold as the bottom of a well. No clouds overhead, as if the sky had known to strip itself of charm. Her metal folding chair is lopsided, its right legs plunging deeper into the grass than the left. That, too, is fine.

Resting on her lap is a black cane with a silver eagle's head. *Too showy,* she'd told Tariq when he'd given it to her as a birthday gift. She'd hung it on the closet rod and hobbled around on shopping trips to Piggly Wiggly and Rite Aid with a plain cedar cane with a rubberized tip. Now, she clasps her son's gift, caressing the eagle's head and regretting how stupid she'd been, how prideful.

Behind the flag-draped casket, the chaplain says something about brotherhood and sacrifice, but his words are too slippery for her to grasp. She stares at the silver eagle until her vision swims out of focus. A movie starts up in her head: Tariq as a diapered toddler chasing their pit bull with a Wiffle bat; her little boy jumping his beat-up Schwinn on a tiny ramp in the street, saying, *Look, Mama, look;* her boy all grown up, posing in a rented tux with his prom date, his smile as wide as Chesapeake Bay.

Sitting in her Sunday finery, she feels as cored out as a jack-o'-lantern. She squeezes the cane, tensing her muscles in an attempt to hold back tears, refusing to cry in front of everybody, being strong for her little boy.

She remembers when Tariq came back from the recruiter, showing off enlistment papers as if they were something to be proud of. *Take it back,* she'd said. *Go on back to Mister Man and take it back.* He'd reached for her arm, saying, *Mama, please.* But she'd slapped his hand away. *Fool, you gonna get kilt in someone else's desert 'less you take it back.* And when he'd run out and slammed the door, she was left in the kitchen with the echoing accusation.

How many times had she replayed that scene? Each time,

her own words stabbing her heart like a dagger. *Fool. Fool. Fool. You gonna get kilt.* If she hadn't made that proclamation, perhaps it wouldn't have come true. If only *she* could take her words back.

Her gaze drifts from the florid-faced chaplain to black-clad mourners with hands crossed in their laps, and then to the cluster of soldiers in dress blues, faces hard as frozen ground, gold stripes down their legs, miniature medals displayed on their chests.

When the chaplain finishes, a square-jawed captain salutes the casket. Seven rifles fire three quick volleys and she jerks each time the shots crack through thin air. When their echoes recede, her shoulders start to shake as something rattles free inside her chest. It's the tide she's tried so hard to hold back finally breaking free. Mustering all her willpower, she straightens her back and stymies the tears. She swears she will *not* make a scene. Not here. Not in front of her little boy.

Two soldiers fold the flag, snapping creases with machine-like precision. Then the captain carries the star-spangled triangle to her and places it in her hands. *On behalf of a grateful country,* he says.

SPECIALIST BRADSHAW

Bradshaw asks the hostess for a table for four. *Somewhere in back, if possible.* As she leads him on a weaving course between tables and past a long curving bar, he's glad to see the few TVs are tuned to sports channels. No chance of this morning's ceremony popping up there. She seats him at a clamshell booth wrapped around a long, oval table, and a waitress comes by moments later to take his drink order. *Just water.*

The restaurant is Catch 31 Fish House and Bar, sandwiched

between Atlantic Avenue and the Virginia Beach Boardwalk. Classier than Bradshaw is used to, but it's their last day of per diem and Sergeant Berkholtz says they should use it up.

Bradshaw admires his squad leader more than anyone else he's ever known. Saddled with life-or-death responsibilities, Berkholtz incessantly drills his men until reactions become second nature. But instead of screaming at them for every little screwup, he goads them on with praise. *Looked real sharp, but we can do it better. Can't have any hesitation. Speed and violence. Hooah?*

But Berkholtz has seemed unmoored since the blast. Bradshaw mentioned it to Faust a few nights ago, but the team leader told him, *It's all good. Sergeant K is the man.*

Berkholtz's first name is Kristian, a Norwegian name passed down from his mother's side of the family. Genetics also gave him pale, smooth skin that makes him seem ageless. Other NCOs in the platoon sometimes call him Sergeant Baby, but Faust isn't dumb enough to do that. Not only can the bulked-up squad leader bench twice his weight, his favorite punishment for men in his charge is twelve-mile road marches in full pack. Berkholtz can be positive and inspirational when the situation calls for it; hard as a rock when it doesn't.

Maybe that's why Bradshaw relates to him so well. Berk's philosophy mirrors his own. In combat, they both act without compunction, performing their duties like machines whenever the whipcrack of bullets rips the air and wounded soldiers cry out for medics. No hesitation. No thinking.

As the war dragged on, walls of Bradshaw's compartmentalized thinking grew thin. In one room of his brain, the absolute certainty of their noble cause began to heed complaints from others. *What were they still doing here when so many locals wanted them gone? When every American death was followed*

*by televised broadcasts urging Muslims in neighboring countries
to take up the fatwa, cross the border, and come fight the Great
Satan?*

Growing up Catholic, Bradshaw had been a choirboy. He'd
held on to his beliefs through basic training and his deployment to Kosovo. But everything changed in Iraq. When they
first charged into combat, he prayed every time there was a
lull. He prayed for the safety of his comrades. He prayed for
compassion to rise up out of the chaos. He prayed he wouldn't
have to take a life. On his third day of combat, he prayed he
wouldn't have to take another. And another. And another. As
his expert aim turned more and more bodies into lifeless meat,
he stopped begging God to sway things in his favor. He prayed
instead for everyone back in the States; he prayed that they
would never know what had become of their husbands, their
brothers, their sons. Eventually, he stopped praying altogether.
He figured God, if he'd ever existed, gave up on man long ago.

Bradshaw and his squadmates may have had their doubts,
may have even bitched about them among themselves, but no
one hesitated when the shit went down. They kept killing and
being killed because it was their job, each man risking everything because he loved the man next to him. Simple as that.

Now, Bradshaw swizzles ice in his cobalt glass, trying to
empty his mind. He's still sipping water when Berkholtz and
Faust arrive. *Hell of a view,* Berkholtz says before sitting down.
The window opposite the booth looks out on the veranda's fire-
pits and the boardwalk teeming with tourists. Looming over
them like a colossus is a thirty-four-foot statue of King Neptune holding a trident in one hand and a giant turtle in the
other.

The three of them sit in companionable silence, Berkholtz
staring glassy eyed out the window. Bradshaw glances from

him to Faust, who merely shrugs his shoulders. Before the silence grows uncomfortable, Mueller comes weaving through the restaurant.

Where's the wife and kid? Berkholtz asks.

Mueller makes a face. *Chrissie's throwing a fit, so the ladies will not be joining us tonight.*

The waitress comes by, and after she finishes taking their orders Mueller asks if she knows what time it is.

Hmm, six-ish, I think.

Uh-uh, Mueller says, *it's beer o'clock. Bring us a pitcher.* When he winks, a smile blooms on her face.

Cute, she says.

So are you.

When she leaves, Bradshaw notices her sashay is more pronounced than before.

Always the life of the party, says Faust.

Argue if I could, Mueller says, palms held up. Then he turns his right hand over and flexes the bruised knuckles. *Last night's kind of a blur. Mind catching me up?* As they recap the previous night, Mueller chuckles at the details he remembers and says, *No shit,* to those he can't.

So you're pounding on this one dude, Berkholtz says, *when his friend cracks a pool cue on your back and down you go. Then the guy gets ready to start stomping on you, but this hard charger over here takes him out and saves your ass.* He claps Bradshaw on the shoulder.

Mueller scratches his head. *I remember that. He smashed a bottle over that fucker's head. Man, I've only seen 'em shatter like that in the movies. That was awesome.*

Yeah, Berkholtz agrees, *awesome.*

Bradshaw has a different recollection. *Yes,* he'd hit the guy with his beer bottle, but it hadn't busted. The guy had fallen sideways into the next table and knocked over some glasses. *Those* had shattered. If he doesn't correct them now, he knows how this story will morph over the years, adding bulk, becoming more heroic with every telling. True details will eventually fade like the memory of a dream surrendering to daylight. But the beer comes before he says anything, and Mueller pours for everyone.

What'll we drink to? Mueller says.

Fallen comrades, Bradshaw says. *To Jackson.*

Berkholtz's face tenses for a moment, then he nods. *Raise a glass,* he says, hoisting his beer.

They all take long slugs. Mueller drains his entirely. He pours another glass, sets the pitcher down, and turns to Bradshaw. *I ever tell you about the time I snuck a fifth of Wild Turkey into a field exercise out on Sicily DZ? We were supposed to just sit around as OPFOR for 3rd Battalion in some mock bunkers, but Jackson got wasted and streaked across the DZ in nothing but his gas mask and a pair of smiley face boxers.*

What I remember, says Berkholtz, *is Sergeant Payne lining everyone up in formation afterwards and ordering us to drop trou so he could identify the underwear.*

Mueller laughs. *Son of a bitch never gave me up for sneaking in the booze. Even after they article-fifteened his ass.*

After that, the stories fly and the pitchers keep coming. *Remember the way Jackson . . . How he used to always . . . What about the time . . .*

Bradshaw listens, wondering which stories are true, but not really caring. What lies they tell and what truths they keep is not for anyone else to dictate. Each man must find his own way home.

Red Legs

STAND UP, HOOK UP, SHUFFLE TO THE DOOR

Anoush loves the industrious way municipal workers scrabble about Richmond wrangling order from chaos, and I love her for that. Our perfect date is not dining at Shockoe Bottom's trendy cafés or strolling through Lewis Ginter's domed conservatory, but setting out well before the morning rush to watch street sweepers scrub curbs, recycling trucks fork up rows of blue plastic bins, and patrol cars nestle their rear ends into nooks, ready to pounce on swervers returning from an all-night binge. To her, these excursions are backstage passes to a favorite show—a blue-collar ballet of men in steel-toed boots removing yesterday's detritus and assembling scenery for today's performance. Most residents have no idea how much sweat it takes to clear away their daily clutter. But Anoush knows, and she revels in the sense that any wrong can be put right. You might, too, if you were dying.

This morning, a Saturday, yellow-vested police are laying cones and sawhorse barricades to block off streets for today's marathon. Crowds of cheering supporters will cluster on Main

Street and Broad, but we take up position south of the James on Semmes Avenue, around mile twenty-one, the point where racers cross over the river and reenter downtown.

It's November, and we huddle together with a tartan blanket wrapped around our shoulders, our backs to a four-story brick apartment building with a row of tiny shrubs. Except for downtown's glass buildings on the horizon, the view is gray. Anoush brought a heel of bread to tear up and toss at ducks or any other birds foraging at this hour. But all we see are a pair of crows perched on a telephone wire. Anoush throws the bread into the street. Nothing happens for a beat, then one of the crows falls off the wire and glides toward the bread. The crow stands next to the heel, investigating, its head jerking toward us, then back again. It snatches up the bread and lifts off with its heavy wings beating the air like someone pounding dust from a rug. Then the other crow descends from the wire and gives chase across the river.

From our vantage, six lanes of blacktop stretch north toward the Robert E. Lee Memorial Bridge. It's impossible to go anywhere in Richmond without bumping into a reminder of its antebellum roots. Names of bridges, roads, and fields. Generals mounted on bronze steeds. The ninety-foot pyramid rising out of Hollywood Cemetery, a grand monument erected for the Confederate dead. Everything casting wistful light on a supposedly nobler era, ignoring that it was built upon the backs of the subjugated people. Individual commemorations reveal how tightly residents cling to their Lost Cause. Rebel flags hanging in living room windows. Pebbles and coins left atop headstones. Regiments of reenactors mustering in gray waistcoats and breeches, replaying victorious battles as if repetition were enough to erase the losses.

A rewrite of history was exactly what I wanted a year and a

half ago, medically discharged from the Army and back on the family farm in Montana. I wasn't missing any body parts, so my sudden return was met with suspicion. Neighbors and high school friends cast sideways glances my way. On trips to town, conversations would hush when I came near. And at home, my father couldn't look me in the eye. In Big Sky Country, reasons didn't matter, just results.

I tried to lose myself in swishing fields of golden wheat. I charged into them in the big green combine, heads popping off their stalks and rattling in the bin like distant gunfire. When I wasn't working, I hiked the flatheaded Rimrocks rising out of the south until my muscles burned. Long ago, I loved scaling the steep cliff face to get to the top; but that version of me died in the skies over Fort Bragg. The version that came home took the gentle path winding to the top. Once there, I would dare myself to stand on the edge with my boots hanging over the lip. But I never came close.

One day, I packed my meager possessions in a rattletrap Honda and drove cross-country for three days straight. Landing in Richmond, I found work on a construction site. By day, I drove a backhoe and chewed holes in the earth. Evenings and weekends, I explored my new home and soaked up the culture, the way a honeyed drawl could stretch any conversation into a story without end, the way modern towers rising along the north shore received less attention than the old, faithfully restored stone buildings that made up the city's heart. It was comforting to settle into a place that cared less about this generation's wars than those fought by their grandfather's grandfathers.

I did my best to fit in. Traded my cowboy hat for a ball cap. Ordered the house special at Southern restaurants. Appended "y'all" to every other sentence. No matter how I dressed or what I ate, I still felt out of sync. Then I saw Anoush in the Fan District and everything changed. She was standing in front of a Panera Bread, gazing over the parking lot with her head tilted to one side, looking in her oversized bomber jacket like a sun-dazed bear just out of hibernation.

You all right, miss? I asked.

Her gaze flicked at me, then back to the parking lot. She said, *Ever wish you had a little more spine?*

Her words cut through me, straight to the heart of all I'd been running from and the nightmare that wouldn't let me escape no matter how far I ran. *What did you say?*

That car, she said, pointing at a Porsche in a handicap spot. *It parks there all the time, but I never do anything about it. I've even seen the driver getting in and out, one of those thousand-dollar-suit types whose time is more important than everyone else's.*

I didn't yet know about her terminal condition, just that she was a woman unhappy with the world as it was. Looking at the spotless Boxster, yellow with a black convertible top, I said, *So maybe today is the day you do something.*

She turned to me with a radiant smile, a look that knocked everything loose in my mind, a look that over the coming weeks would replace my recurring dream and grant me peaceful sleep.

I think you're right, she said.

We exchanged names. It still felt unnatural to say *Lou Parker* without first saying *Corporal*.

Anoush dug into her purse and pulled out a bottle of cobalt-blue nail polish. Squatting by the driver-side door, she brushed shaky block letters onto the bright paint job. The tip of her tongue peeked out as she worked. She was on the "o" in "Asshole" when the suit came barging out of the café.

Hey, what the—

I blocked his way and shoved him back with a stiff arm. If he wanted to square off, I was good to go. I was always ready for a fight. *Let her finish,* I said.

But that's my fucking car.

Yeah, and look where your fucking *car is parked.*

His face flushed. He pulled out his phone, stared at it, then put it back in his pocket and crossed his arms.

Another patron came out clutching her purchase in a small white bag. When she saw what was going on, she stuck the bag under her arm and clapped. I joined in. Anoush finished the "e" and stood up, waving at the applause like an actress taking a curtain call.

Don't forget the other side, I said.

Beaming, she skipped around the car and set to work on the passenger-side door.

AERODYNAMICS

Please tell me you brought something to warm us up, Anoush says with a tipping motion toward her mouth. She's shivering slightly in her ripped jeans and windbreaker. No makeup, dark crescents under her eyes, long hair knotted behind her head and held together with a rubber band.

I retrieve a thermos of coffee from the back of my Civic and a puff of steam escapes when I unscrew the cap. Filling two paper cups, I hand one to Anoush. She holds it close to her mouth, blowing across the black liquid before taking a sip.

Was kind of hoping for something with a little more kick, she says. *You know, hair of the dog.*

Last night, we had dinner at Cafe Gutenberg, where a wild-haired poet recited erotic poetry to the titillated diners. We came home with the poet's new book and a bottle of Hpnotiq, a blue liqueur made from vodka and cognac. Passing the book back and forth, one of us read aloud while the other sipped and stripped off a piece of clothing. Once the bottle was dry and our bodies naked, we made love on the couch, then retired to the bedroom for a repeat performance.

No hair of the dog, I say, *just coffee.*

Probably a good thing. I'm still a little drunk.

She takes another sip and scans the surroundings. Not much to see, but Anoush is content. We haven't visited this spot before and that's all that matters. She's lived in Richmond most of her life, but until her terminal diagnosis she never explored the city beyond her own neighborhood. Now she seeks out its hidden wonders, trying to cram into her remaining time as many experiences as possible. Eating in the dark at a blacked-out restaurant served by a blind waitstaff. Walking atop the pipeline on the north bank of the James, following it past spits of beach and beneath elevated train tracks. Strolling through Jackson Ward and Hillside, snapping pictures of the homeless with her 35mm Canon. I always ask her not to venture into rough neighborhoods until I get back from work, but she hates to wait. She goes alone and tells me about it afterwards, giddy from the thrill of her solo journey.

One time, she got mugged on Franklin not far from the main library. She'd been admiring the architecture of Greek revival row houses, the Doric columns and elaborately carved cornices, when a man in a gray hoodie stepped out from a shadowed doorway. *Your purse and camera,* he said with a jut of his chin, holding out his hand, unhurried, like he was asking the time.

Knowing this day might eventually come, Anoush had rehearsed defiant retorts in her bathroom mirror. But that night she said nothing, handing over her possessions without a peep. The mugger sauntered off with his prize.

He didn't even have the decency to run off, she told me later, after the shaking stopped and her initial shock morphed into rage. The next week, Anoush vented on a series of customer service reps when she called to cancel her cards. On the fifth night she threw a fit in the kitchen, breaking dishes and hurling utensils across the room. I wrapped my arms around her until she stopped struggling and started crying. *I hate being weak,* she said into my chest.

I heard the hurt and fear in her voice, but mostly the shame. Shame of submission. Shame of her mute response. Shame of not living up to the strong self-image she'd created for herself.

Holding Anoush in my arms, I searched for the right thing to say to set her world straight again. The only cure I could think to offer was my confession. The story of my last true day as a paratrooper.

The Army has slang terms for everything, I began. *Rows of medals are "fruit salad." Someone down on the ground doing push-ups is in "the front lean and rest." There's even a term for jumpers falling into the propellers of the plane behind them. They call it "Red Legs."*

* * *

The nightmare always begins the same way, with sixty-four paratroopers crammed into a C-130, sitting shoulder to shoulder in the cupped mesh of four rows of bench seats. I'm fourth in the stick, behind Jankovic, Zeke, and Toomey. The plane is stuffy and our grease-painted faces are flecked with sweat. Parachutes on our backs force us to lean forward against rucksacks that are tied into our harnesses and sitting on our laps. Loaded like mules, we rock in sync with each of the plane's judders as it rumbles toward the drop zone.

Toomey is telling me about a surprise birthday party being planned for his girlfriend. He wants me to come along. Says there will be other girls who are hot for paratroopers. *C'mon, Parker,* he says. *Live a little.* Beneath his Kevlar, Toomey's smile stretches from one jug ear to the other.

I'm smiling, too. And why not? Parachuting is an adrenaline rush like no other. Especially night jumps. The thrill of stepping into pitch black. The prop blast throwing you sideways. The sudden jerk as the static line yanks your parachute open. Then floating under silk as the roaring planes recede and the ground rises up out of the dark.

Inside the plane, the only interior lights turned on are in the back, two red globes by the side doors. When the doors slide open, cool air tongues the suffocating tube, and jumpmasters lean into the howl of night, camouflage fabric of their pants snapping in spastic glee. They check for anything that might snag a static line, running hands along the door's trailing edge as if caressing a lover. Turning back toward the seated men, the jumpmasters give hand signals and scream orders to be heard over the engines. *Stand up. Hook up. Check equipment.*

We rise from our cargo seats and fasten snap links onto the overhead cable. Each jumper examines the parachute of the man in front, tracing the yellow static line zigzagging down his back like bootlaces, the last check for knots and tangles. Missing one could cost the life of the man in front. Though these umbilicals will not be tonight's fatal error. That will be the orientation of the staggered V of planes. The one behind ours should be at a slightly higher altitude, but this is its pilot's first parachute run, and he's flying low.

When the interior light turns green, the jumpmasters scream, *Go*, and we all shuffle forward in our shiny Corcorans. Time slows down as I step to the lip of the door and leap. I can see each of them—Jankovic, Zeke, Toomey— falling into the churning blades. As I tumble after, the trailing plane noses up enough so that the rotors barely catch my chute, shredding the canopy and slapping me against the fuselage before I fall away. In real life, I pulled the rip cord on the reserve parachute and only suffered a concussion, a dislocated shoulder, and a few broken ribs. In the dream, there is no reserve strapped to my belly and I fall into bottomless black.

*   *   *

That night in the kitchen, revealing my nightmare to Anoush had been like ripping off a scab. But the true wound lay beneath. Anoush had stopped crying, her mugging forgotten for the moment, her whole focus turned to me. I could have kept my secret and let it scab over again. But I continued.

Whenever someone dies on a jump, everyone else has to go back up the next day. It's like falling off a bike, you know—you've got to hop on right away if you ever want to ride again. So everyone in the stick packed into another plane and jumped. Except for me. I was in the hospital getting my arm set. After healing up, I just couldn't do it anymore. Couldn't jump. Couldn't even load onto the trucks going to the airstrip. When Sergeant Berkholtz tried to make me, the whole world started spinning and I fell to the ground shaking like an epileptic.

That's terrible, Anoush said.

The Army made me see a psychiatrist. He'd read my file and

knew everything about the incident that left me unable to perform my assigned duties; still, during our sessions, he asked me to replay the scene over and over as he jotted on his notepad. His job was to determine if I was faking, not to offer me any sort of comfort. He eventually diagnosed me with psychosomatic vertigo and aerophobia, a fear of flying. Then he signed off on my medical discharge.

How'd your buddies react? Anoush said. *Surely they had your back.*

I barked a short laugh. *Faust told me to suck it up. Mueller called me chicken.*

But, you got hit by a plane! *That's got to count for something.*

You don't understand. We were deploying to Afghanistan, but I couldn't get on the plane. Half the guys in my platoon had Purple Hearts and they *were going back. But not me. I was useless. Worse, I was a coward.*

And there it was—"coward," the word that had dominated my waking mind and haunted my sleep. For so long, I'd imagined how others would react to my phobia, if their faces would show disgust when they heard how the mere thought of flying was enough to make me curl in a ball. But Anoush's face showed no contempt. She pulled me into a hug and kissed my neck.

When we broke the hug, I grabbed her hand and led her toward the living room. I scooped up her new purse from the coffee table and handed it to her. Then I grabbed her jacket from the hook on the door and held it out for her to slide into its arms.

What's that for? she said.

You're getting back on that bike. Tonight.

She didn't argue as I prodded her out the door, leaving her tantrum and the broken dishes behind.

TERMINAL VELOCITY

It's been almost an hour since the marathon started. We've been following its progress by the slow approach of helicopters tracking the lead pack. *Wish they'd hurry up and get here,* I say.

Not for another forty- to forty-five minutes, Anoush says. She'd run track in high school and still enjoys calculating race pace. The cancer in her lungs makes it too difficult for her to run anymore. Instead, she walks all over the city, people-watching and admiring old architecture, pausing every few blocks to catch her breath.

Waiting is the toughest part, I say.

She arches her eyebrows. *You talking about the runners or something else?*

I shrug.

Thought we were done with that.

When I don't say anything, she grabs one of my arms and drapes it over her shoulder. Then she squeezes in next to me. *Nothing but good times, remember?*

She'd first explained this logic when we'd only been dating a couple of weeks. She told me in the same conversation as the one about her late-stage adenocarcinoma. *With treatment,* she said, *doctors give me a thirty-three percent chance of survival with a ninety percent chance of recurrence; but even if I'm one of the lucky few, I'll still be tethered to an oxygen tank for the rest of my life.*

And if you don't get treatment?

With no chemo or radiation wearing me out, I might actually enjoy my life.

She made me agree not to tell her parents about the cancer. A condition to her moving into my place. It was fast for both of us, but she was eager to get away from home and I wanted to be with her as long as possible, to stretch out whatever time she had left. Anytime I mentioned chemo, surgery, or even holistic treatments, she shut me down with four simple words: *My body, my choice.*

Now, she says, *You know, the Buddhists believe all that matters is the present moment.*

I'm not a Buddhist. Might be easier if I was. But I want a future with you. Is that so wrong?

It's not wrong. It's just—well, it's not going to happen. So why torture yourself like that?

Stepping in front of me, she cups my face in her hands. *Listen, if you want to go, then go. I won't think any less of you. I'll have nothing but beautiful memories.*

Plenty of times I'd thought how much easier it would be if I packed up and disappeared one day while she was out on one of her walks. But I wasn't going to quit on her like I had my squad.

Uh-uh, I say. *You're not getting rid of me that easy.*

MALFUNCTION

After my discharge, I checked in every day to a website that tracked military deaths in Iraq and Afghanistan. For every blip in the rising body count, I scoured news outlets until I was certain the dead soldiers weren't anyone I knew. And when they were, I drank myself into oblivion and picked fights with anyone who didn't shrink from my glare.

Near the end of my unit's rotation, just one week before wheels up, two men from my former squad were blown up by a suicide bomber, one killed and one with his face ripped to shreds. These weren't just soldiers I knew; these were team members I'd trained, buddies I'd barhopped with in Fayetteville. Now Jackson was dead and Pearson was disfigured.

When I heard that Pearson was getting facial reconstruction surgery at Walter Reed, I made plans to visit. But every day I found an excuse to stay at home. On his next-to-last day in the hospital, I worked up enough courage to drive to Bethesda. Walking through his door was one of the hardest things I'd ever done.

He lay in a wide hospital bed with bandages covering half his face. A curtain sectioned the room in two. On a counter beneath the wall-mounted television was an assortment of get well cards. A balloon that said MY HERO was tied to his bed side rail.

Hey, Bryce, I said. *Brought you some reading material.* I held up a copy of the *Sports Illustrated* swimsuit issue.

Parker, he said, *never thought I'd see your sorry ass again.* He winced a little when he talked. The skin where his lips protruded from the bandage was red as stewed tomatoes. He thumbed the hand control and the bed's motor whirred, the back portion rising and pushing him to a seated position. *Long way from Montana.*

I'm in Richmond now.

Hmm. Way you went on about that farm, I thought you'd never give that up.

Needed a new place. Somewhere I could start over again without everyone comparing me to who I used to be.

He picked up a glass of water from his rolling table and sipped through a straw. Keeping his gaze fixed on the glass, he asked if I'd had any bad dreams.

When I said yes, he looked up. *Me, too. Mine aren't so much about the blast, but the moments leading up to it, all the things I should've seen and done. I wake up screaming sometimes. Freaks my mom out. She's in the cafeteria right now. Keeps going down and bringing up more food. Says they're not feeding me right in here.*

I remembered his stories about his mother, about growing up in Louisiana, all that spicy Cajun cooking. I wanted to tell him that going home might be good for him and not to base anything on me. But I couldn't get my mouth to move.

Pearson broke the silence. *You were smart to run away,* he said. *Wish I had.*

As if on cue, the patient on the other side of the curtain began moaning.

SLIP INTO THE WIND

They should get here in another fifteen minutes, Anoush says, *maybe a little less.*

The helicopters are still too far away for their tail numbers to be legible, but close enough that their buzzing is like gnats pestering my ear.

How about a story? Anoush says. *Something to pass the time.*

Imagining life in foreign lands is her favorite pastime. She subscribes to *National Geographic* and dog-ears pages of places she'd like to visit. Her parents encourage Anoush's wanderlust up to a point. Europe and Africa are fine, even the Orient, but not the Middle East. That region is taboo.

Both sets of Anoush's grandparents had come to America after the shah of Iran was deposed, fleeing Khomeini and his warped view of sharia law. By the time Anoush's parents were dating as teenagers, Reagan had freed the hostages from Tehran, and terrorists had bombed the Marine barracks in Lebanon. The young couple grew adept at ignoring suspicious stares. When they married and set up house on the East

Coast, they took it as a chance to start over. They bought Bruce Springsteen LPs, flew an American flag on the front porch, and packed away anything that proclaimed their heritage.

Anoush gleaned what she could from books and web searches. Countless times she ventured into the attic to dig through steamer trunks where the past was buried. She'd step into her mother's embroidered thawbs and wrap her face in her father's red-and-white-checkered keffiyehs. She'd unfurl the tasseled wall hanging of an Arabian stallion and imagine clinging to its mane as it reared. She would unwrap ceramic cups and bowls painted with blue flowers and set them aside to study the Arabic script of newspapers that had swaddled them. Although she couldn't speak the language, she imitated what she'd seen in movies, the sinuous babble slipping from her tongue like water over slick rocks.

Whenever she asked her parents about the items stowed in the attic, their reply was always the same: *We don't talk about such things.* Memories of how things used to be were too difficult for them to reconcile with how they are now.

Which is why Anoush loves my firsthand accounts so much. I skirt around my combat experiences and reminisce about the Middle East like a world traveler back from vacation. I describe sandstone buildings with courtyards shielded by protective walls; tightly packed bazaars selling everything from prayer rugs to pirated CDs; Bedouins who trek across the desert in caravans rather than set down roots. Today I tell her about digging wells around Nasiriyah.

It was part of this new policy of "winning hearts and minds." None of these villages had running water, so a well in the center of town was a big deal. We'd come in early one morning, the engineers towing a machine that looked like a mobile oil derrick. Once they marked off the area and set up, it took less than an hour to drill to the water table. Then they'd bore out the hole, set a screen and a submersible pump in the bottom, and slide in a casing tube for support. All that was left was to cap off the drop pipe with a spigot and show everyone how to use it. They could knock the whole thing out in a day.

But we had to keep going back to this one village because the pump kept breaking down. The brass thought it was Al Qaida mucking things up. After the third time, we set up a night ambush to catch them in the act. But it wasn't terrorists; it was the village women filling in the well. Even though the Euphrates was a couple of klicks away, they wanted to walk there and back to wash clothes and fetch water. It was the only time they could talk with each other. Otherwise, they were forbidden to leave their homes.

Trapped, Anoush says. *Yeah, I get it. I would've filled it in, too.* She's lost in a far-off gaze, and I can't tell whether she's picturing drawing something worthwhile out of a hole in the ground or falling into it.

I tap her shoulder and point west where the blue lights of police motorcycles have crested the hill about a half mile back. Anoush stands on tiptoe, craning her neck to get a better look. Soon motorized trikes bearing swivel-mounted TV cameras rise over the hill. As the vehicles come down the slope, we can see past them to the lead pack, a tight knot of seven runners. Closer and closer they come, striding like gazelles, their faces slack, as if their minds are elsewhere, as if this incredible feat comes at no cost and hasn't been built on thousands of miles of painful practice.

As they rush by, we applaud and shout encouragement. *Way to go. You can do it.* Clap, clap, clap. *Way to go. You can do it.*

After a couple of minutes, there's a large gap in the runners. The heads and shoulders of the next group are visible over the crest, slowly growing taller as if pushing their way out of the ground. Anoush turns to me with a devious expression. *Follow me,* she says. Then she takes off running toward the bridge, her purse slapping against her hip.

I chase after and come up alongside. *You're bouncing like crazy,* I say.

She cups her breasts. *You saying I should've worn a sports bra?*

I meant your purse, dummy.

Sure you did. She slows down to pull the strap over her head and hand me the purse. *What would I do without you?*

STEALING SOMEONE ELSE'S AIR

Anoush's coughing began in early spring. As an allergy sufferer, she attributed it to the heavy pollen count, the yellow film that coated cars and benches and collected in gutters in heaps. But spring turned into summer and the cough persisted. By the time she went to the doctor, the cancer had spread its filaments through both lungs. The morning I saw her standing dumbstruck in front of Panera was the day after her diagnosis.

When Anoush moved in, I thought I knew what to expect. But the force of her coughing shocked me, the way it wracked her chest and left her sucking air in loud, straining drags. Mornings are the worst, her first waking breath setting off a barrage of explosive hacks that sounds like her body is ripping in two. After the fit passes, she takes the wastebasket outside and dumps wadded tissues into the rolling trash bucket, ridding the evidence like a thief wary of being caught.

On days she's too wrung out to explore the city, she sits in a padded armchair with an old sketchbook in her lap, flipping through pencil drawings of fig trees and juniper bushes, of women shopping in an open-air market, of massive boats laden with containers and men working the docks. They'd all been drawn by her aunt Fatima, a self-taught artist who once dreamed of hanging her paintings in galleries. Then an auto-immune disease inflamed her joints, ulcerated her skin, and slowly caused her organs to fail.

Fatima lived with them in America until Anoush was eight. Anoush's father stayed late at work and went in early, leaving his wife to care for Fatima and deal with her temper. The crippled woman seemed to take glee in making her caregiver miserable. One time, peeking in from the hallway, Anoush saw her mother on hands and knees scrubbing up a mess by the bed. She saw Fatima stretch her trembling hand to intentionally knock over her cup of tea. And she saw Fatima's wicked smile as Anoush's mother shrieked and ran to the bathroom, scalded.

Whenever Anoush asked why such a spiteful woman was allowed in their home, her father would say, *Sickness does this to a person. She was once loving and kind. Just like you.*

FLOATING UNDER CANOPY

The runners quickly catch up and pass us on the bridge, most of them wearing spandex leggings, all of them thin as straw. Our own pace decelerates to a slow trot and then a shuffle. Anoush sucks in ragged breaths, but she won't give up and I don't make her. I just jog alongside, ready with a bottle of Gatorade.

When she finally stops, we're three quarters of the way across. She coughs for a while and I hold her steady, handing her tissues from her purse and stuffing the phlegm-filled wads in my pocket. When the coughing passes, I hand her the Gatorade and she sips from the bottle between breaths.

Leaning on the railing, Anoush looks east to Belle Isle, a

clump of land in the middle of the James where wedding parties like to pose for pictures. She points at the island surrounded by rocky outcrops and churning foam. *Used to be a prison camp right there. Hundreds of Union prisoners and just a few guards, but no one ever escaped. Know why?*

The rapids?

She nods. *All they had to eat was moldy bread riddled with maggots. A bunch of them starved to death.*

So it was a real shithole.

Yeah, but look how pretty it is now.

I'm standing a full arm's length from the railing. Even so, I feel a flutter in my stomach as I stare down at the island. I try to imagine happy couples beginning their lives amid all that turmoil. I want to step closer to the edge but I can't make my legs move.

Just beyond the froth, a cormorant scrabbles atop one of the rocks and studies the water. I can tell by its eager posture that it wants to dive in and snap up a meal. But even the bird knows some things are too risky.

PREPARE TO LAND

Whenever Anoush and I visit her parents' house, they speak to their daughter as if I'm not there. It's not just that I'm the guy who stole their daughter away; it's that they were hoping for someone better, someone who worked in an air-conditioned office instead of a construction site.

But her father called me last week, making nice, asking about my work and plans for the future. Eventually he got to the purpose of his call. *Anoush has been talking about backpacking through Europe,* he said. *Have you told her how dangerous that is?*

I could see the trap, how he wanted to win me over to his side and convince her not to go. But she wasn't going anywhere. Not Europe. Not Florida. Not even Virginia Beach.

Her plan, once she becomes too sick to get around, is to check into a hospice and let the disease run its course. No parents by her bedside. Me, either. The trip is her cover story, something to explain being off the grid. She purchased postcards on Amazon to send to her parents. The Sistine Chapel, the Coliseum, Venice's gondolas, and a dozen other iconic scenes. On the back of each one, she invented stories about the wonderful time she was having. As for the foreign stamps and postmarks, that was my job.

This is for you, she told me one day, pressing a round-trip ticket to Rome in my hands.

I agreed to take the trip, to visit the destinations on her cards, and to mail them at the proper intervals. I'd go on the great adventure she'd always dreamed of for herself while she lay heavily medicated in a hospital bed. Alone.

She gave me a sealed letter to deliver to her parents. I'd seen enough of these in combat to know what it was. The final good-bye. *You can just mail it,* she said, giving me the out.

I promised to deliver it in person to her parents and to take the full brunt of their blame. Until that time, though, I'd maintain the deception. So I told her father over the phone that Europe was safer than America. *Don't worry,* I said. *I'll be there to keep her safe.*

Pah, he said, *what can you do?*

I can try to make your daughter happy. The only honest statement I gave him.

DROP ZONE

We're walking west on Cary, part of the onlookers now instead of the race crowd. After a couple of blocks, Anoush stops and shakes her head.

Done in? I ask.

Yeah, she says, and looks back toward the bridge. *At least we made it over the river. Can you imagine having to be rescued out there?*

We find a gap in the crowd lining the streets and squeeze in, Anoush leaning against me for support. She claps but doesn't have the energy to cheer. So I yell twice as loud. The bouncing mass of bodies is mesmerizing, all those pistoning limbs, everyone rushing in the same direction, certain of their purpose, determined to make it to the finish line no matter the cost. A chubby man comes lumbering along at the same pace we'd had on the bridge. *Good job,* I shout. *You can do it.*

The man lifts his gaze from the pavement to flick me a look. It's the same one I've seen in the mirror. The expression of a drowning man. Then he rumbles forward and is swallowed up by the crowd.

My focus blurs and the runners swim out of view. I can see the rolltop desk from our hallway as if it's right in front of me. I see letter slots stuffed with bills and other papers. And I see my hand reaching into the one filled with postcards, pulling them out, flipping through them one by one. I see the Eiffel Tower, and there I am standing at its base, weighed down by a big blue backpack, too scared to step onto the elevator and ride it to the top. I feel the Earth spinning beneath my feet and suddenly it's as if I'm falling from the aircraft again. The spinning rotors beneath my feet. Toomey's face there one second, gone the next. For a moment, I feel like I can't breathe. And then Anoush is tugging on my sleeve.

Hey, she says. *Where'd you go?*

I shake my head and the noise of the cheering crowd rushes back into my ears. I look at her, blinking.

She takes my hand. *You okay?*

Yeah, I say, *fine.* I look to the west but all I see now is the bobbing mass of runners. The finish line is four miles away, too far to distinguish the checkered banner from here.

Anoush follows my gaze and smiles. *It's all right,* she says. *We're close enough to know how it ends.*

Dead Man's Hand

STEALING THE BLINDS

Bryce Pearson seldom talks about his scarred right cheek, those two puckered lines jagging from his mouth to his neck, another one slicing across his right cheek. When people ask, he shuts them up with one-word answers. *Prison*, he says. Or, *Dog*. Both are lies. The truth he keeps to himself.

He used to shy away from encounters with the unblemished public. Now he confronts them like a form of combat. In the tightly packed crawl of eastbound traffic leaving LA, he feels the stares from neighboring cars and knows what's coming. A blond woman in a metallic-blue Prius turns her head, a ripple creasing her brow, eyes widening in alarm. Pearson looks over and she looks away, focusing on the road ahead, her face settling into a façade of nonchalance. Pearson taps the horn of his Chevy Silverado, and she looks over again. He gives a ghoulish smile and the woman's head jerks back as she yanks her wheel to one side. Then she corrects her course and slows down, dropping back out of his field of vision.

Ever since a bomb in Afghanistan peeled his face open like

a banana, Pearson's become adept at reading micro expressions, those facial tics and trembles that betray a person's inner thoughts. When people first meet him, before they can spout the soothing platitudes demanded by good manners, their faces reveal what they truly think of his scars. The pouty mouth and pinched brows of sorrow. The wrinkled nose of disgust. The raised corner of a lip signaling contempt.

At first, this new skill did little more than aggravate. Whenever friends tried to lure him out of his trailer park, Pearson would read the pity underscoring their attempts. And though he dreamed of days hanging out with the guys and nights flirting with women, he knew those days were dead and buried. Trips into the world meant dealing with strangers and their probing eyes. He became a recluse, holing up in his ratty double-wide, shopping midweek in the predawn dark at Walmart, his face hidden in the dark folds of a hoodie as he scanned items in the self-checkout lane.

That all changed when he discovered California's poker rooms, where the blasted terrain of his face put other players off their game and turned a night of cards into a profitable venture. His usual spot is Hollywood Park in Inglewood, but today he's headed to the Agua Caliente Casino in Rancho Mirage, 120 miles east of LA.

The long drive on Interstate 10 is relaxing. As overlapping freeways disappear in the rearview, thinning lane by lane, tension seeps from his muscles. The blacktop almost seems to dissolve as the surroundings take on a hazy shimmer. The passing blur is an endless stretch of scrub-dotted desert punctuated by an occasional cactus or Joshua tree. "Kiss from a Rose" wafts through the speakers. His playlist is a string of songs by Seal. He feels a kinship with the scarred artist, though Seal's disfigurements are not from injury but from lupus.

When he cuts through the San Jacinto Mountains, the colossal white towers of wind farms in Palm Springs tell him he's almost arrived at Agua Caliente. Weaving through Rancho Mirage's palm tree–lined streets, he enters the resort's lush oasis, pulling up to the hotel with a pool fed by a cascading waterfall.

The day's dry heat disappears as Pearson enters the grand casino, the whir of air-conditioning greeting him like the cool grip of a meat locker. He's dressed in studied grunge—frayed jeans and a coffee-stained T-shirt, a down-on-his-luck look meant to make other players think they can steamroll him. Not that he needs a costume here. The resort's casino throws its doors open to everyone, and the crowd that passes through is dressed like a bus-station mob. Bleary-eyed men and women feed the slots with coins from plastic tubs and pull the silver arms like automatons. Wild drunks cluster around the craps table, high-fiving and hollering until the dice finally turn and kill their mood. And frantic men in wrinkled business suits race from the cash-advance window to kidney-shaped blackjack tables, gambling away their mortgages one withdrawal at a time.

Pearson ignores the cacophony as he passes through to the poker room in the back. Instead of the icy pros of Vegas, what he finds here are desperate, slump-shouldered submissives with sour looks and downcast eyes. Penny-wise players more concerned about earning hourly bonus points for the buffet or gift shop than protecting their dwindling stacks of white one-dollar chips and red fives. Their gamesmanship goes no further than catch phrases like, *Got to play the hand you're dealt.* These are sheep ready for shearing. And Pearson has come to slaughter the lambs.

The pit boss directs him to a no-limit hold'em table against the far wall. Seated at the long oval table are a half dozen middle-aged men and one young woman with half the table's chips stacked in front of her. The sweetheart neckline of her snug, cropped shirt showcases her bra's lace trim. *Someone else who knows how to maximize assets,* Pearson thinks, making mental note to pay attention when she's involved in pots.

Pearson sits, and after a round of nodding hellos, everyone but the woman looks away, busying their hands with chip riffles or picking their nails, anything to avoid staring at his scars. But the woman looks right at him and smiles. *So what's the story?* she asks, pointing at her own cheek and swirling a finger in the air. *Dog,* he replies, waiting for her reaction. But she doesn't even blink, her gaze remaining constant as a noontime sun. *Well,* she says, *hope you took a bite out of that bitch as well.* It's been years since a good-looking woman flirted with Pearson, and all he can do is grin. He's glad the others don't notice the blush creeping up his neck and burning his ears.

As the dealer flicks cards across the felt, Pearson sits back to study faces. For two revolutions he folds every hand except for the blinds, and he folds those whenever someone raises. He plans to change gears as soon as he learns the players' habits and tells. There's no rush. No-limit hold'em is a game where you can build fat stacks for hours and lose everything with one unwise bet.

He's noted only one aggressive player at the table, a balding man dressed in a blue pin-striped tracksuit. The man takes long pulls from the highball in the cupholder near his elbow and shreds napkins between deals, their remnants scattered at his feet like confetti. Pearson is in seat one to the left of the dealer and Tracksuit is in seat five at the middle of the table. The "sweetheart"—Ruby, as he has since learned—is in seat six, just to the left of Tracksuit. Great position. While Tracksuit bullies the table and rakes in small pots for a half hour, she tangles with him when he overbets and carves off a sizable chunk of his winnings in one go.

Having studied the other players, Pearson focuses his hatred on them, amping himself up and heightening his senses. Same as Afghanistan. To be an effective cog in the military machine, you had to embrace your hatred. Hate for the Hajjis who wanted you dead. Hate for the populace among whom they hid. Hate for the godforsaken country where you were deployed. The only way to not let down your guard was to hate every damned second you were there, every inch of roadway that might conceal a bomb, and every civilian who might trigger an IED with their cell phone. If you embraced the hate, you were always on high alert, always looking for something wrong, and never surprised when you found it.

But you couldn't just turn off the hate when you came home. It crawled into your bunk and whispered in your ear: *Everyone's staring. Talking behind your back. So why hold it in? Free the hate. Explode.*

Poker provides an outlet for his anger. The felt tabletop is his new battlefield, the other players his enemy. Every chip in front of them is like something stolen from his own stack. They are playing with *his* money, and he wants it back.

Pearson is ready now, his mood keen for blood. As he starts to play, his bets and raises have little to do with the power of his hole cards. What matters is *knowing* when the other players are worried about their own shortcomings. When he sees their tells, he raises and reraises until they fold. It helps that they're so easy to read, every move a sham. Acting strong when a hand is weak, weak when it is strong. Everyone but Ruby. He hasn't got a fix on her yet. When he tries to study her, she catches him and smiles in a way that sets off fireworks in his brain.

Most players fold to Pearson unless they've got a monster

hand. But not Tracksuit. He plays in almost every hand. Each time Tracksuit loses a big pot, he curses the winner or grabs a handful of his black, Brillo-pad hair and tugs while saying, *Stupid, stupid.*

Sometimes, when Tracksuit splashes the pot with an obvious bluff, Pearson lets him win the small victory. Pearson even flashes playable cards before tossing them away. A long con for the big payoff. He wants Tracksuit to think he can push Pearson around with his masterful skills. Each time Tracksuit lays a trap, betting light on made hands to induce a big raise, he sits still as a statue, as if the mere act of breathing might scare away victims. His bluffs are so transparent he's almost invisible.

Now, for instance, as Tracksuit's fat hands tent over his hole cards and he leans down for a peek, his lip corner twitches for just a moment and Pearson knows it's a winner. When the cards snap back on the felt and Tracksuit feigns indifference before raising the blind, Pearson figures it's aces or kings. When he says, *Eh, I'll take a stab at it,* Pearson tosses his pair of 7s into the muck.

A few players call. One even reraises. Tracksuit calls and lets the others limp in. The flop is a rainbow, and Tracksuit continues his slow play. An 8 of clubs on the turn pairs another 8 on the board, and Tracksuit finally makes a strong bet. Everyone but Ruby drops out. The final card is a 2 of clubs. Ruby bets, Tracksuit raises, and when she calls, he turns over a pair of aces, giving him the "dead man's hand," black aces over 8s. Wild Bill Hickok had been holding that now infamous hand when he was gunned down in a saloon in Deadwood. Ruby flips her cards, a suited 6–7 of clubs, cracking his aces with a flush.

You lucky little bitch! Tracksuit roars, pounding the table. *The hell you doing calling with that piece of shit?*

Ruby lowers her chin and gives a pout. *I didn't think you had anything, either.*

Tracksuit is steaming now. Emptying his wallet, he pushes the bills across the felt. The dealer lays out the hundreds in a show for the overhead cameras. She counts the money and uses a Lucite paddle to push it through a slot in the table into a metal lockbox. Then she slides a fresh stack of chips to Tracksuit. *All right,* he says, *you want to gamble? Let's gamble!* He clenches his jaw so tightly that the cords on his neck stand out.

Pearson tries not to laugh, thinking to himself, *You got to know when it's time to leave.* Not that he'd actually warn Tracksuit. Not while he's still got chips to fork over.

A few hands go by with Tracksuit betting large and raking in nothing but the big and little blinds. Then Pearson calls one of the bets. As the dealer lays out the flop, Tracksuit's lip corner twitches again. He checks and Pearson bets strong. Tracksuit calls. This goes on until the river. The community cards on the table are ace of hearts, 8 of hearts, 3 of hearts, 2 of clubs, and 2 of diamonds. When Pearson checks, Tracksuit slides a third of his stack into the pot and holds his breath. Then he props his chin on his hand in a display of boredom.

Pearson riffles two stacks of chips, pulling up on the inside edges to create gaps, then squeezing the stacks together so the chips become one big stack. Then he cuts them in two and repeats the process, over and over, replaying the hand in his head and dissecting Tracksuit's play. Tracksuit probably figures Pearson for a straight or a heart flush, and obviously has that beat. Which means he's holding a higher flush or a full house. There's also the slimmest possibility that he has four of a kind. Quads would be unbeatable. So Pearson's mulling over whether or not Tracksuit has the 2s. It doesn't make sense with the way he played the hand.

Raise, Pearson says. *All in.*

Tracksuit's face is an explosion of delight. He shoves his remaining chips into the pot and throws his cards faceup on the table. *Nut flush,* he yells, turning over the king and jack of hearts.

Pearson flips pocket rockets onto the green felt, a full house, aces full of 2s. Tracksuit looks gutshot. His chair topples over as he jumps to his feet. *This is bullshit,* he yells, jabbing the air with his finger. His face is crimson. He pounds the felt and chips jump all around the table. Then he turns and storms off.

Damn, Ruby says, *you beat me to it.* They both chuckle as Pearson gathers his winnings and stacks his towers ever higher. Three other men collect their chips and exit, leaving only four players at the table.

Might as well pack it in, Pearson says. He leans over his winnings and asks Ruby, *Care to join me for dinner?*

Ruby's smile flattens into a bloodless line. She stands up and throws her jacket on, zipping it to her neck. *Keep it in your pants, buddy. I'm just here for the cards.* She scoops her chips into her purse and heads off for the cashier cage.

RAILBIRDS

Back in his trailer, Pearson zones out as *Survivor* plays on the television. Ruby is stuck in his head, that impish smile that almost made him believe he was normal. He should know better by now.

Rising from his armchair, Pearson opens the cabinet beneath the TV stand. The top shelf holds an ancient VCR and the bottom a row of VHS tapes with handwritten labels. These videos of poker tournaments he's taped are the only reason he hasn't upgraded to a DVD player. He regularly rewatches them and analyzes their fine points, the small details that changed players' fortunes. Today he chooses the 2003 World Series of Poker and pops it in the player. That was the year Chris Moneymaker won it all. Pearson loves everything about the guy. His name, his gear-changing style of play, and the fact that Moneymaker won his seat with an eighty-six-dollar buy-in at an online satellite game. The normal entry fee is ten grand. He went up against professional players and walked away from the final table with $2.5 million.

Before the World Series, Moneymaker had just been a chubby accountant in Maryland. But the poker room doesn't care about pedigree. Weekender or pro, executive or janitor—everyone is the same once they belly up to the table. All that matters is your skill and how much you're willing to risk. The year after Moneymaker's big win, small-time players crept out of the basements and garages that hosted their regular poker nights, rolled up stakes, and headed out to Vegas. *If he can do it,* everyone figured, *so can I.*

Pearson dreams of entering the tournament. The only thing holding him back are the cameras, the close-up shots of players making stone-cold bluffs. He's not up for that kind of scrutiny. He could care less what morons like Tracksuit tell their buddies about the mutant they saw at the casino. But anyone making it past the opening rounds of the World Series is memorialized by ESPN's cameras, recorded by grinders who examine their play the same way Pearson does with greats like Daniel Negreanu, Phil Ivey, and Gus Hansen. Every time he convinces himself he's ready, that he doesn't care what anyone else thinks of his face, someone like Ruby comes along and knocks his dick in the dirt.

Turning off the TV, Pearson steps onto his back stoop with a Heineken and plops into an Adirondack chair. Behind his home is a scrubby vista of pinyon trees and juniper bushes. Cutting across his view is a concrete culvert that stands dry most of the year and roars with water the few days they get rain. Today it's dry, and a handful of teenagers from the trailer park are skateboarding in the culvert, riding up and down the sloped sides and practicing ollies on the flat bottom.

Pearson remembers belonging to his own pack of rough boys. When he sleeps, his old life in the Army fills his dreams. He misses it all. The brotherhood. The strutting confidence. The knowledge that someone always had your back. He even misses 6 a.m. PT and Sergeant Berkholtz's endless training exercises, rehearsing simulated combat until responses burned into muscle memory. Pearson knows full well the cost of war but he'd go right back without hesitation. If only they'd take him.

What he really misses is being part of something bigger than himself. The importance of it all. He misses *mattering*. Now, if he oversleeps—or doesn't get up at all—no one gives a shit. *He* certainly doesn't. But in Afghanistan, every moment and every action mattered.

Most combat patrols were uneventful but nerve-wracking. Setting out on missions, they shed nonessential gear like MREs and ponchos, wedding rings and pictures of home. They only brought items that harmed or healed. Weapons, ammo, Kevlar vests, aid kits. Whenever contact occurred, after the confusing rush of battle was over, each safe return to their compound became a celebration. The thrill of survival coursed through their veins, each soldier feeling more alive than ever before.

When you're part of the pack, you're invincible; but when you're cast off, you're like those pieces of discarded equipment, unnecessary, unwanted. As the machine keeps churning without pause, without even hiccupping from your absence, the feeling of inconsequence wells in your chest like a black hole. It's an emptiness Pearson knows well. The feeling of zero. Immaterial as smoke from a fire.

The boys in the culvert haven't noticed Pearson yet. He's still as a sniper, hidden in the five o'clock shade hanging off the back of his trailer. On days when he walks out to the mailboxes nailed to the split rail fence at the trailer park entrance, the kids stop dribbling as he passes the basketball courts. They lean toward each other with jokes and laughter, and though he can never hear their words, he imagines it's something about him being half human. The kind of thing he and his own jackass friends might have said at that age.

Pearson tosses his empty beer bottle into the wheeled trash can. It clatters, and the boys look over. A short kid named Darrell points in Pearson's general direction. He says something and the others chuckle. This time Pearson doesn't ignore it. He acts like a monkey, hopping up and down, grunting and scratching his head and under his arms.

The kids stare. Then they make a point of ignoring him, going back to their skateboard tricks. After a few minutes, Darrell face-plants on the cement to a chorus of jeers. Pearson stands up and claps, and the kids all quiet down again. As they glare at him, Pearson forms a gun with his forefinger. Then he cocks his thumb and fires.

BAD BEAT

Pearson is coming back from a late-night gaming trip, his first in a week. The tires of his Silverado crunch along the gravel road that winds a loop through his trailer park. When the car's headlights splash across his home, he slams the brakes.

Spray-painted in bright orange across the front of his trailer is one word: *Freakenstein.*

He slams the car in park and jumps out without turning the engine off. The trailer's front door is ajar, the jamb buckled in several places. Being all too familiar with forced entries, he recognizes the work of a crowbar.

He rushes inside and flips the switch for the overhead light, but the bulb has been smashed. Even in the gloom, he can tell the place is a wreck. He goes to the kitchen and tries that switch. No luck there, either. Then he opens the fridge and the spilling light throws tall shadows across the living room. Everything that once stood on the counter or was shelved in the wall unit is now strewn about the floor along with clothes from his bedroom and spooled-out ribbons from VHS tapes. Food from the kitchen is smeared on the walls. The TV screen is spiderwebbed. The table lamp and a handful of dishes are smashed. The couch is sopping from an emptied gallon of milk.

Eyeing the mess, he fixes on one item: the 40" × 30" framed print of Pearson with his squad. Back when Pearson had been whole. Back when he'd had purpose. Now, the picture is torn, a long slash decapitating his buddies, a flap of canvas drooping from the frame like a dog's ear.

Pearson races out to his car and pops the trunk. He roots through a go bag packed with cash, MREs, and survivalist gear. He pulls out a rubber-banded pack of zip ties and looks for a weapon. He'd left the Beretta in his sock drawer before tonight's trip—gone now, he's sure—so he settles on a folding knife with a four-inch blade.

Then he's running down the road toward Darrell's home. The front is dark except for the blue light from a television dancing in a curtained window. Pearson bounds up the wooden steps and yanks the storm door. He pauses long enough to think, *Maybe the kid didn't do it.* Then he shakes it off. He's in the zone, operating on instinct. He kicks the door with a pent-up force that has been building inside of him for the past year.

Rocketing inside, he launches himself at Darrell's father, a beer-gutted man in boxers and a wifebeater whose only reaction is to scream and stand halfway up from his recliner. They tumble over along with the chair, and Pearson quickly has the man face down on the carpet. He flex-cuffs one wrist, then the other, and as he's cuffing a link between them, the man shouts, *Jesus! Take whatever you want!*

A light snaps on and Darrell appears from the hall. *Get off!* he yells. He's holding Pearson's gun in front of him in a shaky, two-handed grip.

Pearson looks over his shoulder and smiles. When he lets go of his prisoner and stands, the father squirms sideways and rolls over, catching sight of his son. *You little shit,* he says. *What have you done now?*

Darrell's eyes flick toward his father and Pearson notes the contemptuous tic. Pearson steps forward and Darrell yells, *Stop. I'll shoot. I swear.*

I'm sure you will, Pearson says as he keeps coming.

Darrell takes a half step back, his eyes wide. *I mean it!*

Pearson lunges forward at an angle and loops back to grab the kid's wrist, pushing the muzzle away. The gun goes off, blasting a hole in the television, stifling Jerry Springer and his angry studio mob.

Wrestling the gun free, Pearson straight-arms the kid against the wall. He reads Darrell's face. Defiance. Hate. All things he's seen before. Pearson points the gun at his chest, and the expression turns to fear. That, also, is nothing new.

The father starts to rise awkwardly from the floor. *You*

stupid little shit! Look what you've done to my TV. He falls back in a heap.

The fear in Darrell's face morphs into a hateful resignation. It's a look that tugs at Pearson's memory, but from long before the Army. Pearson pockets his weapon and signals Darrell to stay put. All the fight seems gone from the kid. Turning to scan the living room, Pearson steps over toward a beige love seat beside the knocked-over recliner. The love seat's fabric is faded through in spots, but it's in better shape than his milk-soured sofa. He leans over the padded arm and knocks the remnants of a Hungry-Man dinner from the cushions onto the floor. *Okay, kid, come here.*

Darrell steps forward and stands with his arms crossed.

Well, go on, Pearson says. *Grab a side.*

BETTING ON THE COME

After the adrenaline ebbs, Pearson sleeps better than he has in a long time. It's still dark when he wakes. Thrashers and sparrows have just begun their predawn chorus from the sagebrush outside. Pouring himself a bowl of Apple Jacks, he settles into his new love seat, propping his booted feet on the coffee table. The floor sparkles with smashed glass so the boots are a necessity. He'll be wearing them until the kid comes to clean it up this morning. *If* he shows.

Last night, it seemed like Darrell took Pearson's threat to call the police seriously. But now, after a night to think on it, the kid might reconsider. He might realize Pearson would have even more to lose from that phone call.

Whether the kid shows or not, the thought of it is enough to make Pearson smile. He plans in intricate detail the many ways he'll make the experience as shitty as possible. Just like boot camp. Except this time *he's* the drill instructor, not the buzz-cut private. He pictures the kid scrubbing until his joints are sore, then scrubbing again after Pearson inspects his work and says, *Not good enough.* The cereal grows soggy as he daydreams. He's giddy by the time a knock on the door pulls him from his reverie. But his joy dies when Darrell steps inside.

The left side of Darrell's face is purple and swollen so fat his eye is a slit. Bruises stand out on his arm and neck as well. He shuffles toward Pearson with his hands in his sagging shorts. Hard to read his puffy face, but a kindergartener could understand his dare-you-to-say-something stance.

Hefty bags on the counter, Pearson says. *Broom and dustpan in the slot by the fridge.* Then he turns his attention back to his bowl and scoops another spoonful in his mouth.

As the kid cleans up the wreckage, Pearson aims for nonchalance, flipping through a copy of *Card Player* magazine. The boy never bitches, never slacks off. Whenever he seems unsure where to put something, Pearson interjects. *Stack those on the counter. Put that on the shelf.* When Darrell cuts his hand on some glass, he says, *Band-Aids in the medicine cabinet.*

Once the trash is picked up and everything in its place, he says, *Vacuum is in the bedroom.* And when the vacuuming is done, he says, *Okay, kid, time to head to the store.*

My name's not kid. It's—

I know what it is. Get in the truck.

They drive to Lowe's, and Darrell pushes a long dolly through the store. Pearson leads him to the paint section and loads the dolly with brushes, an electric paint sprayer, paint guards, masking tape, and a power-wash hose adapter. Beside the rows of five-gallon cans is a rack of color swatches. *New start deserves a new color,* Pearson says, *don't you think?*

Darrell shrugs.

You're the one who's gonna paint my trailer, you should pick the color. Something that'll stand out from everything else in the park.

Darrell looks sideways at him, trying to decide if he's having him on. Then he scans the rack's gradations of hue and steps over to the purple section, judging the colors carefully. After a few moments, he nods to himself before pulling one out. *Here.*

Pearson reads the name on the swatch: FEATHER FALLS. *You think my trailer should be purple?*

Darrell shrugs.

Uh-uh. I need more than that. What's special about this color?

Again with the sideways glance. Then Darrell mumbles, *Was my mom's favorite color. Made her think of grapes.*

Pearson has never seen Darrell's mom or any other woman at their trailer. He wonders what happened, why she's gone, but knows better than to ask. *Grapes,* he says. Then he flicks the swatch with his fingernail. *All right then.*

THE FLOP

Darrell power-washes the trailer while Pearson spreads a sheet over the balding yard and sets up the electric paint sprayer, squinting as he reads the tiny print on the folded sheet of directions. By the time Darrell finishes, Pearson has lubed and primed the sprayer and dipped the siphon hose into a fresh bucket of paint.

When Darrell hands him the garden hose, Pearson threads the gun tip onto its nozzle and points it into an empty bucket, readying to prime the line with paint. As he turns the machine on and squeezes the gun handle, a gush of water ricochets from the bucket up into his face, nearly knocking him over. *Whoa, wasn't expecting that.* He looks at the kid, whose bruised face momentarily splits with a gap-toothed grin before he winces and brings a hand to his cheek.

Pearson spreads his feet in a shooter's stance and squeezes the handle again, ready for the hose to buck, but a smooth stream of paint flows out. After he screws on the tip and tip housing, paint sprays out in a five-inch band.

It takes nine gallons of the extreme-weather paint-and-primer to cover the aluminum exterior. They split the duties, Pearson spraying while Darrell holds the cardboard paint guard, then swapping positions every half hour. They paint everything but the windows and frames, from the rusted bottom edge to the cracked gutters.

They finish up at dusk and stand in the yard admiring the now-purple trailer. As they do, the background thumping of a basketball stops, and Pearson looks over his shoulder. Out past the old couch, now sagging at the curb, past the line of trailers where finger holes in blinds suddenly snap shut, the neighborhood gang of kids stares back from the basketball court.

Was it just you, Pearson says, *or did those assholes lend a hand?*

Darrell turns away and scoops the hose from the grass, coiling it around his arm.

Yeah, I wouldn't rat on my buddies, either.

DRAWING DEAD

Overnight, Pearson fixes the torn print of his comrades, stitching the canvas together with black silk. When he finishes, a knotted seam curls across the group like a scar. Pearson studies it and decides he likes it even better this way.

Everyone seems so confident in the picture. Jackets loaded down with Kevlar plates. Tinted goggles strapped to their helmets. Weapons slung across their chests. The picture had been snapped just before they left on patrol, one of a hundred others just like it.

Pearson presses his hand on the print and rubs a slow circle over the surface, knots scraping his palm like the past clawing out of a grave. His gaze stops on his buddy, Tariq Jackson. Jackson had died in the same blast that minced Pearson's face. Knocked unconscious and not waking until days later in a hospital, he'd never seen Jackson's body. But that doesn't stop him from imagining it.

A thousand times he's envisioned the tattered corpse lying in the sand. Now though, he thinks of a time when Jackson was alive and their squad paused near a line of street vendors hawking flatbread and pirated CDs. Jackson bought two stacks of bread and passed them out to some emaciated kids playing soccer with an empty soda can in the middle of the street. When the patrol started to move on, the kids ran over to the vendor and sold the bread back at half price. The whole squad hooted with laughter, even Jackson, who took their ribbing good-naturedly as they marched off into the desert beneath a sky so blue it seemed to stretch forever.

CHECKING BLIND

The following day Darrell doesn't arrive until 9 a.m., giving Pearson time to look up trim-painting tutorials on YouTube. The research reminds him of the way Berkholtz assigned the role of instructor to the person who knew the least about a particular subject, forcing him to become an expert to avoid embarrassing himself in front of the squad.

The splattered sheet from yesterday is spread on the lawn by the time Darrell arrives with a pillowcase slung over his shoulder.

He sets it down on the sheet and Pearson roots through it, pulling out his laptop, a pair of Nike cross-trainers, and a dozen green boxes, each containing an Army medal.

Pearson looks at the returned booty and raises an eyebrow.

Darrell toes the grass and mumbles into his chest. *Rounded 'em up last night.*

Pearson is itching to ask which of Darrell's friends took what, why they bothered with his medals, what the fuck they were thinking. But then he remembers his own dad, the way he made him feel smaller than a bug. He stuffs the items back in the pillowcase and sets it aside. Then he points at the paint cans. *Why don't you pop the top on those and I'll show you what to do with this masking tape.*

Once the kid has the hang of it, Pearson gets out of his hair. Inside, he leans back in his love seat while the 2004 World Series of Poker plays on the new flat screen he bought last night. In 2004, Greg Raymer won the Main Event wearing a pair of holographic sunglasses that befuddled opponents trying to read his face. Pearson seems dazed, too, not really seeing the cards, the bluffs, the bad beats. He's looking through the screen at his childhood, Mom locked in the bathroom, Dad pounding on the door, wasted on Jack Daniel's, pounding until she let him in or he tired of it and turned his attention on his son.

His thoughts skip from his biological family to the one he'd joined. The soldiers in his team were his brothers in every sense but blood. Upon discharge, the only question his father had asked was what kind of pension he was going to get. When Pearson revealed how small it would be, his dad said he didn't think there was space for him at home. Not that Pearson would have ever moved back in.

When the poker tape ends and static fills the screen, Pearson doesn't even notice.

VALUE BET

Pearson's finger hovers over his mouse. The World Series isn't for another month, but a ten-thousand-dollar seat to the Main Event is just a click away. He's got plenty of cash stashed away, more than enough for the ticket and a hotel room for the full week. Enough to buy a new suit for each day he plans to be there. Maybe even a purple suit for the finals, something that says, *I'm done lurking in shadows.*

He thinks about Ruby, how she made him feel whole one minute, eviscerated the next. That had been a couple of weeks ago, but it seems like a year. That night, when the loudmouth in the tracksuit had been beaten down, Pearson had thought, *You got to know when it's time to leave.* He smiles. "Leaving" has a whole new meaning now.

Pearson wonders if, like Tracksuit, he's letting emotion get the better of him. No, it doesn't seem that way. This isn't a rash reaction. It's a sense of peace. He clicks the mouse and a confirmation number pops up on screen. Above that is a single word: *Congratulations!*

TURN AND BURN

Life can turn on a single moment—experience has taught Pearson this lesson over and over. The enlistment papers he signed, marking the end of boyhood. The bomb blast that shredded his face. The cold, hard truth of Ruby's flattened mouth. Every turn has taught him that as bad as things might be, they could always get worse.

Which is why last night felt so strange, the hopeful flutter in a stomach used to acid. *Congratulations* tinged everything he touched, every place he looked. And the sensation didn't diminish when he woke. It might even be stronger now in the light of day.

Pearson is done being the hard-ass. When Darrell comes over this morning, he'll free the kid from his remaining obligation. All that's left anyway is spot cleaning and replacing broken items. He can take care of that on his own.

But life isn't done with its surprises. When Darrell shows up, he's clutching a trifold pamphlet that Pearson recognizes. On the front is a bearded man in a top hat, the words WE WANT YOU stamped above his head in bold print.

Pearson feels the world tilting on its axis. Years ago, when his mother had dropped him at the bus station to go to boot camp, she'd been sobbing. He kept telling her not to cry, that this was a moment to celebrate. *I can be proud and sad at the same time,* she'd said. Now, he finally gets it.

Like to ask you something, Darrell says, holding out the glossy pamphlet.

Later, Pearson says. *We got work to do.*

He drives them to the Pomona Walmart to buy replacements for all his destroyed items. When they get there, Pearson gives Darrell a legal pad and tells him to tally the prices. *Ten bucks an hour sounds fair for the work you're doing. This'll show us how much time you owe me.*

Each time Pearson pulls another item from a shelf, he checks with Darrell to see if he agrees it's a fair substitute. *Don't want you to think I'm cheating you.* Occasionally, he points out a row of housewares and tells Darrell to pick out which lamp, mirror, clock, or set of dishes he should buy. Darrell checks prices and lingers over the cheapest ones, but never puts them in the cart. Same for the most expensive.

Now, with the new purchases loaded into the Silverado,

Darrell studies the pad in his lap, looking over each item. And its cost. *Why didn't we just use the total?*

Uh-uh, Pearson says. *Everything has a cost. Sooner you learn that, the better.*

Darrell returns his attention to the pad, calculating hours in his head. Thirty dollars for the Better Homes and Garden lamp—three hours work; fifteen dollars for the Mainstays shower curtain—an hour and a half.

Forgot one thing, Pearson adds. *The TV I bought the other day was a hundred and eighty dollars.*

Darrell squeezes the edges of the pad as if trying to rip it in two. Then he plucks a pen from the center console and adds the television to the list.

ALL IN

Where we going now? Darrell asks.

It's a surprise, says Pearson.

I'll bet.

Darrell is still sulking from yesterday's shopping trip, the accounting of debits in his ledger. When Pearson pulls his truck into a strip mall and parks in front of a Mexican restaurant, Darrell asks, *Gonna make me pay for this, too?*

Pearson laughs. *Got any money on you?*

He shakes his head.

All right then.

Pearson shuts off the engine and opens his door, but Darrell doesn't budge. He squints at Pearson like he's reading fine print on a warranty. The bruise on his cheek has darkened to tar black, but the puffiness is gone and Pearson can read the mistrust written on his face.

Christ's sake, Pearson says, *it's no trick. Lunch is on me.*

They're quiet in the booth, Pearson eating his chicken and sausage paella bowl, Darrell, two shrimp avocado tacos. When Darrell finishes, he turns sideways in the booth, staring out at the parking lot and absently touching his bruised cheek.

It won't always be like this, Pearson says. *You'll get away from him soon enough. A new beginning is out there waiting on you to come round.*

The fuck you know about it.

Pearson looks down into his paella and sighs. His voice, when he speaks, is somber. *When I was a kid, I'd lie awake at night listening for my dad to drop off to sleep. I kept imagining all the things I could do to make sure he never woke up again. Poison in his Jack. Cut his throat. A hammer to his head. But I never did any of it, never lifted a finger. Just took it and took it, till one day I escaped.*

Pearson knuckles the brimming tears from his eyes and wipes streaks across the thighs of his jeans. *I never figured out how you can hate someone so much and still love them.* Gathering himself together, he slips a hand into his jacket pocket. What comes out is a key chain with a single house key fastened to its loop. He sets it on the table between them.

What's this? Darrell says.

Just want you to know you got options. The Army's not your only way out.

What, like you gonna be my new daddy now?

No, you're stuck with that son of a bitch for life.

So what then?

Like I said, just giving you options. You want a safe place to call home, you got it. You want something else—Pearson hooks a thumb over his shoulder—*recruiting station's two doors down.*

Darrell looks out the window and his face takes on the same

contemplative cast from the paint aisle. *Thought you were taking off for Vegas.*

I can go another time.

Pearson shovels another spoonful of paella in his mouth and chews slowly, as if luxuriating over the taste. He feels like one of those players in the poker videos trying hard to disguise what's truly burning inside. He wants to jump up, shake Darrell about, and yell, *Come to your senses.* But he just keeps chewing.

The kid nods to himself and slides out of the booth, his decision made. *Nah, man, go to Vegas. Don't put it off any longer.*

Pearson looks up at the kid, feeling, like his mother, proud and sad at the same time. *You want, I can go in there with you, make sure the recruiter's not feeding you a line of bullshit.*

Darrell shakes his head. *Uh-uh. I got this.*

He walks out the door and Pearson watches, ready to nod encouragement. But Darrell never looks back, striding out of view like all boys eager to become men. And Pearson, no longer hungry, stares at the glass door and everything beyond. Nothing left to do but wait.

Replacements

They come when soldiers fall, when the ones you've trained, fought, and bled beside no longer breathe. They come to fill holes before emptiness becomes desolation. They come to occupy vacancies in squads before squadmates can think too long, before grief rises from its pine box. They come to seal the gap with putty and Spackle, to slather fresh paint to convince you the gap never existed. They come to remove the pall and restore weightlessness to the squad. They step onto one side of a scale, a counterbalance to the anchor in the other dish, which refuses to rise off the ground. They come and step in line so the unit can march on. Everyone has a job to do. One stenciled name on a footlocker is as good as another. The roaring machine must churn.

They come, at first, to Fort Benning, home of the infantry, a word derived from the Latinate "infant," a clue that soldiers are little more than children turned to men too soon. Teenagers when they come, smooth-faced youths fresh from high school, from football fields and proms, from fumbling attempts in back seats to prove their manhood. Zahn with his hard fists and quick temper. Tefertiller with his map of the constellations folded up in a square and shoved in his pocket. Trawick with a chip on his shoulder the size of the trailer park he left behind. They come to the hard clay of Georgia where drill instructors in brown rounds scrub away individuality. They come and learn how to take apart a weapon, how to hide in the mud, how to dig a hole and crawl inside like returning to the womb. Mostly, though, they come to kill, to feed that base impulse, the fight-or-flight instinct passed down through generations of men thirsting for others' blood. They come to learn how to shoot, how to stab, how to silence breath with bare hands.

They come with swagger and confidence in jeans and shaggy haircuts. They come from Maryland and Texas and Alaska. They come from subdivisions and urban projects. They come with high school diplomas or GEDs. They come with black and brown and white skin but leave wearing green.

They come to new units in clean uniforms with ironed creases, faces hopeful as lilies turned to sun. Names printed atop orders, stenciled on duffel bags, stamped on dog tags. They sew patches on shoulders and stab into their chests unit citations proclaiming past glories. They come to dress-right-dress, to stand at attention, to vacuum up the voids in formations.

They try to share their stories, the reasons why they came. Zahn seeking a useful purpose for his anger. Trawick earning the respect of the scar-faced man who'd urged him to sign up. Tefertiller wanting to find his place in the universe. But no one seems to care, not these men with combat patches and hollow eyes. They've come, and that's all that matters. Not the reason, not their pedigree, not even the names stitched in black thread on their chests. A person can be loved and grieved, but a serial number is just a number, digits not much different from those before or after.

They come to understand their role as spare parts, like tie-rods and nylon strapping, like butt springs and handguards, like Corcoran boots and bloused ACUs. They come and bide their time. They deploy and drive trash-littered streets like moving targets on a range. They kick down doors and zip-tie the hands of men, women, and children behind their backs. They search for weapon caches that rarely hide where Intel predicts. They fight and kill as they've been trained to do. They stop thinking so much. They act on instinct. They core out their hearts and come home changed. Or else, like those before, they die and are briefly memorialized. Until others come to take their place.

Even after war, after rotating Stateside to families, to girl-friends, to barracks or apartments, even then, more replacements come. They come when others process out. They come when others get promoted or transfer to different units. They come when others retire or simply tire out. They come when others swallow muzzles and pull triggers. Like the wind scrubbing away history of all that's come before, like the ceaseless rising of the sun, like the endless spinning of the Earth beneath our feet, they come, and they come, and they come.

Dog Is Not a Palindrome

THE BLEEDING EARTH

The rottweiler snarls at the end of its chain as soon as the backhoe arrives. Two hours later, it's still barking, disrupting the harmony of this otherwise quiet subdivision of Colonials, Georgians, and Regencies where every yard is pristine and professionally landscaped. Tied to a tree two houses down from the pool dig, it strains against its bonds and snaps the air as silvery ropes of drool shake free from its mouth.

The backhoe has already dug the shallow end and is working on the deep. Dave, the crew boss and owner of Crystal Pools, stands at the edge of the pit and spits in the hole. Looking over at the dog, he says, *Wish someone would shut that bitch up.*

Love to, says Zay. Five feet seven and wiry, he holds his shovel like a baseball bat and chops the air, halting midswing and vibrating his arms as if connecting with something solid. *Bong, out like a light.*

Sick, Curt says.

That's why you love me.

Cut the grab ass, Dave says. A former wrestler who used to jog in a sauna suit to shed pounds and make weight, Dave now has a paunch that rolls thick over his belt. In their three-man crew, only Curt and Zay are lean from hard effort. Dave doesn't labor until the floor is being poured and all hands are needed to race the concrete before it sets. Otherwise, he's reading instruments, chatting up the customer, or driving off in the truck to *see to other business*. Stepping down into the shallow end, he sets up a tripod-mounted level to take elevation readings.

In the deep end, Curt stands dangerously close to the toothy bucket as it carves out plugs of earth the size of a washing machine. A veteran of five combat tours, he doesn't scare easily. Waving for the operator to pause, Curt sets a ten-foot rod on the lowest point of the scraped earth. The pole is marked like a ruler with sixteenth-inch hashes.

Dave peers through the level's eyepiece and uses hand signals to show how much needs to come out. He holds up five fingers, drops them, and then makes a slashing motion across his index finger. Five and a half inches to go.

The pool's low point, the hopper, needs to be eight and a half feet deep. Whatever earth the backhoe doesn't remove, the crew must shave off with shovels; whatever extra the backhoe cuts away, the crew must backfill and tamp down. Each inch removed by the big bucket would take a half hour of hard digging for the crew.

Getting the closest dig out of the backhoe is an art form. Now that they're close to target depth, Curt signals the backhoe to cut long, thin slices from the bottom, then steps back to watch. The ground is blue marl, a lime-rich sediment whose crumbly texture near the surface becomes more like hard-packed clay the deeper they dig. All the while, the dog keeps barking. Just like the wild dogs that scavenged the littered streets of Tikrit.

These days, Curt tries not to think about war. The IEDs, the shredded bodies, the sudden firefights clapping away silence and leaving ears ringing for hours. All that death and ruin are locked in a strongbox deep in his mind. But with the dog's incessant barking, the box cracks its lid. The gouged-out hole resembling a bomb crater, the rumble of the backhoe like a Humvee's diesel roar, the smell of oil and gas like the lingering odors of a firefight—it all combines to send him back to the days of sand and blood.

He remembers the raid where they waded through a sewer line to approach their target house undetected. But the wild dogs weren't fooled. They howled the squad's approach better than an early warning system. An AK opened fire, tracers splitting the night like lasers, and everyone dove for cover in the shit-filled ditch. The LT had come along that mission, and he was all kinds of pissed after submerging himself in sewage. After that, it was open season on dogs. Patrols hunted them down and soldiers made necklaces from their teeth.

As the backhoe makes a thin pass on the ground, clay slices off like cheese from a grater, spooling into the bucket in long curls. The earth has become soft and pliable, gleaming with a sloppy slickness. Curt signals the backhoe to halt and he yells to Dave, *Looks like the water table.*

The last breach had cost three extra days. Without compensation, since Dave pays the crew by the job, not the hour. Great money when all goes well. A goose egg when it doesn't. It normally takes four days to put an in-ground pool *in the ground.* Dig Day, when the hole is dug; Footer Day, when a cement truck pours its mix down a long chute into the trench surrounding the pool walls; Floor Day, when the concrete floor is poured and smoothed; and Liner Day, when the vinyl liner is snapped into the walls and trapped air suctioned out with a vacuum. Soon as that's done, a running hose is dropped into the pool. Four days, start to end. Homeowners never believe it when the crew marks the pool's outline in the grass. *Four days?* they say. *Impossible.* On day four, they're standing with their mouths agape as the pool slowly fills.

The money is the best that Curt and Zay have ever seen. Still, when something goes wrong and they have to eat a day or two, Zay bitches nonstop about the arrangement, how unfair and lopsided it seems, how the Man is always sticking it to the little guy, and how they need to shove it right up the Man's ass.

Dave stares into the hole, tugging on his thick blond moustache. *What you want me to say,* he yells at Curt. *We got to make depth.* He makes a rolling gesture and the backhoe revs up with a belch of black smoke, stretching out its long yellow arm.

The bucket scrapes the ground again and water bubbles up like a sucking chest wound. Down in the pit, soft clay and blue marl transform into mucky swamp.

Shit, says Dave, his hand dropping from his moustache. *You guys stay with this. I'll go get us some rock.*

As Dave drives off and the backhoe shuts down, the barking seems louder than ever.

VANDALS

Zay steers the work truck aimlessly through quiet subdivisions as dusk creeps into the sky and crickets fill the warm air with chirping. Fog is rolling in from the shore, blanketing Virginia Beach in its haze. *Ain't fair,* Zay says. *We're stuck in that hole shoveling slop and Dave's driving around in air-conditioning.* He slaps the steering wheel with the heel of his hand. *Ain't fair.*

When they'd dropped Dave at his house, he'd told Zay and Curt to hang on to the truck and go to the site without him tomorrow. *Rock'll be there at noon. You guys know what to do.* Zay has been fuming ever since, ranting and banging the wheel. Curt could talk him down—nothing he hasn't done before—but the barking echo in his head has him feeling fractious as well. Instead of offering comfort, he pokes what he knows to be a tender spot. *Sure, Dave could've been driving around in air-conditioning. Could've also been at the club.*

Six months ago, Dave took the crew to a strip club for a long lunch break. They ate barbeque sandwiches washed down with tap beer and watched bored women shake their tits on stage. *My treat,* Dave said, paying the tab and handing Zay a fistful of ones to stick in the strippers' G-strings. From then on, whenever Dave drove away from the work site, all it took was the slightest nudge for Zay to be certain Dave was headed to the club.

Damn straight. Dave was hanging with the honeys while we were busting our asses. Just ain't fair. He grabs the 40 of King Cobra in a paper bag between his knees and takes a slug. *Should fuck his truck up. That'll show him.*

Sure, sure, Curt says. *Least wait till I'm out of it.* He sips from his own 40 as Zay exits suburbia and aims toward downtown. Curt knows what's coming. They'll keep cruising and looking for trouble, slowing for any rowdies with a swagger in their step. Then Zay will lean out the window and yell, *The fuck you looking at.* If they respond in any way other than backing down, it's go time. Curt and Zay will jump from the truck and charge into God knows what. "Head hunting" is what they call it. Cracking skulls or getting theirs cracked—either is fine with Curt as long as it shuts up the dog.

Before the Army, Curt avoided embrace; now he's a junkie, addicted to the almost orgiastic pleasure that comes from a good beatdown, the purge of built-up tension, the euphoria that immediately follows, and the liberating sense of calm that comes on slowly after that. Most nights, he paces through his apartment with dread pumping through his veins, but brawling helps bleed it off and give him a good night's sleep.

He's not sure what Zay gets from their head-hunting sessions, but he suspects it has something to do with family history, early abuses that left him looking to even the score as a man. They never talk about things like that, but sometimes he'll tighten up when he sees a dad horsing around with his kids. *They don't know how lucky they got it,* he'll grumble; other times he won't say anything, just stare right through them with his face gone slack.

One time, while Zay was shopping at the 7-Eleven, Curt waited out in his Jeep, nodding along to Tim McGraw on the radio. Just as Zay came strolling out with a couple of 40s, some guy at the pumps leaned in through the back window of his car and smacked his son on the head, yelling at him, *Because I said so, that's why.* Zay shot toward him like a rodeo bull loosed into the ring. He swung the plastic bag of beers like a flail against the man's head, knocking him to the ground. The man cowered as Zay screamed for him to get up. *How 'bout picking on someone your own size.* When Zay came back to the Jeep, his face was slick with tears.

Curt doesn't know which of them is more fucked up. All he knows is that even if he and Zay didn't work together, they would've gravitated toward each other like two black holes swallowing up and destroying every bright star around them.

Zay coasts down Lynnhaven Parkway, cruising past an Olive Garden, TGI Fridays, and other family-friendly establishments whose neon signs blaze through the fog like a string of lighthouses. A half mile farther, he reaches the lesser lights of LoanMax Title Loans and a host of pawnshops with barred windows. Nothing offers relief for their combative urges. It's Tuesday night, and no one's hanging on the corners. Even if they were, neither of them can see well enough through the thick soup to tell.

They continue past a series of low, clustered row houses, and then a monolithic structure materializes from the mist like a creature from a horror movie. Gothic spires and turrets appear first, then a massive oak door fit for a castle. Our Lady of Charity Catholic Church. Curt has been here once before and now the hairs on the back of his neck stand on end. *Hold up,* he says, and Zay pulls to the curb.

In his youth, Curt had been a true believer. Church every Sunday, religious retreats in the summer, prayers before every meal and each night before bed. In the Army, he never pushed his beliefs on others, but he attended worship circles, wore a cross taped to his dog tags, and carried an extra pocket Bible for any comrade who needed one. Then came the wars, and life stopped seeming so sacred. In witnessing the many ways a body tears apart, he lost his sense of wonder. It seemed ridiculous to believe an invisible soul piloted our movements. A more likely explanation was that each Earthly form was animated meat in search of a bullet.

The first time he'd seen Our Lady of Charity, the grand façade stirred memories that tugged like a fishhook in his brain. He'd stepped inside and slipped into a back pew, unprepared for the shock to follow. The priest was the same one from Curt's former church. Seeing Father Tony had been like a sign from God. But as the priest offered up a sermon that had galvanized Curt's childhood faith, the story of Jesus multiplying fish for the masses, Curt now listened with the ears of a cynic. He saw the miraculous story as a fabrication packaged with a good moral and delivered as fact. The epiphany sparked something inside that threatened to burn the whole damn church to the ground. The fire still burns within him. Turning to Zay, he says, *Grab the ladder and follow me.*

As Zay unlashes the telescoping ladder from the roof rack, Curt roots through the cargo bed for the orange spray paint. It's what they use to mark the grass and show the backhoe where to dig. Once he finds the can, he strides up the wide steps, Zay following without question, the ladder under his arm. *Set it up there*, Curt says, pointing to the wall beside the door.

Zay plants its feet on the ground and pulls the extension rope, closing the lock bar when the ladder reaches its full height. Then he leans it against the wall and holds it steady. *Want to tell me what's up.* When Curt does, Zay says, *Fuckin' A. I love it.*

Curt climbs to the third rung from the top and stretches out to the left. He begins spraying his three-word message, inching back to the center and then leaning as far as he can to the right for the final letter. Back on the ground, he stands next to Zay and admires his handiwork. Above the great door in letters four feet tall is the accusation: *LIARS AND RAPISTS.*

PURGATORY

On the drive home, they're flying high, stratospheric. Curt, so often quiet, hangs out the window and howls into the fog-shrouded night, *That's what you get! That's what you get!*

Too soon, Curt's adrenaline ebbs and thrumming blood settles into the calm pump of habit. Then comes the inevitable drop, the plunge from peak to valley, the approach of all-encompassing black. Shapes loom out of the fog and fall away. Zay is lead-footing it and Curt wonders, without really caring, what it would be like to smash headlong into something solid.

Only thing would've been better, Zay says, *is if we'd hung around for the fog to burn off, you know, just waiting for all the looky-loos to check out what we done.*

Yeah, would've been something.

I mean, just picture it. All them holier-than-thou churchgoers trying to apologize for those kiddie fuckers. "Oh, we never knew, we never knew." Ha. Just picture it.

Curt *did* picture it. He could think of little else but the predictable consequence of their actions. The fog would indeed burn off. Crowds would gather. And his painted words would draw blood. News would spread and people would come, regarding the ornate building through slit eyes, imagining what depravities might be going on beyond its gilded gates.

When Curt had climbed the ladder, his only thought had been to paint *LIARS* on the wall. But as Zay held the ladder, propping him up in more ways than one, he'd added *RAPISTS* to lash out against his friend's demons as well. Not that it mattered. With sex abuse rampant in the Catholic world, *LIARS* would have drawn the same conclusion—that this church harbored another fallen angel, a sinner of the most grievous sort, a shepherd who abused his flock.

Curt knows differently. When Curt had been an altar boy, Father Tony had been kind and caring. His virtuous example made Curt eager to kneel before God and offer up all that he was and all that he ever would be. *That* is what Curt meant to attack, the lie of organized religion, the assurance that good deeds beget good results, the promise that the meek will inherit the Earth.

As they soar through the fog, Curt pictures Father Tony at the center of the angry crowd, the mob tightening around him like a noose as he denies the spray-painted words, orange as the purifying flames of purgatory. And all the while, like a soundtrack accompanying his inner thoughts, the dog keeps barking.

STEAK AND STEEL

In his apartment, Curt changes into a terry-cloth robe. Usually a shorts and T-shirt guy, tonight he needs the robe's deep pockets. Tucked into one of them is a snub-nose .38, its weight a comfort against his leg. At any moment, if he feels the need to shoot something, all he has to do is reach into that pocket and squeeze.

Even caressing the revolver is reassuring. The finger-grooved grip. The short, firm barrel. The cylinder's five furrows notched in steel skin. The hard-edged hammer jutting out like a thorn. And the trigger with its slight give, as if aching for a curled finger. His other gun, a .308 Winchester, is stowed in the bedroom closet. Something to hunt deer. The pistol is for game of a different sort.

Curt itches to pull the trigger. He tries to blank the thought from his mind as he shuffles in circles around his apartment, through the tiny living room, hallway, kitchen, and back again. Shuffle, shuffle, the growling dog following one step behind.

Stopping at the sink, he runs hot water, then centers the handle and plugs the drain. From the freezer he takes the rib eye he'd been saving for the weekend and drops the frozen steak into the flowing water. Soon it's floating in a warm bath. At least a couple of hours to defrost, Curt figures, so he shuts off the water and resumes his shuffling course.

Curt is a dog guy. Loves them all, especially the big ones, the ones you can roll around on the ground with and wrestle. Before his commander's edict, Curt used to dump out MRE pouches for the pack of mongrels shadowing their squad's movements. But that was nothing compared to Tefertiller. Tee was a nerdy guy, a replacement who joined the platoon after Jackson died in Afghanistan. A whiz with the radio. And with dogs. Every day, he fed this one mongrel with a scarred face and fur matted in clumps, and the wild dog came closer each time. Finally, Tee rigged a trap using a poncho liner as a net over an open pack of beef slices. Everyone laughed at the Wile E. Coyote trap, but it worked. At first. When Tee pulled the squirming dog out of the liner, he wore leather gloves to protect his hands and spoke in a calm, reassuring voice. But soon as the dog's head was free, it clamped onto Tee's calf and tore out a chunk. Ran away and never came close again.

Years ago, Sunday school teachers told Curt that dogs have no souls. Same thing his commander said. Curt never disagreed, but each time he followed orders and zeroed his reticle on flea-bitten ribs, he always wondered. If any creature possessed a soul, it would be dogs. Obedient, protective, faithful to a fault. Lining up his sights, he'd pause to say, *Forgive me,* under his breath. Even though he'd stopped praying to God for anything by then.

Curt keeps shuffling, caressing the gun in his pocket. He remembers how the squad used to wear flea collars on their ankles to keep sand fleas away. That makes him bark a short laugh. *Not so different from dogs after all,* he thinks.

He shuffles into the bathroom and opens the medicine cabinet. The bottle of Klonopin calls out to him, its blue pills with a K stamped through the middle promising to calm him down. Beside it is the blister pack of Lexapro, its white tablets meant to even things out when his mood hits rock bottom. But both leave him feeling like a passenger in his own body, so he shuts the cabinet and returns to pacing.

This time, as he circles through the living room, he stops

at the coffee table and picks up a glass globe his sister, Darla, made. Called a suncatcher, the globe has thin, green glass with silvery streaks threaded across the surface. She'd explained how she'd spun a molten blob on the end of a long, hollow rod inside a blazing kiln, then blown through the rod and watched glowing mass expand into a bulb. Recounting the experience, her face lit up like a kid at Christmas, and Curt was left wondering why he no longer felt such simple joy.

The globe had been a housewarming gift. It was meant to catch the sun and send green-and-silver sparkles dancing through his apartment. But he never hung it in the window. He set it on the coffee table where it has stayed ever since, something for his eyes to fix on when they tire of sitcoms on TV and his mind aches for the happy home he'd enjoyed as a child.

One day, he went to the studio where she'd made the suncatcher and picked up a pamphlet listing times and prices for glassmaking classes. He never told Darla, even though she'd urged him to give it a go. *It's like therapy without words. Perfect for you.*

Now, dropping onto the couch, he cradles the globe in his calloused hands. His eyes swim through a green ocean that pulls him down, pulls him down, down. When he snaps awake, he's unsure how much time has passed. Returning the globe to its spot, he goes to check the steak. Its sides give a little under his squeezing grip. Firing up the stove, he slaps the rib eye in a pan, shakes salt and pepper over the meat, and waits for it to sizzle.

FEEDING THE DOG

The next morning, it's still dark outside when Zay picks Curt up. They arrive at the work site just as dawn breaks over the horizon, shadows of boxy homes stretched long across the sub-division's quiet street, streamers of mist curling off the grass. Soon as their truck parks at the curb, the dog starts barking.

That bitch again, Zay says. Stumbling out of the truck, he yawns and scratches himself as Curt piles tools in a wheelbar-row. Shovels, a sump pump, a 150-foot extension cord on a reel, a fifty-foot hose fastened in a figure eight, a five-gallon paint bucket, hammers, rebar, a foldable measuring stick, a thick spool of string, two pairs of gum boots, and a rake with thick, sturdy teeth.

All right, Curt says. *I loaded, so you haul, barrow monkey.*

That's Mr. Barrow to you. Zay juts out his chin in mock defiance.

To the untrained eye, the backyard hole is a sloppy mess, but Curt and Zay can visualize the 18' × 36' oval pool it will become. But for now, the pit is a mess, the deep end a murky pond. The hole is wider than the pool's dimensions to allow space for a concrete footer to be poured. The footer will anchor the three-foot liner walls that delineate the water's edge.

There's plenty to do before the load of rock arrives at noon. Zay unspools one end of the hose toward the wood line while Curt attaches the other end to the pump. Curt places the pump carefully in the water before plugging it into the extension cord. The pump hums immediately, and moments later the hose is spewing dirty water into the woods.

Yesterday, they'd run strings in an X across the shallow end to mark its target elevation, showing which humps needed to be shaved down with shovels and which divots needed back-filling. Now they do the same trick over the deep end, except this X hovers five feet above the target depth.

After the water is drained, Curt slogs through the mud and hammers rebar at the four corners of the hopper. The sludge tries to suck the boots off his feet, making his progress slow and laborious. At all four corners, Zay holds the measuring stick against the overhead string and Curt marks the target elevation on the rebar. They connect strings to those marks to create another X. If not for the over-dig, these strings would cross two inches above the ground, the thin strip to be packed with concrete, then smoothed over to make the floor; instead, the gap is ten to twelve inches above the wet ground. By filling this space with rock, the water table can continue to flow without building up to a floor-cracking pressure.

Grabbing shovels, they level the muddy earth by shaving off the high points and packing them into the hollows. Every ten minutes or so, Curt climbs out of the hole and looks over at the rottweiler, still barking like mad. When he finally sees its owner leaving for work in a blue Ford F-150, he tells Zay he needs a short break.

Sounds good to me, Zay says, dropping his shovel in the mud.

Removing a Ziploc from his cooler, Curt marches across the intervening yard, Zay by his side. The sun is still low enough for loblolly pines to throw a blanket of shade over the circle of worn earth surrounding the chained dog. As they approach, its barking heightens to a frantic pitch. Without pause, Curt hops the waist-high, chain-link fence and Zay follows. The barking stops, replaced by a low growl and raised hackles. Eighty pounds of snarl aching to be released.

Stopping on the fringe of grass just short of biting range, Curt squats down and unseals his baggie. Inside is the cooked steak cut into strips. Curt says nothing to the dog, no sing-songy patter, no *Who's a good boy? Who's a good boy?* He just holds out a strip of steak in a gloved hand and inches forward.

The rottweiler can smell the meat, but it seems more intent on the hand holding it and, if it could break its chain, the neck beyond. It launches forward, snapping the air, gobbets of froth on its muzzle.

This close, Curt can see one torn ear and a scar ringing the dog's neck where metal links have rubbed away its short, black hair and chafed the skin. Several spots are wet with blood. And still the dog strains against its chain. And still Curt inches forward. Threat of pain means nothing to either of them.

When snapping teeth find the outstretched meat, jaws clamp tight and shake the strip back and forth in the air. But then the dog is chewing and the meat vanishes. Immediately, the growl returns. Curt pulls out strip after strip, and the rottweiler swallows them begrudgingly, fighting against the offered meat until it is in its mouth and biology takes over.

While he's feeding the dog, Zay is shooting a video on his cell, adding color commentary. *Damn, boy, that bitch nearly got you on that one.* After the last strip is gone, Curt remains in a crouch, one predator taking stock of another. Who knows how long he would've stayed like that if not for Zay.

Holy shit, Zay says, *check this out.*

Curt stands and Zay turns his phone. The screen shows a clip from WAVY TV 10 about last night's graffiti. As the picture zooms in on the church and *LIARS AND RAPISTS* fills the screen, a voiceover remarks, *Vandalism has marred a Virginia Beach church leaving community leaders wondering why.* The reporter's tone clearly states that *he* knows why, and you should, too, but he cannot say so outright. The view cuts away to a plump man in a porkpie hat standing before a crowd of protesters waving signs. *We shall not turn a blind eye*, the man says, his jowls rippling with indignation. *Like any wayward soul, the Church must be held accountable for its sins!*

Dude, we're famous, Zay says, pumping a fist in the air. There's a bounce in his step as he strides across the neighbor's yard, Curt lumbering behind. And as he follows his friend into the pit, the dog resumes barking.

PENANCE

Curt is shuffling through his apartment again, the green ocean in his hands, the dog in his head. Shuffle, shuffle. In his mind, the rottweiler yanks at its chain until one of the links pops free. Then its jaws clamp onto the hand holding out a strip of meat, ripping it off and leaving behind a bloody stump. Curt thinks about how "dog" backwards is "God," and the odd digression almost makes him laugh. Something he so rarely does anymore.

Digging back through time, he searches for the memory of what it was like to be carefree. What he uncovers instead is being a choir boy, wearing the white linen surplice with its square neckline over a long black cassock. In those days, everything was black or white, colored by either blessing or sin. He can picture himself with his hands pressed together in prayer, but he can't remember how it felt to actually *believe*. If only he could grab that scrawny kid by the shoulders and shake some sense into him. *Wake up*, he'd scream in his face. *The world is gray.*

Curt also remembers coming to church the first Sunday after the towers fell. He'd been a teenager and filled with the susceptibility of youth. When light streamed through one of the stained-glass windows, he viewed it as a beam personally directed by God, a divine message instructing him to become a holy soldier. He doesn't want to merely shake this version of himself; he wants to punch him in the face, knock him into the aisle, and kick the stupid out of him.

His minds drifts, transforming his old surplice into one of

the long white thawbs that men wore in Iraq. The way they dressed, the way they bent over rugs to pray—everything about the Middle East made him feel out of place. Returning home was no better; he'd become a stranger in the land of plenty as well. He'd brought back too much from the desert. He was aimless, adrift, except his sea was one of sand.

In Iraq, squadmates in boxy flak jackets used to mock the skinny men in long robes, calling them ragheads and Hajjis. The soldiers wrapped T-shirts around their heads and mimed having sex with goats. Curt never joined in, but he never said anything to stop it, either. Whenever minaret speakers broadcast a muezzin's wails, he'd watch the faithful kneel and press foreheads to unfurled rugs, facing south toward a block-shaped mosque as unyielding as an Abrams tank. He'd lost his own faith by then, but he was still impressed by theirs. He always wondered what Iraqis would think if they visited Fort Bragg during taps or reveille as traffic came to a halt, soldiers standing at attention by their cars, blades of their right hands affixed to brows, spouses and children beside them with palms holding hearts and every devotion that beat within.

WORK RITUAL

By the time the rock arrives, Zay and Curt have set the main drain in the hopper and attached a long PVC pipe to serve as a suction line. They're careful not to jostle the drain out of position when packing rock around it. At the bottom of the drain is a flutter valve. Once the pool is full, water pressure will keep the valve closed. And if the water table's pressure becomes greater than that of the pool, the valve will "flutter" open to allow groundwater to seep through; otherwise, the thin concrete walls would crack.

After packing the rock and raking it flat, they resume their routine, constructing the top portion of the pool's shell, screwing polymer walls together with plastic bolts and adjusting for height. That afternoon, after five cubic yards of concrete is poured into the trench to lock the walls in place, Curt rechecks their elevation and signals Zay to either pound them down with a sledge or lift them up with balsa shims under the bases.

By the time the pool's shell is complete, night is coming on and fireflies are etching the sky with sudden streaks. Zay pulls himself out of the hole and looks over at the dog, curled quietly in sleep. *Thank God,* he says, flopping spread-eagle on the grass.

Curt lies next to him and stares up at the sky.

Zay lights two Marlboros and passes one over. They both take long drags. *Man,* Zay says, *think I'm just going to lie here and wait for the sun to come up. No reason to go home.*

Well, there's one. With Dave taking the truck back, it's your turn to drive tomorrow. Got to pick me up.

Yeah, that. Zay sketches the glowing tip of his cigarette in front of him and makes a buzzing sound. *Look at me,* he says. *I'm a firefly.*

The next morning, Zay picks Curt up at eight in his black Camaro and tells him to look in the back. Sitting on the rear bucket seats is a tinfoil package. Curt unwraps it and finds three hot dogs. Holes are poked in the side of each one. Probing, Curt finds white powder packed in the holes. *What's this?*

Crushed-up Ambien. Zay sticks his tongue out the side of his mouth and lolls his head to the side for effect.

Looks like you put enough in there to kill a horse.

Zay shrugs. *You saw that bitch. Be a mercy to put it down.*

Curt rewraps the tinfoil and tosses the package out his open window.

What the fuck, man.

Just keep driving, okay.

When they get to the work site, Dave is already there, standing by the cement truck in his kneepads, his tight white T-shirt straining against his gut. *Give him one of those chef hats,* Zay says, *he could be the Pillsbury Doughboy.*

Curt is glad to hear Zay wisecracking again. No hard feelings about the hot dogs. The rottweiler is barking, but it's hoarse, not nearly as insistent as before. Curt slips on his own kneepads and joins Dave in the pit. Zay dumps the first load of concrete at their feet, then runs off with his wheelbarrow for more. All day, Dave and Curt trowel the floor on their knees, broiling as the smooth, gray surface reflects the sun and magnifies its heat. Zay feeds them loads of concrete from the truck. And when he's not running back and forth with the wheelbarrow, he's laying plumbing on top of the footer, sawing PVC pipes to length and gluing them together. Floor Day is a nonstop ballbuster, and they're all dragging ass by the end of it. No lingering this time to stare at the sky.

Curt stumbles into his apartment feeling drained. The dog is still barking in his head, but he's too damn tired to care. He collapses into bed without showering. It reminds him of coming in from patrol and crashing on his bunk, grabbing a little shut-eye before Sergeant Berkholtz shook him awake. The thought of his muscle-bound squad leader brings a smile to his face. The man had a saying for everything. Curt pictures him now pointing at the barking dog. *Mind over matter,* he says. *You don't mind, it don't matter.* The barking doesn't disappear, but the volume lessens and in a few moments Curt is fast asleep.

The next day is their last on this job. Zay mixes vermiculite in a wheelbarrow and Curt scoops it out with his trowel. He uses it to patch rough spots on the floor. Then they roll out the heavy vinyl liner and snap it into a ridge at the top of the walls, pushing out air bubbles as they go. An industrial vacuum sucks out the last of the air, flattening the blue vinyl and fitting it to the floor and walls like a second skin.

As if on cue, Dave arrives in his truck. He walks around the pool like an inspecting general. *Okay, boys,* he says, *load up the tools and you can clock out for the day.*

They follow orders, then jump into Curt's Jeep. Dave stays behind, dropping the homeowner's garden hose into the blue hole and turning on the spigot. He stands there with his arms crossed and waits. Moments later, the homeowners are there beside him, clapping him on the back.

There he goes, Zay grumbles. *That fat bastard taking credit for all we done.*

Curt could wind him up in hopes of cruising by the bars to look for a fight. Not tonight. For once, he's not in the mood for cracking heads.

REPENTANCE

Approaching the church, Curt is relieved to see the paint scrubbed off, the picketers gone. Checking on the graffiti was why he'd come. Or so he told himself. Now, standing outside the arched doors, he feels a familiar tug pulling him inside.

He shuffles through the vestibule in the same daze that overwhelms him on late nights in his apartment. Shuffling over the nave's gleaming marble, passing the neatly ordered pews with hymnals and Bibles in their slots, passing the stained-glass saints peering down at him with pity, he arrives at the base of the steps leading up to the altar. Adorning the altar are scenes in bas-relief of apostles accepting communion, and standing on both sides are five-foot golden candleholders bearing thick tapers. And beyond, on the wall, is Jesus looking down on him with sorrowful eyes.

Glancing sideways, Curt notices a rosewood confessional recessed in an apse. On one side is a wall hanging with the words I WILL PRAISE YOU LORD FOR YOU HAVE RESCUED ME. The same sentiment is repeated on the other side in Spanish.

Long ago, confession had nourished his spirit. Now, the thought of it puts a sour taste in his mouth. Even so, he pulls the black curtain aside and enters, dropping to the padded kneeler. As he does, a panel slides open in the dividing wall to reveal a latticed screen. Behind that is the outline of Father Tony.

May the Lord be in your heart that you may know your sins and be truly sorry, the priest says.

Curt knows what's expected of him. He resists the urge to speak, but his tongue operates on muscle memory and words spill out of his mouth, fulfilling his side of this ritual compact. *Bless me, Father, for I have sinned. It's been eight years since my last confession.*

Go on, my son.

As the penitent, Curt is supposed to list whatever mortal sins he's committed and then the venial, those minor faults and impure thoughts that plague all men. Instead, he repeats, *Eight years, Father. That's how long it's been. Last confession. Last time you granted me absolution.*

Curt, is that you? Curtis Bradshaw? How wonderful to hear your voice, my son. You know, the whole congregation prayed for you in Iraq.

They shouldn't have. I'm a lost cause, Father.

No one is truly lost, my son.

Curt gives a strained sigh.

You can't have changed that much. I know what's in your heart.

No, Father. My heart is black.

It feels strange for Curt to be so casual with a man of the cloth instead of fawning over his every word. As a child, he'd been mesmerized by Father Tony, the mouthpiece of God. Older now, his brown hair gone gray, he's become a frail man, no different from anyone else. Just one more lie exposed.

If it's the killing—

No, Curt says, *not that.*

When he'd first come home from war, high school classmates kept asking how many insurgents he'd killed, what it had been like. They wanted gory details. But death is nothing like the movies. On the scale he'd seen it, day in, day out, death had become as ordinary as lacing his boots. One moment, a man would raise his rifle to aim at Curt; the next, he'd rise up as if struck by an idea, then crumple to the ground, lifeless as the sand and rocks that became his tomb. Nothing glorious. Nothing exceptional. Just one more spurt of gunfire as Heaven turned a blind eye and the sun boiled in a sky so stark and nearly white it could be made of bone.

Because God can forgive taking a life for a holy cause.

I'm the one, Curt says to change the subject. *I'm the one that spray-painted the church.*

There's silence from the other side of the screen. He expects Father Tony to yell at him, maybe even threaten excommunication. Instead, after a pause, the priest says, *I see. Anything else?*

Isn't that enough? All this week, that mob out front—that was because of me. I did that to you.

If it's me you're worried about, there's no need. I forgive you, my son. But it seems something else is on your mind, something weighing you down, something you haven't told anyone else. As you said, eight years is a long time. Unburden yourself. Set yourself free.

Tears well in Curt's eyes. He sniffles, takes a deep breath, but he doesn't cry. *Nothing else,* he says, *just the paint. That's what I came to confess.*

Father Tony sighs. *I see. Well, if you will not confess before the Lord I cannot convey absolution. Come back when you are ready. Until then, I suggest you look outwards and search for a way to do good unto others. In helping those in need, you will in turn help yourself.*

Curt leaves the church in the same daze he'd entered. But at least now he knows what to do. He must set the dog free.

ACT OF CONTRITION

Parking his Jeep two streets over, Curt heads into the woods that snug up to the subdivision like a glove. With a screen of clouds hiding the half-moon, he blends into foliage in his old fatigues like a shadow. His face is camouflaged as if he's out on patrol, the hollows lightened, his brow and cheekbones colored dark green. The old habits come back without thought. Creeping forward, his head swiveling side to side, stepping toe-heel, toe-heel for silence.

He nestles into a comfortable spot with good vantage. From here, he can see the rottweiler lying on the ground, its massive head resting on forelegs. It hasn't detected his presence yet. Nor have the trio of children splashing about in the pool he built, their tiny, exuberant shrieks filling the air. The in-pool lights turn the oval into a giant blue beacon. He settles down to wait for them to leave, not wanting any witnesses.

Turning his attention to the rottweiler, this creature whose temperament mirrors his own, he wonders how things might have been different if it had been freed from its chain. *Could it have ever been anything else but a weapon?* The question circles his mind like the dog orbiting its tree. Time passes and the children eventually go inside. A moment later, the pool lights snap off. When the clouds shift, the moon gives him all the light he needs.

He uncaps the Winchester's sights and lines up its crosshairs on the sleeping rottweiler. Though his aim is true, his finger won't cooperate. It stays rigid outside the trigger guard. Closing his eyes, he whispers, *Forgive me.* The knot in his gut unravels and his finger works again. He aims, letting out a slow breath, the voice of Berkholtz in his head. *You should be surprised when the shot goes off.* As Curt's finger starts its slow, steady pull, he watches the dog and waits for the kick.

River Crossing

The platoon plods through Fort Bragg's forest, afternoon sun streaming through towering pines and oaks, the thorny claws of wait-a-minute vines snagging their ACUs and occasionally biting through to skin. Tangled scrub blockades their path toward the river, which they must soon cross. The Kevlar helmets bending their necks seem heavier than when this field exercise began two weeks ago. Today is the last day, and each time the weaving line of soldiers halts, those farthest from Platoon Sergeant Stackhouse whisper in twos and threes among themselves about the coming weekend. They'll still have to clean their weapons one last time, turn them in to the armorer, strip off their mud-caked ACUs and hose themselves off in a hot shower. But those are mere formalities, a nuisance of the linear flow of time. In their minds, they've already jumped ahead to tomorrow.

The rising sound of burbling water and the thickening of the briar screen lets them know they are nearing their final obstacle—a river crossing through enemy-controlled territory. When the platoon finally stops, it forms a cigar-shaped perimeter, every other soldier facing opposite directions before seeking cover behind trunks and lying prone. They unbuckle web gear and loosen the ruck strap on one shoulder so their packs slide sideways onto the ground while still remaining linked to their bodies.

Here it comes, says Private First Class Zahn, eyes the color of Jack Daniel's glinting amid the loam-and-green camouflage paint slicked on his face. Raised in a waterfront community, he knows before Stackhouse says a word that he'll be the one called upon to swim the rope across the river and tie it to a tree on the other side. Everyone in the squad has their particular role to play. Specialist Bradshaw, with his linebacker's physique, is hauling an extra PRC battery and a mortar round in his ruck. Corporal Faust with his explosives training handles the demo. Private Banks, a five-jump cherry fresh from Fort Benning, the youngest, least experienced, and most expendable member of the squad, is the resident guinea pig. After a chemical alarm goes off and the testing team finally declares the air safe to breathe, Banks is the one who must crack the seal on his gas mask and suck in a sip of it to be sure.

And sure enough, Sergeant First Class Stackhouse, barrel-chested, hard as granite, with striated scars slicking his neck and face, *does* call on Zahn. The PFC pushes up from the soft matting of pine needles, says, *Yes, Sergeant,* and trots forward. Zahn's left forearm is puckered with smooth dots from shrapnel. Half the squad has some nick or other from their tours in Afghanistan and Iraq.

Staff Sergeant Muñoz, their new squad leader, is one of the few without a combat patch on his right shoulder, a fact that irks him as much as he imagines it does his men. When his last unit deployed, a torn ligament in his knee forced him to stay behind as a garrison commando. Then orders transferred him from another battalion into this squad just after they rotated home from Iraq. Minus a couple of men. The former squad leader, Berkholtz, and a private named Ramirez, had both been killed in a friendly fire incident. The men still adore their old squad leader, still quote his sage pieces of advice. Some even tattooed their shoulders with BERK'S MERCS. Muñoz hopes to one day earn that kind of respect, but he knows it will take time.

With the platoon leadership's attention focused up front, security loosens up in the middle. Rifles and machine guns still point out from the halted cluster, but soldiers' eyes turn inward. Two days earlier, they'd been tasked as OPFOR themselves and know that the attack won't come until after the platoon crosses the river and slogs up the other bank, weighed down with waterlogged clothes and tired from their exertions. When the time comes, they'll all perform their duties. For now though, tonight's promise tastes too succulent on their tongues to ponder anything else.

Private First Class Tefertiller takes off his helmet, pours canteen water over his head and down the back of his neck. Next to him, Specialist Mueller, with a thick plug of Red Man in his lip, says, *Gonna break some laws for sure this time. Yadkin won't know what hit it.* The weekend before the field exercise began, Mueller had been tossed out of The Bottoms Up, one of the strip clubs on Yadkin Road. But with payday recently passed and the prospect of a wallet full of cash, they'll welcome him back without qualm.

MPs get you, Corporal Faust says. *I'm not picking you up till tomorrow.* Faust's wife, Olivia, is eight months pregnant with their first baby, and Faust carries a sonogram image in the webbing of his helmet. Faust is smiling until suddenly, Banks screams and jumps up. Faust's mouth becomes a snarl. He whips around with his rifle, ready to fire, his reactions honed from multiple combat tours. Same with everyone else in the squad, everyone back in their proper positions, covering their sectors. Everyone but Banks.

Get your ass down, Private! Muñoz bellows.

But Banks is oblivious. He whirls in a circle, slapping his skin and cursing. The moldy log he'd been leaning on is home to a nest of hornets, and the black-and-gold insects are getting their revenge for his intrusion. The rest of the squad looks over to see what's going on, why the break in security protocol. Their constricted pupils take in Banks and they can't help but laugh. *Dance, Banks, dance,* yells Mueller.

The tittering grows into howls. Even Muñoz is laughing. But then the hornets expand their range and find more victims to sting, and everyone shifts positions, jumping up and resetting.

Stackhouse runs up and takes a knee near Muñoz. *What the hell's going on here?* he says through clenched teeth. And when the squad leader tells him, he can't help but chuckle himself. *Well,* he says, *guess y'all better get your dumb asses up to the river.*

So third squad rises from their positions, hustling toward the burbling water, toward the enemy they know lies up ahead.

Sacrifices

BENEATH A PINK CANOPY

Sophia mouths a silent *Thank you* as we stand on the threshold of her old bedroom at her parents' house in Princeton, New Jersey. In a guest room down the hall, our three-year-old daughter, Chrissie, is bouncing on a king-sized mattress big enough for the three of us. Her bed at home with the Little Mermaid headboard is only twice her length, but that's plenty of space for her and George, the stuffed panda she only sets down to take a bath or go potty. Two or three times a week, she'll shuffle into our bedroom with George dangling at her side, climb into our double bed, and snuggle between us without a word. On those nights, I'll kiss her forehead and study her heart-shaped face, a duplicate of her mother's, thinking, *What I wouldn't do for you.*

Sophia says I spoil Chrissie, but what choice do I have? Absent half her life, I have to work twice as hard to make the time count. A paratrooper in the 82nd Airborne Division, I go where the Army sends me. Serving my first tour while Chrissie was growing in her mother's belly. Eleven months in Iraq while she was nursing, then six more months in Afghanistan as she took her first steps. Each time I come home, I'm a stranger to my own daughter. When I'm gone, I live in hallway pictures and on the computer screen as her mother Skypes. When I'm finally there in the flesh, it's hard for her young mind to connect the two-dimensional image with the three-dimensional reality. My face might wear the same brown hair buzzed high and tight and the same scar bisecting my left eyebrow, but it still seems foreign, it still seems wrong. Her tiny body will squirm when I hold it against my wiry frame, her own arms squeezing George in a death grip as she struggles to break free. Months later, after she's grown used to me being around, I'm off again. Then it's my leg she's clutching as she wails, *Don't go, don't go,* George tossed aside in a heap.

Another deployment is coming up and Sophia and I have a big decision to make, one that could take me away from war and allow me to be a full-time father and husband. Which is why I agreed to this trip. Even though it rubs against my fiber. Even though I want to lock my legs like a defiant dog as Sophia's mother, Gloria, pushes us into her daughter's old bedroom.

We kept it just as you left it, Gloria says. *Didn't change a thing.*

I shouldn't be stunned by the room's splendor, but I am. I'd pictured it as a slightly larger version of our own but with the same cozy feel. I maintained this belief as we rolled up the circular drive in our Honda Prelude and parked behind twin BMWs; held on to it as I scanned the acre plot with manicured cypress trees. Even after entering the grand foyer, whose crystal chandelier glinted like an accusation, I clung to the hope that the life she'd chosen to live with me had been no different from the one she'd led before.

Since eloping three years ago, we've been living on Fort Bragg in a two-bedroom duplex with particle-board bookcases and a threadbare sofa. The living room as small as the trunk of my car. Growing up in a trailer park, cramped quarters suit me fine. But seeing where Sophia came from, I'm surprised *she* never complained. Everything in this grand room makes me feel small. The vaulted ceiling. The antique, claw-footed vanity with its gilt-edged, triptych mirror. The mahogany four-poster bed that looks like it cost more than my annual salary.

So this is what we fought for, I say.

Shut up, Bren, Sophia says, slugging my shoulder, but smiling. She's been giddy since I agreed to this trip, hoping it might bring me and her parents closer together. Fat chance. We've only mingled twice, and they made it perfectly clear that was two times too many. The first was right after our wedding when they rushed to North Carolina to push for an annulment. The second was five months later when I was home on emergency leave for Chrissie's birth. The timing, so soon after the wedding, galled their sense of propriety, but they said the right things even if their faces didn't agree.

I'll let you two get settled, Gloria says, closing the door as she exits.

The room is a time capsule commemorating an era when Sophia conformed to expectations. Pinned to a corkboard are prize ribbons from horse shows and photos of Sophia and her girlfriends in jodhpurs and bright satin tops. Stacked on shelves are thick textbooks of molecular biology, organic chemistry, and principles of genetics—premed courses she'd been taking before dropping out of Duke to have the baby. And arching across the wall behind her desk is a rainbow mural topped with three all-capped words glitter-painted gold: *DREAM. BE-LIEVE. ACHIEVE.*

Setting my duffel and Sophia's suitcase on the floor, I go to the desk. Spread on top is her high school senior yearbook opened to an inscription. *Sofi, Glad we were chem lab partners. You + me = a perfect bond. Love, Ken.*

Hey, who's Ken?

Sophia's eyes flare before she regains composure. *Just an old boyfriend.* Snatching the book from my hands, she snaps it shut and laughs. *This is* not *how I left everything!*

She tosses the book on a leather wingback in the corner and jumps onto the bed. *Come here, you,* she says, pulling me down and rolling me on my back. She curls against my side and throws a leg across mine. *Have I told you how much I appreciate this?*

Only a thousand times.

Well, make it a thousand and one. She unfastens one of my shirt buttons and slips a hand inside, teasing the whorls of my chest hair.

What if I wake up screaming? Ever consider that?

It's been two weeks since the last episode. I think you're over it.

My nightmares seldom reproduce the deaths and disfigurements I've witnessed—Jackson blown up by a suicide bomber, Pearson with his face shredded, Berkholtz and Ramirez cut in two by friendly fire. Instead, my mind invents other horrors, faceless fears that coat me in night sweats and strangle me in tangled sheets. The Taliban once overran another unit's outpost, but in my dreams, it is *my platoon* being attacked, the skinny, bearded insurgents scrabbling over rocks and sandbags with AKs and RPGs, an endless horde that I mow down with a .50 cal. This is my most frequent dream, my mind's eye panning across like a slow-motion scene in a movie. While comrades fall on the periphery, the focus zooms in on my ammo belt as the end of it draws up into the machine gun and the weapon halts with a loud *ca-chunk.* And still the enemy keeps coming.

Sophia squeezes my shoulder, her fingers kneading tense muscles. *Relax,* she says. When I let out a long breath, she traces the outline of the BERK'S MERCS tattoo on my shoulder.

It sucks what happened to your squad leader. I know you two were close.

After the friendly-fire incident, Army shrinks told everyone, *These things happen,* and other such nonsense. Then came the prescriptions. Klonopin for anxiety. Zoloft for depression. Ambien for sleep. And, when it was time to head back outside the wire, Dexedrine to keep us alert. The aphorisms did little to heal our psyches, but at least the pills let us do our jobs. Even now, there's a bottle of benzos in my duffel. I haven't taken any in weeks, but it's nice to know they're there.

And about tomorrow, Sophia says, *don't feel guilty. It's just an interview.*

Her father had set it up. The job had something to do with security at the lab where he works, but he's been vague on details. All he'll say is, *It's perfect for you. You'll see.*

Last time I'd interviewed for a job was right after high school when I applied to Pizza Hut. I lied to the manager, promising I had my own car. Instead I had to borrow my mom's Chrysler LeBaron to make deliveries. She worked as a hairdresser at Supercuts, and at shift's end she either walked home from the salon or caught a ride with me, the steaming boxes in padded sleeves stacked on her lap. Ours has always been a family used to making do.

This job, Sophia says, *it could be a new start for us. So play nice with Daddy. Okay?*

I nod again, knowing better than to start another fight. Our last one, two nights ago, had been epic. *I can't believe you want me to abandon the guys just as we're going back to the shit,* I'd yelled. Then I'd shattered my WORLD'S GREATEST DAD mug on the kitchen wall, coffee splashing across the buttercup wallpaper.

Sophia had hollered back, *What about abandoning your*

family? Every time you're gone and there's a knock on the door, I start shaking. One of these times some damn chaplain will be standing there telling me how sorry he is. No. Three combat tours is enough!

I've only been in the Army four years. If I re-up and ship out again, I'll have as many combat tours as years of service. And who knows what the next four years will bring.

Don't worry so much, Sophia says now. *If Daddy didn't like you, he wouldn't set you up with this job. It's going to be fine.* She kisses me on the lips, then rolls out of bed. *Gonna go check on Chrissie. Love you.*

My eyes follow her out of the room, then veer to the walk-in closet with posters on the door. Spice Girls and NSYNC back in their heyday, before the bands broke up and their music grew dated. Appropriate to the room's theme. A glitzy snapshot of the cush life. Maybe her parents maintained this shrine because they knew all along their little girl would return. And they were right. She has come home. With unwanted baggage.

Grabbing the yearbook from the chair, I flip to the page with Ken's inscription. *Love, Ken.* My left hand rises unbidden to my eyebrow's smooth scar. As I rub the glossy surface, my vision starts to tunnel and time seems to slow down. Like it always does just before battle.

BREAKFAST WITH THE IN-LAWS

Trapped at the breakfast table, I'm not sure which utensil crowding my gold-trimmed plate to use. And what about this lacy napkin in my lap? I can't imagine blotting my mouth or sopping up a mess with it. I'd sooner use my sleeve.

Silence is contrary to my nature, but I refuse to say anything before my father-in-law speaks. It's like we're playing our own version of chicken. As Lord of the Manor, he sits at the head of the table, back straight, balding crown gleaming, thin lips pressed flat as a sheet of hammered tin.

I remember the first time—*the only time*—we shook hands. Feeling the lotion-softened texture of his palm against the thick scuff of calluses ringing my own, I was careful not to squeeze too hard. His nose wrinkled from the touch, and when he pulled away he wiped his hand on his pocket square. Left me regretting I hadn't crushed his tiny bones.

I remember when my battalion landed in Jalalabad, it took a few days to organize a convoy to our forward operating base near the Pakistan border. Nothing we weren't used to. "Hurry up and wait" is the Army's unofficial motto. In the lull before shipping out, I bullshitted with guards at the detention center and finagled my way inside. Teasing prisoners seemed like an amusing distraction. But once I saw the naked Afghans squatting on cardboard squares in chicken-wire cages, their sunken eyes like hot coals, my good humor evaporated. In the months that followed, I wondered what the prisoners had been thinking, what retributions burned within their hearts. Now, twisting the lace napkin in my lap and glancing at Sophia's prig of a father, I think I know.

If Sophia would just come back to the table, I could relax. But she's in the kitchen leaning against the center island, chatting with her mother. Gloria is going on about her current teaching load at Princeton and minor spats between faculty members. When she pauses, Sophia mentions how she is reading the same Winnie the Pooh books to Chrissie that Gloria had read to her twenty years ago. Both women are practically aglow. As much as I want Sophia to bail me out, I won't ruin her moment.

Breakfast consists of a split English muffin topped with an

egg sunny-side up and blueberry yogurt swirled into a porcelain ramekin. I sip coffee without touching the food. In the center of the table is a basket of cut fruit, a plate of triangular-cut toast, and a small ceramic bowl filled with orange marmalade. I consider grabbing a piece of toast and chewing on the corner. My stomach is in knots and I doubt I could eat much more.

Chrissie doesn't share my worry. She clutches a muffin in one tiny hand and bites the egg, runny yolk dripping down her fingers to her wrist. The other arm is looped around George's neck in a stranglehold. When she looks up, her oblivious smile eases some of my tension.

Yummy, isn't it? I say.

She nods, beaming.

Sophia's father lowers his head and regards me over the horn-rimmed glasses perched on the tip of his aquiline nose. *How would you know? You haven't tasted it yet.*

My ears burn. *You're right, Mr. Bisset.* Sophia keeps telling me to call him Dad, but no way that's happening. Same with calling him by his first name, Jules. Since he's a scientist with a doctorate, I could call him Dr. Bisset. But that would bestow more respect than I'm willing to confer.

Cutting into a muffin, I fork the gooey wedge into my mouth and turn to Chrissie again. *Yummy.*

Sophia's father clucks his tongue and dissects his muffin into tiny pieces. Without looking up, he says, *Does she know how to use cutlery, or is this how you always eat at home?*

My first inclination is to leap across the table and punch him in the throat. Army training has honed my aggressive tendencies to a sharp point and shown me how to stab through any problem. But Mr. Bisset, however spiteful and pompous, is still my father-in-law, so I keep my fists on my side of the table.

Yes, Chrissie knows how to use a knife and fork. She also knows when they're not needed. Dropping my silverware in a clatter, I pick up my nibbled muffin and shove the remainder in my mouth, snuffling like a hog as I scarf it down. Then, eyes fixed on Mr. Bisset, I repeat the earlier sentiment. *Yummy.*

Chrissie giggles.

Mr. Bisset utters something in French, which I'm sure is a curse. Then he cuts his eyes toward Chrissie. *Now I see where she gets her manners. The least you can do is wipe her off.*

Chrissie's smile disappears and she glances at her yellow-smeared hand and arm. It looks like she's about to cry.

Hey, sweetie, let me get that for you, I say. I lick the goo on her arm, making slurping sounds until she starts to laugh. Then I use the lace napkin from my lap to wipe her hand. As I ball up the napkin and tuck it under the rim of my plate, Sophia enters with a pitcher of grapefruit juice.

What'd I miss? she says.

Not much, I say. *Just a discussion on fine dining.*

THE PRINCETON PLASMA PHYSICS LAB

Mr. Bisset's job—developing fusion as an energy source—seems like something out of science fiction. If he were someone else, someone I didn't want to choke, I might ask about the possibilities of light-speed engines, laser weapons, and personal jet packs. But I'm mum on the drive to the lab in Mr. Bisset's BMW 530d sedan. Classical music fills the cabin. Not to my liking, but I won't tell him that. I won't say anything that gives him further reason to brand me a hick.

Too bad Sophia's not here to act as a buffer, but she and Chrissie are with Gloria today. The girls are brunching at the Cherry Valley Country Club, then browsing upscale stores at

Palmer Square. Clothes shopping is torture to me, but I'd gladly take it now to get out of this car.

Mr. Bisset breaks the silence. *Let me be straight with you. You're not good enough for my daughter. You know that as well as I. But she chose to be with you, so it seems I'm stuck with making the best of it.*

Finally some honesty. *Yeah,* I say, *you're not my first choice, either.*

I don't relish the thought of you working at my lab, but being a father means making sacrifices. Same with being a husband. You do things you wouldn't otherwise for those you love.

Right. I'm tracking.

Good. I'm sticking my neck out by recommending you for a position. I have a reputation to uphold. Please don't soil it.

Hey, it's not like I'm going to pull my gun every time someone's ID doesn't check out.

Mr. Bisset titters. *Oh, no worries. I don't think you'll be carrying a gun.*

I can tell I'm the butt of some private joke, but have no idea what it is. I promised Sophia that I'd play nice, but I didn't agree to sit still while he shits on me. *One last thing,* I say. *You ever talk like that to my daughter again, I'll break your nose. How's that for straight talk?*

THE INTERVIEW

Their first stop in the lab compound is Mr. Bisset's office, where he slips into a white lab coat. *I'll just be a minute,* he says, flipping through a stack of memos and binder-clipped papers in his inbox.

I figure this detour is another act of intimidation, one more jab at my lack of formal education. Running the length of one wall is a whiteboard filled with complex formulas. A few boxy machine components are spread on a table, red, green, and black wires sprouting from their innards. And the shelves behind a massive oak desk are lined with three-ring binders, spines labeled *Magnetic Resonance, Beam Dynamics, Plasma Nano-synthesis, Lithium Tokamak Experiment,* and other equally convoluted titles. Waiting in the open doorway, I lean against the jamb in the new sport coat Sophia bought for the interview.

If I get the job, I figure the only time I'll have to see this asshole is at the beginning and end of each day. And that's only if I'm positioned at the guardhouse. The campus has scores of buildings spread across ninety-one acres; who knows where I'll end up.

Okay, let's get you to that interview.

As we march down the marble hallway, colleagues offer passing pleasantries. Mr. Bisset doesn't introduce me. He doesn't even slow down to say hello. Apparently he's a prick to everyone.

Walking in silence works for me. I'm mentally prepping for the interview, psyching myself up, running possible questions and answers through my head. With the right spin, my military experience could be a transferable skill. I've done guard duty, crowd control, search and seizure, and even detainment, using plastic zip ties instead of metal handcuffs to bind prisoners' wrists. While questions scroll through my mind, my eyes automatically scan everyone who passes, flicking from face to hand and back again, checking for anything out of place. It's a habit born of a thousand patrols where one slack moment could kill or maim you; or worse, kill or maim a squadmate.

I should probably warn you, Mr. Bisset says without looking at me, *that this interview is for an entry-level position.*

No problem. Just like the Army. Got to put in the time before you get your stripes.

Indeed.

I hear that same snarky bemusement in his tone, and it puts me on alert. Even so, I'm not prepared when we reach our destination. I feel like I've been funneled into the kill zone of an ambush. Seeing the nameplate on the door, I finally get the joke.

Here we are, says Mr. Bisset, holding the door open for me. *Good luck.*

In the small office, a stocky man with salt-and-pepper hair rises behind a metal desk. He's holding a clipboard and wearing gray overalls. *Dr. Bisset told me about you,* he says amiably. *Was in the service myself. Navy. Please, have a seat.*

My father-in-law retreats into the hall, smirking. Before the door swings shut, I get a second look at the nameplate. JANITORIAL.

LAST NIGHT BEFORE ANOTHER FAREWELL

Thanks, hon, for what you were willing to do, Sophia says. *For me. For us. For our family.*

No problem.

And thanks for not popping Daddy in the mouth.

It was harder than you know.

Two weeks have passed since Princeton. We're back at Bragg, back in our small duplex. Chrissie is asleep in her room, snuggled up with George, and the two of us are lying in our own full-sized bed.

I didn't want to tell you until you'd calmed down, says Sophia, *but Mom pulled a fast one on me, too.*

How so?

That brunch at the country club—my old boyfriend, Ken, was there. He came up to the table and was like, "Oh, wow, what a coincidence." Mom asked him to join us, and I could tell she'd planned it out. She never touched her salmon. She just kept going on about how successful Ken is and what a cute couple we'd make.

I slap my forehead and groan. *Man, what a pair.*

Them or us?

Both I guess.

Pulling Sophia close, I bury my face in her neck. *You aren't pissed, are you? About me reenlisting and all?*

As soon as we returned to North Carolina, I signed the papers. The two weeks since have been filled with hectic preparations, and this is my last night at home. Tomorrow, the battalion goes on lockdown, gearing up for the flight to Iraq.

No, not pissed, she says. *Not even a little.*

You ever think this is all I'm good at? Going to war? Killing people?

Instead of answering, she rolls out of bed. *Give me a sec.*

The first time I deployed, both of us had been nervous wrecks right up to the end. The last night had been the worst, Sophia crying through most of it, me repeatedly promising not to be a hero. We both regretted not making love. If I never returned, that wretched night would have been her last memory of us together.

Now she comes back from the bathroom in a pearl-white chemise with black lace trim. She dims the light and says, *There's one more thing you're good at.* Approaching the bed, she slips one spaghetti strap off a shoulder. Then the other.

Come here, I say, grabbing her waist. Then we stop talking altogether.

Exodus

FUGUE

Pounding, pounding on the door, Daniel knows how easily he could knock it down and stifle his wife's hysterics. He can't remember why Olivia locked herself in the bathroom with their two-year-old son, Magnus. Barefoot in the carpeted hallway, enveloped in the same fog that rolled over him in battle, he acts without thinking, his body on cruise control. All he knows is he must get in.

Whenever Daniel reflects on his four combat tours, it's not the desert he sees, but the kicked-down doors. Adrenaline-fueled forced entries. Blasting sawed-off shotguns into locks. Kicking with heavy boots. Bursting in with rifle snug to shoulder, selector switch on SEMI. Never knowing what he'd find until he rushed inside. Never knowing if he'd have to shoot or be shot at himself. Nothing before or since has thrilled him as much as the celebration of survival the moment a raid was complete.

Fear never froze him during firefights. It came in the aftermath, when time stretched and he reflected on close calls—the supersonic whipcracks of bullets passing overhead, the chalky puffs of sandstone near his face. Now, blinking back the red veil, Daniel unclenches his fists and stares at his hands. The drumbeat of blood in his ears dwindles to a percussive throb. Coming back to himself is like a long fly ball falling into an open glove. He could press his mouth against the door to beg forgiveness, but Liv has heard it all before.

So many sweaty nights when Daniel wakes tangled in sheets, it's his wife who eases him back from chasm's brink, her smooth hand on his chest, his racing heart in her palm. Wordlessly, she kisses his shoulder, her fingers skimming circles through tiny hairs on his breast, the rhythm of the universe traversing its grooves.

Retreating down the hall, Daniel passes wedding pictures, Olivia's nursing certificate, a black-and-white photo of Daniel's squad in full battle rattle posing in front of a Humvee. At first, Humvee doors had no locks and anyone could grab the handle and yank them open. Schiller from Third Brigade disappeared like that—there one moment, gone the next. When mujahedeen posted a video of him gagged and kneeling on a blanket, everyone knew what was coming. Schiller, too, his crazed eyes wide and rolling in his head. Afterwards, two steel plates were added to Humvee doors that slid down over the frame so troops could combat-lock them from inside.

Hovering in the framed glass atop the photo of his squad, Daniel sees his current reflection, hooded eyes dark as caves. Eyes, he's heard, are windows to the soul. But where on the body is the door? Is it the mouth, open and shut so easily, filled with words, most of them lies? The heart, that industrious sac, its echo thumping backbeats to every murderous thought? Or the brain, that way station for dreams before they're prodded onto cattle cars and carted over dissolving horizons?

Beyond his reflection are the grim faces of his squadmates. Half of them now dead or disfigured. The other half, he figures, as screwed up as he is. Most of the time, he hopes not; but in his darkest moments, he wishes them stuck in the same purgatory if only for the company. Comrades till the end.

Turning away, Daniel comes to the end of the hallway, to the cross with Jesus nailed to it. The crown of thorns. The beseeching eyes. Even they can't get him to pray again.

Down the hall, behind the bathroom door, Liv's whimpers call out like a form of salvation. He could beg one last time, promise to go to a therapist, to release all the memories bottled inside. Instead, he continues down the stairs, out the front door. Doesn't bother with shoes. Walking around back, he enters the woods where wild things fight for daily survival. An environment he understands. A place he knows he belongs.

QUESTIONS

When Olivia asked which he loved more, the Army or her, Daniel had stood there dumbfounded. *Phone me when you figure it out,* she'd said. Then she took Magnus and drove to her mother's house. That was four days ago.

Daniel has picked up the phone a hundred times since and set it back down without dialing. He wants to call but can't give Liv the answer she wants. She knows him too well. She can tell when he's lying.

Alone now except for faces of squadmates floating in the gloom, Daniel hears one question whispering in the dark. *Why? Why?*

Three tours in Iraq and one in Afghanistan, yet Daniel was never hit with an IED. Always a different vehicle in the convoy. Or another convoy altogether. Rolling in afterwards as part of the quick reaction force, he'd cordon off the area as medics stuffed QuikClot into broken bodies and wrapped them with gauze. Then came the doors, kicking down doors, kicking, screaming, searching for someone to blame, racing in circles like a dog chasing its tail.

Now, the memories gather weight and walk beside him. Each day, he plods through the mindless motions of garrison life on Fort Bragg. And each night, he paces a circuit through his empty house, furtive creaks and groans transforming into the wails of ghosts. *Why?* they moan, *Why us and not you?*

SOMETHING BIGGER THAN YOURSELF

After a week, Olivia tires of waiting and calls the house. *You know I'm serious about this, right?*

I know.

You've done your time, Dan. You've served your country. It's someone else's turn. You're not the only one who can do this job.

He's told her a hundred times before that it's not a job, it's a calling. Giving yourself completely to something bigger than yourself, being driven by purpose. This isn't the time to bring it up again, so he stays quiet on his end of the line.

It gets worse with every tour. You bring the war home with you, but you never talk about it. You just let it build up until you explode. Well, I'm not raising our children in that kind of environment. I'm not going to sit quietly while you tear the house down around us.

You're right, he says. *This shit has got to change.*

So change it. Your enlistment's up. Sign the papers and get out.

It's not that easy though.

Yes, Dan, it is. She waits a couple of beats for him to respond, and when he doesn't, she huffs in frustration. *How's this for simple—either put in your papers or we're through.*

WHAT ONCE WAS POSSIBLE

His unit has been home for three months, yet Daniel still jerks awake at the slightest sound, coiled and ready to fend off an attack. He feels uneasy entering the bank, the post office, the grocery without someone guarding his six. Can't help swiveling, scanning corners, looking for anything out of place. In the back of his mind lurks the memory of how easily he once did it, sauntering through glass doors with a bop in his step.

The thought of that younger, carefree version of himself fills Daniel with pity and disgust. How could anyone be so naïve? But then he snags on the barbs of his cynicism and starts to wonder if he was defective *then* or *now*. If he's broken now, the kindest thing for him to do would be to stay away from Liv and Magnus. All he can do is hurt them more.

Back home, Daniel ambles through the house cradling the picture of his squadmates. Where it used to hang is a fist-sized hole in the wall. He wanders past the downstairs fireplace with potted ferns huddled on the brick hearth. In the guest bathroom he strokes the fancy towels and soap. In the master bedroom he studies the ruffled duvet and mountain of throw pillows. How had *this* become his life?

Opening his wife's teak dresser, he rifles through her clothes. In the sock drawer, he comes across the blue clay casting of Magnus's baby handprint. The moment he picks it up, he feels the vise gripping his chest begin to loosen.

He'd been in the delivery room for the birth, watching the miracle happen, home on emergency leave from Afghanistan. Back in the desert, he'd shown off the photos of his son. His favorite showed a swaddled Magnus in his wife's arms, her face a mixture of exhaustion and joy. *Keep it close,* SSG Muñoz had said. *That's what we're fighting for.* The picture rode in his helmet lining for the rest of the deployment, something to gaze upon whenever he took off his Kevlar.

Carrying the clay handprint to the hole in the hallway wall, Daniel holds it up against his knuckled outline. He fingers the ragged edge. *One or the other,* he thinks. Then he pulls out his phone and punches in a number, holding his breath, waiting for Liv to pick up.

First Drunk Night Back

BENEATH THE BRIGHT RIBBONS

Wound tight and hyperalert, Royce Tefertiller moves through Atlanta's crowded terminal feeling naked without his body armor, without his weapon. Every day for the past eight months, his M4 has been strapped to his body. On patrol. In the chow hall. Even in the shitter. *Think of it like a third arm,* Sergeant Berkholtz told him. *Anywhere you take the other two, got to bring this one as well.* Except now the weapon is racked in the company arms room and he's out in the open. Defenseless.

Home, he reminds himself. *This is home.* His rational mind knows this swarm poses no threat, but his body hasn't caught up to his new reality. Muscles tensed for action, his body and all its interconnected nerves say vigilance is required as his eyes flick from faces to hands, so many holding cell phones, each a potential detonation device.

For its part, the jostling crowd is lost in their own affairs, rushing to different gates or texting updates to coworkers and loved ones. The few people who make eye contact with Royce seem slightly surprised by his Class A uniform, the green jacket's rows of ribbons, the combat patch on the right sleeve. Invariably, surprise turns to pity and their voices take on a funeral-parlor tone. *Thank you for your service,* they say. And though Royce nods his recognition, he never stops moving, never stops scanning hands.

Once he reaches the gate, Royce drops into a seat. With his momentum halted, the coil in his gut winds tighter yet. He wonders if hushed conversations are about him. In uniform, he's not an individual; he's a symbol, a representation of some larger ideal. The body inside this uniform is not his to own; it belongs to the crowd.

Lowering his head, he shuts his eyes and thinks of home. His actual home in Luzon Heights, the quiet subdivision in Pensacola with Japanese maples and crepe myrtles carefully placed in well-tended yards. He wants to stroll down its wide streets, smelling the salt air from the nearby Gulf and its white sand beaches, tilting his head back, no reason to be on guard.

He feels a moment of peace, then the tension returns. *What if it's all changed?* He thinks of Thomas Wolfe's *You Can't Go Home Again* and what the title implies. It's the kind of thought he kept to himself in the barracks. The other guys' reading didn't go far beyond *Playboy* or Army field manuals. Royce buried his books beneath neatly folded T-shirts and towels in his footlocker. When Berkholtz found them, he said, *Never be ashamed for being smart. It's the smart ones that save everyone else's ass.*

Royce's high school buddies flipped out when he enlisted. He was supposed to be the guy who stayed in school till he got his doctorate and landed a job with some tech giant where he invented a widget or computer program that changed the world. And it wasn't just his friends who were shocked. The cool kids invited him to their parties. People who hadn't noticed he existed began high-fiving him in the halls.

Then there was Sabrina. She pulled him into a bedroom at a graduation party and took his virginity in a furious few minutes. He pegged it up to drunken happenstance, but the following week, his last before reporting for duty, she came back for more. They did it in her frilly room. They did it in the back seat of his father's Buick. They did it in the bathroom at Wendy's. He couldn't get enough of her. She, more than anything else, made him want to stay. But his leaving was the only reason she was interested. If he found a way to wiggle out of his commitment, he would go back to being a faceless physics nerd and she a cheerleader who only had time for those in the spotlight.

On their last night together, she said, *I might be the last woman you ever touch,* rocking on top of him with a hungry smile on her face. She gave him an envelope filled with pouty photos of her in skimpy lingerie. *To let you know what you're fighting for,* she said.

He tucked the photos in the webbing of his Kevlar helmet and thought about her every day. But after three weeks, she stopped replying to his emails. And the promised care package never came. His best friend Greg told him she was spending all her time with Wade Bristow, a football player who'd become a fireman.

Royce wasn't the only soldier ghosted by a once-true love. Outside the mess tent was a billboard with photos of girlfriends and wives tacked to it. At the top of the board was a banner reading, RAN OFF WITH JODIE. Royce found a bikini picture of Sabrina, wrote *Bitch!* across it in black marker, and added it to the board.

Approaching movement snaps his mind back to the present. A middle-aged man in an expensive suit is coming his way, smiling, and Royce gets his battle squint on, cataloguing soft spots to strike if the man makes a sudden grab. Stopping in front of Royce, the man holds out a ticket and says, *Wanna switch? It's first class, like you deserve.* Royce doesn't know *what* he deserves. He takes the ticket anyway.

The first-class seat is plenty wide, but Royce can't get comfortable. At least the woman next to him is wearing a sleep mask. The sense that everyone else is looking at him prickles his skin like an itch he can't scratch. He feels like he should be standing at attention. Soon as he gets home, he's going to change into his favorite Levi's, the ones with the seat and thighs worn soft. Maybe then he'll feel normal.

Someone touches his elbow and he jerks away. It's the flight attendant, a red-and-white chiffon scarf snug around her neck. *Hey, look,* she says, *we're twins.* She taps a set of silver wings on the lapel of her navy blue jacket and gives a thousand-watt smile. Her smooth, unblemished face is an advertiser's wet dream. This close, her perfume fills Royce's head, the scent of fresh-cut lilies, the sweetest thing he's smelled in months.

You seem a little on edge. Like something to drink?

I'm good.

You sure? It's free.

Royce shakes his head. *Better not. I've been dry for eight months.*

A concerned look ripples the pond of her face.

No, no, Royce says, *I'm not an alcoholic or anything. It's just booze is illegal over there, you know.*

Her serene expression returns. *Okay, hon. Just let me know if you need anything.* Then she glides off to the next passenger.

Some soldiers had ignored the war-zone edict against alcohol, sipping from mouthwash bottles filled with gin and green food coloring that loved ones sent over. Others distilled gasoline to create high-octane moonshine. Rumor had it that a whole squad had gone blind from the stuff. Royce didn't believe that, but he still obeyed the prohibition, staying dry as desert sand.

Royce squirms in his seat, wishing that either his back was against a wall or someone he trusted was guarding his six. It isn't until he touches his breast pocket that a sense of calm washes over him. To anyone looking, he's posed like a schoolchild about to recite the Pledge of Allegiance. For once, he doesn't care what anyone else thinks. All that matters is what's hidden beneath the bright ribbons on his chest.

WHAT LURKS OUTSIDE THE FRONT DOOR

As Royce nears the concourse exit, he sees his parents just beyond the metal detectors. His mother is leaning against a rope barrier causing the stanchions into which it's clipped to tilt forward at a precarious angle. She seems ready to bolt into the restricted area, TSA be damned. The past year has aged her a decade, the gray streaks in her hair now overtaking the brown. But youth returns to her taut face when it unclenches in an expression of glee. *Royce, Royce, over here,* she calls, waving frantically as if he might miss her otherwise.

She races around the rope barrier and runs to her son on a collision course. She almost disappears in her son's chest as his arms envelop her. Then he lifts her in the air and her scream in his ear is louder than an RPG. Someone applauds and it spreads through the terminal. More than ever, Royce feels like a bug beneath a microscope. He tries to set his mother down, but she clings to his neck, one hand cupping his buzz-cut head. Crying into his shoulder, she keeps saying, *My little boy, my little boy.*

When she finally lets go, Royce sees his accountant father standing a few paces away in a brown cardigan, filming the scene on his camera. *I'm really proud of you, son. You just don't know,* he says in a choked voice.

He seems ready to burst into tears, which is strange for Royce to witness. His father is usually so reserved, so quiet and pensive. Wanting to drain the high emotion from the moment, Royce says, *God bless us, every one,* intending the line borrowed from Tiny Tim to inject a little humor into the situation. Instead, his joke becomes the tagline that turns the video into a viral sensation.

But for now, his father turns off the camera and steps toward his son. He claps his shoulder and leaves his hand resting there. *Let's get you home, son.*

After Royce stows his duffel in the Buick's large trunk, his mother insists he sit in the front seat. On the drive home, she keeps reaching through from the back to touch his arm or his face, saying, *I just can't believe it.*

When they pull into his subdivision, he's relieved to see the neighborhood hasn't changed, and he relaxes a little. But on the last street before their own, Mr. Johnson stops mowing his yard and stands at attention, saluting as they drive past. As his father turns into their cul-de-sac, Royce sees yellow ribbons wrapped around the black olive trees in their yard and a WELCOME HOME banner hanging above the front door.

As he unloads his duffel from the trunk, he feels the stares from every window on the street. It's the terminal all over again, feeling like a marionette dancing on someone else's strings. Soon as his father unlocks the front door, Royce rushes inside, saying he needs to change out of uniform and wash off the travel stink.

Okay, hon, his mom says. *Get yourself settled and I'll call when dinner's ready.* She cups his cheeks with her hands and stares. *I'm so glad you're back. I was certain that—* Her voice catches and she slaps a hand to her mouth before turning away.

Royce kisses the top of her head and retreats upstairs. Nothing in his old bedroom has changed, but in a way everything has. It's as strange as an alien landscape. A soft world with no hard corners. On the wall behind his desk are three posters, one of Albert Einstein bracketed by two with supermodels in underwear. His closet door is covered by a mosaic of techno-pop album covers. Model rockets and launcher stands blanket his desk. Affixed to the ceiling are glow-in-the-dark stickers that map out an accurate depiction of the night sky, while strung below them are plastic models of *Star Wars* X-wing and Y-wing Starfighters. Royce drops onto the quilted comforter on his queen-sized bed and can't recall anything ever feeling so plush.

Turning to the nightstand, he grabs the framed photo of Sabrina. She's wearing her cheerleader outfit and posed with her hand on her chin, long, blond tresses cascading over her shoulder. A tug of desire stirs in his gut, and he chuckles. *Yeah,* he says to himself, *like that'll ever happen again.*

He removes the picture from its frame and drops it into the trash can. Then he unbuttons his breast pocket and pulls out a charcoal sketch. It shows an Arabic girl he's never met. Retrieved from the severed hand of a bombing victim, Royce carried the drawing with him through the rest of his tour. He isn't quite sure why; maybe to remind himself how fleeting love and life can be. All he knows is that nights when he lay rigid on a bunk in his CHU waiting for the next random mortar blast to rock the compound, he would stare at her exotic face and feel his tensed muscles unknotting.

When Royce comes back down for dinner, he's changed into a plaid button-up shirt and his worn Levi's. The meal is sumptuous. Fried chicken, okra, corn on the cob, whipped potatoes fashioned into a bowl, then filled with steaming gravy.

He wolfs down as much as he can, but his mother keeps heaping more on his plate.

Mom, listen, I can't fill up. I'm meeting the D&D crew at Harpoon Larry's.

Springing to her face is an expression he recognizes too well, the same fear that plagued her face throughout his childhood. Fear whenever the phone rang. Fear of what might happen to those who weren't cautious. Fear of what lurked outside the front door.

As Royce stands, she looks smaller than ever. *Please don't stay out too late,* she begs, looking up at him with mournful eyes.

I won't.

And if you drink anything, call for a ride.

I will.

Doesn't matter how late. I'll come at any hour.

Royce can't help but smile. He knows the forestalling commentary will string along until he either leaves or succumbs to the gathered, guilt-inducing weight and sits back down. And for that, he's grateful, pleased to see *something* hasn't changed. But tonight her soft-pedaled worries are not enough to restrain him.

As he turns to leave, his mother jumps up, nearly knocking her chair over. She grabs onto his waist and buries her face in his back. *My little boy,* she says, squeezing. *My little boy.*

ROLE-PLAYING

All through high school, the D&D crew met on Friday nights except when family obligations intervened. Sometimes the gaming sessions would go all weekend. Its three members, Royce,

Greg Fuller, and Charlie Radinsky, would hole up in one of their houses to play old-school Dungeons & Dragons with campaigns that ran on for weeks. Multisided dice, grid-lined dungeon maps, bulging Trapper Keepers holding player histories tracked and tabulated for years—these were what they obsessed over during the week. Not that they didn't dream of girls; but girls were more fantastical creatures than the elves and orcs in their game. Until Royce hooked up with Sabrina and skipped out on the boys his final Friday at home.

Now, entering Harpoon Larry's, Royce looks around for his friends, half expecting them to be dressed in costume as wizards or paladins. The barroom is packed with boisterous drinkers, the long bar two rows deep with patrons yelling orders at the two bartenders. They don't card anybody, which is why the crowd is so young. When he spots his friends seated at a booth, he sees that time has passed for them as well. Greg is wearing a Mötley Crüe T-shirt with a torn-out neck hole and has a chain tattoo encircling one skinny bicep. And Charlie is sporting a patchy beard that makes him look like he has scurvy. They both rise when Royce approaches.

Yo, Roy, my man. Greg gives him the bro handshake, pulling him close, and patting him hard on the back. Charlie, ever the follower, does the same. Royce slides into the booth opposite his friends.

You hear about Brian? Greg asks.

Brian had been the one who'd dropped out at seventeen to join the Army and bugged Royce to do the same until he finally promised. But Royce's parents wouldn't sign for his early enlistment, so he'd had to wait another year. A grunt in the 10th Mountain Division, Brian had replied to Royce's emails during his first month of deployment to Iraq. Then one day he'd stopped. Royce never knew what to make of it, but he stayed true to his word. Now the hairs on the back of his neck bristle. *No, what about him?*

Aw, man, I would've told you earlier, but your mom thought it might screw with your head. Anyway, you're back now, you should know. He got blown up by an IED. Lost both his legs and one arm. Spent, I don't know, a year or so in the hospital. His parents split up and he went with his mom to Texas. Nobody's heard from him since.

Royce feels a vise squeezing his lungs and then Berkholtz is in his head. *Shit happens, soldier. Don't think on it. Just focus on your breathing and nothing else. Your training will tell your body what to do.* And so he takes a deep breath, looks dead eyed back at his crew, and says, *Shit happens.*

Yeah, man, Greg says. *Sure does.* He drops his head and stares down into his beer, and Charlie follows suit.

I think we need something stronger to drink, Royce says. *How about I get us a round of shots.* He starts to get up to go to the bar.

No, no, Greg says, *sit back down. Wait for the waitress.*

But, I—

Trust me.

Royce drops back down and soon enough the waitress comes by in a tight white tank top and even tighter shorts. It's Sabrina.

Hey, handsome, she says, sliding in next to Royce, hugging his neck, and giving him a wet kiss on the cheek. *Love that video your dad posted on YouTube.*

You saw that?

Well, yeah. Like, ten times. Everyone has.

Just breathe, Royce hears in his head. *Just breathe.*

Hey, listen, I don't get off till one thirty, but if you stick around till then, I can welcome you home proper. She licks her lips with a slow tongue.

The boys giggle on the other side of the booth.

Yeah, Royce says, *sure.*

Okay, so let me bring you all something. And don't worry, drinks are on the house. Long as you don't tell the boss on me. She stands and looks down with that wicked smile from his dreams, the one where she's riding on top of him in the back of his car. *Mmm-mmm,* she says, shaking her head. *So good to see you again. And all in one piece.*

Sabrina takes the boys' beers and brings back a round of Three Wise Men—Johnnie Walker, Jim Beam, and Jack Daniel's mixed together in a strong shot of whiskey—with a round of rum-and-Coke chasers to take the edge off. For Royce, the first sip of liquor packs the jolt of an electrical current. After this long on the wagon, moderation would be wise, but there's no way he'll let the boys outpace him.

So what was it like in the desert? Charlie asks.

Hot and boring, mostly.

Mostly? Charlie says with his eyebrows raised, the connotation of that one word sitting between them like a land mine.

Royce knows what his buddies want. Combat stories. The intimate details. The sounds of bullets ripping the air. The screams of wounded soldiers. The coppery taste of fear. The way sand soaks up blood like a thirsty sponge. He also knows they won't come right out and ask. They'll pussyfoot around the subject and hope Royce fills in the gaps.

So he tells them other stories from the desert. About camel spiders and scorpions. About trying to sleep in 120-degree heat. About working the shitter detail, dragging out pans from beneath the latrines, pouring in diesel, burning the disgusting stew, and stirring it with long paddles until it all burned off.

And he could have gotten off with just those guiltless stories, except Sabrina keeps stopping by, lingering at their booth, sitting next to Royce and stroking his leg. She's the one who pushes the conversation forward. She has no qualms about asking the tough questions. *You ever get shot at?*

Sure. We all did. He tells her about the time he took a round in his vest during a firefight without realizing it until later, when he took it off and saw the slit in the fabric, the spider-webbed indent in his Kevlar plate.

Yeah, but what was it like to kill someone?

Just something you had to do, you know.

Her hand is high on his thigh, her eyes glittering. *C'mon, Royce, you can tell me.*

Much as he wants to, he can't deny her anything. So Royce gulps down the last of his drink and feels its liquid fire hot in his gut. *First time, it happened before I even realized it. It was just instincts. Our squad was patrolling through this village and a guy pops up over a sandstone wall and points his AK at us. We fired at the same time and then he threw his hands up in the air like he was surprised. Then he just fell away. When we got around to the other side of the wall, he was just lying there all crumpled like with a spot of red on his chest. He wasn't even a person anymore. Just a pile of rags.*

Sabrina slides her hand higher and gives his cock a playful squeeze. Even with his stomach knotted, his muscles rigid with tension, her touch sends a thrill through his body.

Be right back with another refill, she says, taking his now-empty glass.

Royce looks down at his hands flat on the table and tries to focus on his breathing. Racing through his head is the compact of quid pro quo, the expectations that accompany every palm-passed tumbler of bourbon on the rocks, every whiskey sour and shot of tequila. In his mind's eye, he sees Sabrina continuing to pick at the scab until blood pours forth and he tells them all about Berkholtz being sawed in half by friendly fire.

He raises his head and looks across the table at his friends who sit hushed and expectant, their faces etched with lustful leers, their thirst unquenchable for the tonic of his sins.

Bright, Inconsequential Things

ENEMY ENCOUNTER

Jerking awake in his living room, Reuben Zahn's first thought is *Mortars!* Then he hears the pounding and his mind turns to a different type of attack: his sister with another dinner invite. Anything to pry him out of his apartment. Once she fixes on something, she's like a tick that won't shake off. Last time, she knocked for fifteen minutes. Then she threatened to get the rental office to do a health-and-welfare check if Reuben wouldn't open up. She knows which buttons to push, how private he is, and how much that invasion would piss him off.

As Reuben rubs his eyes and shuffles around the couch, he realizes the racket isn't coming from *his* door. Putting his eye to the peephole, he sees a stringy mullet and the back of a Harley-Davidson jacket. The hulk wearing it is banging on the door across the breezeway with an open palm. *Open up you little shit,* he yells. *Show your skinny ass.*

Zahn's neighbor Jeremy doesn't have the sense to hunker down and wait out the barrage. He opens his door with a placid look on his thin, goateed face. The image on his light blue

T-shirt shows hennaed hands pressed together in prayer with NAMASTE arched over them in a curly font.

The hulk grabs a fistful of shirt and hoists Jeremy so he's standing on tiptoe, nose-to-nose. *I know it was you, fucker. You're the one turned me in.*

Whoa, dude, Jeremy says. *Chill.*

Zahn knows what's coming before the behemoth cocks back his fist. Just as he'd known his first day in the company barracks, approaching his bunk and seeing the smirks on his new squadmates' faces, that an initiation ritual was coming. A painful one. As two of them pinned him to the bunk, the others took turns swinging a bar of soap wrapped in a towel at his exposed stomach. Hard as they could. Those welts were a badge of entry. But Jeremy has never known this type of brotherhood. To him, everything is peace, love, granola.

When the biker's fist connects with the hipster's wispy chin, Zahn feels a twinge of satisfaction. Half the time, he'd like to do the same. Maybe knock some sense into him. If the biker had left it at that, with Jeremy sprawled on the carpet inside his door, message delivered and received, Zahn wouldn't have intervened. But the biker steps forward, keen to continue his lesson.

Throwing his door open, Zahn rushes out and grabs the guy's jacket, spinning him around. *Hey, Harley,* he says, *I'm the one that turned you in.* Turned him in for what, Zahn doesn't know. He's never seen the biker before. But the goad does its trick.

Harley winds up a haymaker that never lands. Before he can swing, Zahn chops his Adam's apple with the blade of a hand. The biker doubles over and sucks wind. Gripping his belt and collar, Zahn turns him from Jeremy's door and propels him toward the stairs. He stumbles down the first few steps, then catches himself on the railing. He glares up. *You're going to pay for this.*

Sure, sure, Zahn says.

Stomping down to the parking lot, the biker yanks open the door of a Ford F-150. A pissing Calvin decal decorates his back window, a pair of nuts dangles from his trailer hitch, and a specialty license plate wreathed in silver chains reads, BIG DAWG.

As the big truck roars off, Zahn turns to see Jeremy on his feet, one hand cupping his jaw, wiggling it back and forth, testing it out. *Thanks, man. I don't know what I would've—*

Yeah, yeah. Listen, next time some psycho pounds on your door and you let him in, I'm just going to watch the show through my peephole. Maybe grab some popcorn.

Huh? Oh, of course, you're right. Next time. Thanks for stepping in, um—I don't even know your name.

Zahn.

You got a first name?

Listen, Jeremy, we're good here. Just use a little common sense, y'know. Zahn taps his temple for emphasis. Then he backs into his apartment and closes the door. Through the peephole he sees Jeremy standing there, dazed, like an insurgent in a sandstone hovel after a flash-bang grenade exploded at his feet, dust swirling around him as he struggles to understand what just happened. Before Zahn and his squadmates gun him down.

BASIC TRAINING

Zahn grew up envious of people like Jeremy. Soft kids protected from the world's hard corners by doting parents. Zahn's dad drove a forklift on night shift at a fish-packing warehouse. Coming home each morning he reeked of fish and Wild Turkey.

With his truck idling at the curb, he'd take stock of his situation—his dead-end job, his runaway wife, his shitty shotgun shack with its patchwork roof and water-stained ceiling—then he'd stomp up the front steps to confront his son.

An only child, Zahn's job was to take the abuse. Not *physical* abuse, but verbal; the few times Zahn's dad actually hit him were with a sudden backhand that seemed to surprise him more than Zahn. He hammered his son with words, long-winded rants that let Zahn know how worthless he was, how everything wrong was his fault.

Looking back on it, Zahn can only remember the feeling of insignificance, which still burns like a hot cinder. But the actual words from those demeaning tirades are a blur in his mind. His only clear images from childhood are of the rare occasions his dad made a half-assed effort to be fatherly. Once, he gave his son a pair of brass knuckles to take down a middle school bully. Another time, when Zahn was thirteen, his father took him to FedExField to see the Eagles take on the hometown Redskins. When Zahn's dad jeered the Skins and two locals threatened to beat his ass, Zahn kicked one of them in the balls, then jumped on the other's back and bit his ear. He never saw his dad more proud. Not even the night of his fifteenth birthday when his dad bought him a tired whore who took Zahn's cherry in the next room. When they came out of the bedroom, Zahn's father gave the woman her cash and tossed a beer to his son. *You're a man now,* he said, then turned his attention back to ESPN.

Zahn's senior year of high school, his father was incarcerated at Rivers Correctional Institute for running over a pedestrian. His fourth DUI. The prosecutor wanted to put him away for murder, but the inveterate drunk had been the one to call 911, blubbering and apologizing, and the public defender had actually been competent. Once headlines moved on to other stories, the charges quietly pled down to manslaughter, eight years with a possibility of early release for good behavior.

Zahn was seventeen, a younger version of his father, angry at the world for everything. Unlike his dad, he struck with fists, lashing out for any reason—a bumped shoulder in passing, a disrespectful look on someone's face, a hushed conversation that might (or might not) be about him. At a graduation party, Zahn put two kids in the hospital and wound up before a judge who gave him a choice of how to serve his time: in jail or in the Army. Next day, he went to the recruiter and enlisted.

In no time at all, Zahn was thrown into combat, kicking down doors and filling body bags, venting his rage and being praised for it. *You're a born killer,* Sergeant Faust said. *Hooah.*

So it went for years, multiple deployments to Iraq, decorating his chest with medals, then Afghanistan for more of the same. Combat supercharged Zahn, gave him purpose. What changed it all wasn't the accumulation of bodies or the number of times he was nearly killed. It was what happened after Zahn shot a man in the head and screamed his usual victory cheer—*That's how we do it, bitch!* Pumped full of adrenaline, he turned to see the dead man's young son looking on. The killing had been justified. The man had been armed and raising his AK. But all Zahn saw—all he *still* sees of that moment—was the stunned expression on that boy's face, the howl before he turned from his father to glare at Zahn, his brow bunched into a fist above hate-filled eyes.

RETREAT

Months ago, when Zahn started stocking groceries at Jewel-Osco, coworkers tried to chat him up. Now the crew gives him space, idling in aisles he's vacated, leaving the ones he enters. They know how little it takes to set him off, how easily he erupts. It's one of the reasons Zahn picked the night shift. With a skeleton crew, there's less chance he'll rip someone's head off.

Zahn is content to while away the night in shadowless fluorescence. Forking pallets and hauling freight over the waxy gleam of buffed tiles, stocking shelves with all the bright, inconsequential things that matter in a normal person's life. The desert seldom intrudes on this air-conditioned chill. Swaddled in the monotonous bliss of routine, Zahn can actually hold a thought. Sometimes he ponders differences between "stocking" and "stalking"—one, a chore, the other, an art; one lumbering through light, the other embracing dark.

He brings to work the same precision his squad leader admired, focusing on tiny details, straightening rows to right angles, searching for anything out of place. In the desert, soldiers scanned piles of trash for IEDs. But all Zahn finds here are the lunatic smiles of cereal mascots—the leprechaun, the bandannaed tiger, the elves yelping, *Snap, Crackle, Pop*. Such grinning joy, such easily repeated catchphrases echoing in Zahn's head. Almost like real conversation.

The questions don't come until break time when he eats his packed lunch on the loading docks' steel plates, legs dangling over the sides, staring beyond pavement into the woods. *Is it possible to change who I am at the core? Can living a peaceful life now make up for my violent past? Do I deserve anything more than this?* No matter the question, the same answer glares back from shadows in the wood line. The hate-filled eyes of the boy he made an orphan.

BATTLE PLAN

Staring in the mirror, Zahn thinks, *Whoever came up with TGIF can go fuck himself.* Zahn's workweek runs Sunday through Thursday, leaving Friday and Saturday nights as a void in his schedule. Nothing to do but hole up in his apartment, alone except for the ghosts. Berkholtz. Ramirez. Rambali. Jackson. Even their interpreter Kayoosh, that wiry Afghan who traded newspaper-wrapped figs and dates for MREs and rambled on about Khost's history as they rolled through its streets. His bone-handled hunting knife is the only memento Zahn brought home. The day Kayoosh didn't show for duty, a team went to check his home. Kayoosh, his wife, and their two children were flex-cuffed on the floor, sandbags pulled over their heads. Just like American soldiers did with potential suspects on raids. Except these sandbags were splattered with blood.

Most Friday nights, Zahn sits on his floor, lights off, picking at the carpet's pile with Kayoosh's knife, jumping at every little noise. The heater kicks on and the whirring fan blades remind him of Blackhawks. A car door closes and he hears the *crump* of a mortar launching from its tube. He's like a kid all over again, scared of noises in the dark. Except it's not monsters in his closet that he fears; it's the black dog in his heart, longing to be freed from its chain. On long nights when the clock ticks past two in the morning, when the boy's eyes burn in the shadows, and voices of dead squad members whisper in Zahn's ears, the phantom itch of sand creeps beneath his skin, worming into his brain.

But not tonight. Tonight, Zahn has a date.

Jeremy set it up. He came by earlier to ask a favor, said his wife had invited a friend named Aurora for dinner and wanted

Zahn to be her date so she wouldn't feel like a third wheel. Any other day, Zahn wouldn't have opened the door; but it was Friday, and the voices were already whispering.

Now, looking in the mirror, Zahn feels the need to fix something to make himself presentable. Maybe he should shave his buzz cut down to the scalp? Switch shirts to conceal the winged skull tattoo peeking out the neck of his Metallica tee? Shove cotton balls in his mouth to swell up his sunken cheeks? Put on a Halloween mask and pretend to be someone else?

He remembers once embracing the wild impulse of night, the joy of reckless abandon. Every moment electric. Alcohol's fiery tongue down his throat. The hungry pulse of blood. The need for flesh on flesh. Now human contact scares him. As long as he keeps away, he knows he's safe. Everyone else is, too.

Zahn tries on a smile but it doesn't fit the rest of his reflection, the lips turned up but the hooded eyes hard as ever.

Well, boys, he says, *time to tighten up your sphincters.* It's what Faust always said just before the squad set out on patrol. Before heading into enemy terrain.

DAMAGE ASSESSMENT

The foursome stands in the living room, fidgeting, sipping drinks. Whiskey on rocks for the boys, strawberry margaritas for the girls. Aurora is a young woman, early twenties, with a sheet of raven hair that keeps falling over one eye before she tosses it back with a snap of her head. Model skinny with angular features, but with lips too thin and teeth too snaggled to ever be a cover girl. She's wearing Vietnam-era fatigue pants and a dog collar tight around her slender neck. The sleeves and collar of her sweatshirt are ripped out, and printed across the chest in block letters is: THINGS TO DO BEFORE I DIE: 1. BUY MILK. 2. GET THE MAIL. 3. EXPLAIN THIS SHIRT.

Zahn hadn't changed anything from the mirror. Not his Metallica tee, his seat-worn jeans, his scuffed Army desert boots. No need to impress. Seems like she'd had the same thought.

I'll bite, he says, nodding at her sweatshirt. *What's it mean?*

Set your expectations low, you won't be disappointed.

Deep.

No, shallow. That's the point.

She flips her hair back, then invades Zahn's personal space. Normally, a slip of a girl like her would be repelled by his air of menace. But she looks Zahn up and down, surveying, her nose wrinkling like she's about to send an order of bad fish back to the kitchen. He expects her to comment on the string of glossy shrapnel scars on his left forearm, but when her brow unclenches, what she says is, *Like your boots.*

She does that throughout the night, squinting as she studies an object before announcing some peculiar observation. Zahn makes a game of it in his head, trying to figure out what she'll say, but he's wrong each time. When she fingers the plastic lei looped around the stem of her margarita glass, she says, *Ancient Hawaiians made human sacrifices of defeated politicians. Might be something to that.* Studying a painting of a horse and rider, she says, *Stonewall Jackson was shot off his horse by his own men, but that didn't kill him. He died of pneumonia eight days later.* And when she stands in front of a three-foot replica of an Easter Island sculpture, she says, *Did you know that the first dildos were made out of stone?*

Jeremy's wife, Melanie, recoils at the last comment, her nondrinking hand clutching her breast as if shot. *Wherever did you learn such bizarre trivia?*

I was a history major before dropping out. Aurora sips loudly, then smacks her lips. *Is there anything more useless than a degree in history?*

Not if you're a history teacher, Zahn says.

I look like a teacher?

Zahn leans back to give her the same once-over she'd given him. *I don't know. But if you were, I might consider going back to school.*

Aurora's mouth spreads into a genuine smile, her bad teeth showing for a moment before she covers them up with the back of a hand.

Zahn pulls her wrist down. *No need to hide.*

She smiles again, and unlike the eyes in Zahn's reflection, hers show appreciation.

MOVEMENT TO CONTACT

If you're walking me all the way home, Aurora says, *I should warn you about my mother.*

Out past your curfew? Zahn says.

Funny. No, see my mom, when guys come over, she prances around like she's still Miss Naperville. She'll probably hit on you.

Miss Naperville? You mean, like in a pageant?

Yeah, like a pageant. You know, tiaras, world peace, the whole shebang.

Hmm. Never been with a beauty queen before. Something to consider.

She punches his shoulder. But she's smiling and still not covering it up.

Zahn hasn't felt this comfortable this quickly around someone since the Army. There, you jump in a fighting position with someone you've never met before and you're instant brothers. If you had to, you would give your life for him.

The sidewalk they're walking on is treacherous. Dirty mounds of snow piled at the curb overflow onto the narrow walkway in places. Between the white drifts are patches of slick ice. Aurora jumps over one of the icy sheets, her unbuttoned overcoat flapping wide, the sheen of lamplight on her collarbones.

You ever try pageants? he says.

She rolls her eyes. *Much as I hate to admit it, yes. Ugh. When I was little. Before I learned it was okay to say no to Mom.*

An edge to her voice hints not to pry. But Zahn has suffered that same kid-glove treatment, everyone saying, *Thanks for your service*, then giving him that pitying expression that makes him want to slap it off their face. *So what's the deal with you and your mother? I mean, you still live there, so she can't be that bad, right?*

Aurora halts and stares at the crusted snow, her face tight. Zahn waits her out. He knows she's teetering at the lip of a well of pain, wondering whether to pull up a bucket and pour it out.

Picture this, she says, *first thing every morning, Mom has me step on the scale. Then she pinches my waist and says something like, "Guys don't like fat girls." It's not that I believe her or anything. I know I'm not fat, but that doesn't make it hurt any less. And the way she looks at me all day, like she's studying me, figuring out the thing she can say that will cut me the most.*

Again, Zahn feels a moment of caution before saying what she already knows but needs to hear out loud. *You're not your mother. You want to change, do it. You don't want to be skin and bones, then eat a little more.*

At dinner tonight, she'd eaten half her salad, picked at her roasted Tofurky, left the mashed potatoes alone entirely, and forked steamed carrots into her mouth one slice at a time.

Yeah, she says, *I know.*

'Cause if I ever take you out to some restaurant, you got to do more than nibble on garnishes.

What makes you think I'd go out with you?

He feigns a shocked expression. *You're out with me right now.*

Fine. What makes you think I'd go out with you again?

Crystal ball.

She glances at Zahn's crotch. *Just one of them?*

He lets loose a belly laugh, first time in ages. Then he grabs Aurora's gloved hand. The bones are delicate, fragile as a baby bird's.

I almost didn't come tonight, Aurora says. *Glad I did.*

Why did you?

Oh, Melanie said I could meet someone as fucked up as I was.

Melanie said that? C'mon.

Well, she actually said I could meet someone who was perfect for me. But I'm good at reading between the lines.

They walk in silence a few beats.

I'm perfect, huh?

She pulls his hand around her shoulder. *Her words, not mine.*

WINNING HEARTS AND MINDS

Stocking aisle 9 on autopilot, Zahn is thinking of his wars, dredging up dread-soaked memories and wringing them out. Jackson blown up on guard duty. Kayoosh and his family trussed on the floor of his mud hut. The orphaned boy turning to scorch him with his burning eyes.

The Army turned Zahn into an efficient killer, taught him how to sight a moving target, how to stack outside a door, how to double-tap prostrate bodies while racing by to ensure no one shoots you in the back. All those lessons built on endless repetition like Pavlov with his dog. All the blood-spattered knowledge passed from warring father to warring son. All the razor-edged expertise gained from centuries of grief. Skills so dire in the desert now as useless as mantras about *going along to get along.*

Zahn is just about done on 9 when he hears a crash one aisle over. Instead of pushing his dolly to the stockroom for another load, he slides into 10 and sees Toby standing over a dumped load of soup cans and cursing. *Hey, how about I give you a hand.*

Toby's expression flips from irritation at the spilled mess to bewilderment over Zahn's offer. Then he nods, saying, *Yeah, that'd be great. Thanks.*

They scoop up the spilled cans, and Zahn thinks how good it feels to be kneeling on the floor together. Almost like praying.

CONDUCT UNBECOMING

Zahn's second date with Aurora is dinner at Olive Garden. This time he does dress up. After trying on several outfits, he settles on a button-down Oxford and the only pair of dress pants he owns. He's pleased with his choice when he sees Aurora in a clingy blue dress and a white flower in her hair.

At the restaurant, they order the same thing, never-ending pasta, three plates for him, one for her. But she eats every bite. Seated at adjoining sides of their table, they keep touching each other's arms and knees. Her perfume makes him want to lean over and smell her neck every chance he gets.

After dinner, they stroll arm in arm along brick-paved side-walks fronting a procession of bistros and bars whose revelry spills outside to their patios. Other couples pass by, also enjoy-ing the last light of evening on this cool, cloudless night.

Skirting a huddle of smokers in Harley-Davidson jackets,

Zahn recognizes one of them. Big Dawg. Aurora and Zahn keep walking, but the biker must have made the connection, too. *Look who it is,* he yells. *The shitface who jumped me from behind.*

Zahn turns to assess the situation, stepping between Aurora and potential danger. Big Dawg tosses his cigarette and glares. The other two bikers keep smoking, unperturbed. Maybe they know what a blowhard their friend is.

Sorry about that, Zahn says, putting his arm around Aurora and continuing their walk in the other direction.

You better be sorry, Big Dawg yells. But Zahn hears no approaching footsteps and keeps walking.

I see you've bumped into that asshole as well, Aurora says.

Huh? How do you know him?

He shops at the Dollar Store where I cashier. He's always got some lewd comment for me. Ick. She shivers.

Like what?

Doesn't matter.

Zahn nods to himself. She's right. It doesn't matter *what* that piece of shit said, just the fact that he said it. Dropping Aurora's arm, he spins and rockets toward Big Dawg like a heat-seeking missile. *Turn around,* Zahn calls out. *Don't want you telling anyone I jumped you from behind.*

Big Dawg holds up his hands in a placating gesture. Zahn grabs a wrist and twists the arm behind the big man's back. Then Zahn locks a choke hold around his neck. If he keeps squeezing, he can make him pass out; and if Zahn drops to the ground, he can snap the biker's neck like a dry twig. *Apologize,* he says.

Sorry, man, Big Dawg croaks. *Sorry.*

Not to me. Her.

Before he can wrench the biker's head around to face Aurora, she is beating on Zahn's back.

What the fuck are you doing? she screams.

He releases his choke and Big Dawg bends over, wheezing, one hand on a knee, the other at his throat.

Who the hell you think you are? Aurora says. She rips the flower from her hair and throws it at Zahn's feet. Then she brushes past the men, her heels clicking a staccato rebuke.

On the patios, all faces are turned toward Zahn. In each one he sees the horrified expression he's been running from since the war. Anger drains out of him in a whoosh and he stands there, helpless. Big Dawg's friends hook hands beneath his armpits and help him stand up. If he threw a punch now, Zahn would do nothing to stop him. Except Big Dawg doesn't. He just stands there with a smirk on his face.

SCORCHED EARTH

Gus the grocery store manager leans on his desk, shoulders slumped, neck bulging over his collar. On the breast of his white shirt is a U.S. flag pin. Thumbtacked to a bulletin board, a bumper sticker reads, WE SUPPORT OUR TROOPS! A big red heart dots the exclamation point. He's reprimanding Zahn for breaking store policy again, mumbling into his chest instead of making eye contact.

Zahn sits in a hard-backed chair on the other side of the desk, bloody knuckles limp in his lap, wondering if his stocking career is over. His eyes are scratchy like they're full of grit. He only got three hours' sleep this morning, two the day before. His mind is swimming and it's hard to follow what Gus is saying. Something about the hole Zahn punched in the break-room wall. Something about the need for a safe work environment.

Gus suggests counting to ten when Zahn gets mad. *Try to think happy thoughts.*

And what can Zahn say? He's just not that guy. *Nothing* has prepared him to be *that guy*. Not his father's brass-knuckled gift. Not the scores of brawls that showed him the value of striking first. Not the months of training deep in the pines and scrubby dunes of Fort Bragg, where he invaded mock cities, kicked down doors, and shot torsos of plastic targets shaped like men.

Driving to work this evening, Zahn had cracked the windows of his Honda Civic to let the frigid air swirl in. As he cruised side streets, taking the long way in, the scrolling view transformed into sandstone walls and minarets, the plowed snow becoming a blizzard of roadside trash, each piece a potential IED.

Staring at the manager's thin black tie, the way it separates the halves of his starched white shirt like a zipper, Zahn wonders if he ever worries about splitting in two, another person climbing out from the shell that everyone else can see. He'd rather talk about that than the wire coiled in his gut.

Gus sighs and leans forward. *It must be difficult,* he says, *everything you've been through. I can't begin to imagine.* He lets the sentence hang between them, waiting for Zahn to fill the dead air.

As the silence stretches, Zahn remembers how relieved Aurora had been to share those secrets about her mother. He can feel the words on his tongue. But instead of telling Gus about the coiled spring, he says, *No worries, boss. Everything's under control.*

Shaking hands, the two men go their separate ways. Gus

eases his beige Volvo onto a street shaded by elms. When the taillights disappear around a corner, Zahn exits the lot and turns onto the highway, stomping the accelerator to the floor, ready to greet any obstacle with the full force of his momentum.

What Won't Stay Buried

Maybe the ultimate wound is the one that
makes you miss the war you got it in.
—From *War*, by Sebastian Junger

BEFORE THE BLOOD

Before the blood, Daniel Faust's violent past didn't intrude upon his peaceful present. A line supervisor at Widmark Bag, he spent his shift walking circuits on the factory floor, chatting with workers and spot-checking orders. Unflappable in this domain, he was a man who wrung solutions out of every problem.

Before the blood, no one but Faust's wife, Olivia, knew of his military background. Not his coworkers, not his neighbors, not even his children, Magnus, age eight, and Mercy, age six, born shortly after he'd ETS'd from the Army. War and everything he'd seen and done during combat were buried deep within himself. The past had no place in the factory, where he ambled through his day and quashed minor problems, nor outside, where he bobbed along in life's currents, content within a bubble of his own creation.

Before the blood—*long before*—dead comrades floated

through his bleary-eyed days, their whispers reminding him of all he wanted to forget. He pushed them into a pit deep inside himself and shoveled dirt on their faces. But then came the blood, and the revenants crept out of their graves.

ZERO DAYS WITHOUT AN INJURY

From the glass cubicle of the supervisor's office, Daniel scans the factory floor for anything amiss. From this vantage, he views the back ends of a dozen paper bag machines, each twice as big as a farm combine. All the machines are thrumming and everyone performing their tasks—lead operators inspecting bags for quality, machine helpers stacking finished bales on pallets, and waste handlers blowing off machine surfaces with air hoses.

Most workers ignore the paper dust that clots the atmosphere. Floating particulates are too fine to be seen by the naked eye, so it's not until the end of the shift, when they change into street clothes and shove uniforms rimed with a fuzzy brown film into lockers, that they consider the incremental damage to their lungs. On the floor, it's the railcar-sized bag machines that get their hackles up, the insatiable hunger with which they gnash. The most dangerous spot is the open-faced drum, where the web of brown paper fed into one side of the machine is cut and folded into individual bags. The drum is rife with hazards—razor-edged slitters, snapping drum fingers, and folding wings that can easily grab a loose sleeve or an un-netted tress and pull its careless owner into the drum, crushing bones in a matter of seconds.

Daniel has already taped up his wedding band, inserted earplugs, and donned safety goggles, so he steps out of his office and is immediately swallowed by the thunder of heavy machinery. His circuit normally begins near the workers' entrance at Machine Twelve and progresses inward toward One. But today he starts at Machine Three. Lavonna has recently been certified as a lead operator and this is her first order helming the machine. Crowding next to her on the anti-fatigue mat at the inspection station, Daniel pulls a bag from the conveyor. He checks the ink design on the bag's front, then the paste at the central seam and bottom. He checkmarks a page on his clipboard and bends to Lavonna's ear. Even this close, he has to yell to be heard over the constant roar. *Looks perfect,* he says. *Just what I'd expect from you.*

From beneath his clipboard, he pulls a tin of gingerbread cookies that his wife baked. *These are from Olivia. She's as proud of you as I am.*

Lavonna beams. *Thanks, boss.*

Daniel informs her of the bumping priorities, then heads to Machine Twelve to continue his rounds. If he notices bags coming off a conveyor with crumpled corners or long slits, he'll shut the machine down and call an adjuster over for a quick fix. Jamal or Martin will wheel a tool cart to the quiet hulk, and soon enough bags will be spitting off the drum again.

At Machine One, he asks the lead, Tori, how the new hire, Miguel, is working out.

Great, she says, talking over her shoulder, keeping her eyes on the conveyor. *He's real eager. Doesn't speak much English, but you just need to show him something once and he gets it.*

A fat bottom protrudes from the line of marching bags and Tori's hand snatches the bag before it reaches the ram arm and gets pressed into a bale. *Looks like one of the drum fingers is slipping,* she says.

I'll send an adjuster over to look at it after I finish my rounds.

Daniel's next stop is the warehouse. This section of the

factory is filled with two-ton paper rolls that tower forty feet high. He patrols through aisles where clamp-truck drivers sometimes hide in alcoves among the stacks. Finding none, he walks over to the railhead loading docks, the only place where smoking is allowed. Dimitri, one of the waste handlers, sits on the steel plates with a cigarette notched in his fingers. Crisp winter air curls around Daniel as he crouches beside him and pops out his earplugs. The tracks are empty of cars and the rail lines vanish into a blanket of snow. The vista beyond is speckled with oaks, ash, and sassafras, their bare crowns limned in white.

How's Lena doing? Daniel asks. *She kick that flu bug yet?*

Yah, much better. She pretend is not so good. She like me cooking.

Daniel laughs. *You know what they say: happy wife, happy life.*

Yah, yah.

Well, about time to get back to it, Daniel says. He stands up and lingers on the dock.

Dimitri takes a last puff, stubs his cigarette out on the steel plate, and shoves the butt in his pocket. Before Daniel got promoted to supervisor, smokers would toss spent butts all over the docks. Then Daniel made them do "police calls," picking up all the butts and other litter. Now the docks are pristine.

Dimitri rises and grabs his waste cart, pushing it toward the rumbling machines. Daniel peels off as they near Machine One. He sees Tori up on the ladder spraying silicone into the drum and Miguel standing in her spot at the inspection station. Miguel yanks bags with loose bottoms from the conveyor but misses one, only managing to pull the bottom flap out so it droops like a dog's ear outside the marching line of brown. He grabs the flap but it just snags other bags in the stack and makes more of a mess. He tries to straighten the bags, and Tori yells frantically, waving her hand in a stop-it motion. But it is too late. The ram arm shoots up and catches his hand, pulling his arm up into the stacker. Tori clambers down the ladder and hits the Emergency Stop button. The machine crashes to a halt, scorched paper emitting a smell like burnt oatmeal.

Miguel is dangling from the stack of bags, half in and half out of the machine. The thin edge of the stacker has sliced the underside of his upper arm, and blood spurts out, coating his torso, the bags, and the machine. Miguel screams and curses in Spanish. Tori hits the control panel's Reset button, but with the stacker jammed, the ram arm won't reset. She steps back from the panel and stands there dazed and holding her head as the amber alert light flashes above her on its pole.

One glance at the blood spatter and Daniel knows there's no time to waste. Candy-apple red is the harbinger of death, fresh from the heart and full of oxygen. Experience has taught him how quickly arterial bleeders can drain a body dry. Daniel races past Tori, his X-Acto knife in hand. He dives to the base of the hydraulic cylinder and cuts the connecting hose. Dark fluid gushes out and the ram arm lowers with a loud hiss. As Miguel's hand jerks free, he topples and flips over the conveyor, landing hard on the floor. His eyes are wide and he's clutching his forearm, his hand flopping unnaturally. Miguel is weak from loss of blood, but Daniel still has to fight him to pull his good hand away and get at the gash under his arm, which is still bleeding. He squeezes the brachial artery with both hands and yells at Tori to get him some rags. She tosses him a couple of the blue utility rags. He loops one around Miguel's arm and ties it so the knot is right above the gash. He ties another rag higher up his arm, but this time with just one loop. Then he slots a wrench between the tails of the knot and twists them until the makeshift tourniquet cuts off the flow of blood. Then he fastens the wrench to the first knot.

The sides of the stacker look like a red Rorschach. With all the blood Miguel's lost, there's no time to wait for an ambulance. Tori still seems too dazed to be much help, so Daniel throws Miguel over his shoulder in a fireman-carry and hauls him out the employee entrance. He dumps him in the back of his Ford Taurus, then squeals out of the parking lot, racing for Palos Hospital.

Hey, Daniel says, looking over the back seat, *stay awake back there.*

Miguel is limp and glassy eyed, but he gives Daniel a slight nod.

There you go. Stick with me. Everything's going to be fine. Daniel smiles even though he doesn't believe his own words. He's seen enough bodies drained of animus to recognize the gray and gasping end.

SAVING LIVES

Dressed in a nurse's scrub top, his own bloody shirt dumped in a hazardous waste bin, Daniel sits in a plastic chair bolted to the wall outside the surgical hallway. Now that he has passed Miguel off to hospital staff, he's coming down off his adrenaline high. He knows this feeling well from four deployments to Iraq and Afghanistan, from sustained battles and countless skirmishes. After the amped-up, all-encompassing intensity of combat, the thrill of survival always brought full-bodied satisfaction, like the afterglow of a satiated lover.

Pulling out his phone, he makes the requisite calls in a near stupor. The plant manager. The HR department. The Alvarado home to inform Miguel's family. With each conversation, he rehashes and relives the accident, the moments playing out in slow motion on his mental movie screen.

The one call he hasn't made is to Olivia. Tonight is the big Oscar party she's been planning for months, and he needs to let her know he'll be late to help with setup. He's waiting for the excitement to dissipate, for his bubble of calm to rewrap him in its comfortable glow.

The quiet, antiseptic, well-lit hallway is the antithesis of his usual environment. He looks down between his bouncing knees at his steel-toed Red Wings. The paint-flecked leather is one of those tiny identifiers of his industrial work. He takes a deep breath and stares at a six-foot painting hung on the opposite wall. It depicts a herd of antelope bounding left to right through a grassy savanna. Something to inspire tranquility, he supposes, but all he can think of is the predator outside the frame, whatever spooked the herd into their headlong rush.

Turning back to his phone, he scrolls through his contacts list and comes across Bryce Pearson. As a corporal, Faust had been a team leader and Pearson one of three soldiers in his charge. They were the same age and liked each other well enough, but the military adhered to a rigid hierarchy and Faust had been the one in charge. Any command he gave, Pearson had to obey. It meant they could never be equals; not until Pearson received his medical discharge.

Pearson had been blown up in Afghanistan, the bomb tearing away half his face and killing his best friend. The docs put him back together, but he was never the same. He kept calling the barracks, ranting to old squadmates about the soft civilian world. The guys nicknamed him Section 8 and avoided his calls. Easier to do that than ponder how they're going to adjust themselves when the time comes.

They'd all seen news stories of soldiers acclimated to combat returning home, the violence bred into them spilling into their relationships and breaking them apart. And though they'd all been warned with past examples, it kept happening over and over again. Zahn's girlfriend dumped him during his first tour; Mueller's wife divorced him after his second; and Faust nearly lost Olivia after his fourth. Faust had been flying into bouts of sudden, explosive rages, and she was ready to leave him. But she was pregnant with Mercy at the time, so she gave him an ultimatum—her or the Army; he couldn't keep both. He picked family and put in his papers. But it took a full year for the rages to subside. And longer still before combat stopped ruling his dreams, before Mercy's first steps and Magnus's wobbly bike rides took their place.

Now the electricity is back in his veins. Staring at his contact list, he thinks about Pearson, who'd become a professional poker player in Vegas. He was practically the poster boy for PTSD turnaround. Faust taps Pearson's name, unsure what he's going to say but knowing he needs to talk to someone. It goes straight to voicemail. *Hey, buddy,* he says, *saw you on ESPN last year at the World Series tournament. You did awesome. Bummer you didn't make the final table. Sure came close though.*

The double doors swing open and a smooth-faced surgeon in green scrubs steps through. He looks young enough to be a new recruit.

Hey, listen, Faust says into the phone. *Got to run. I'll call you later.*

Faust stands up and asks about Miguel. The doctor's forehead furrows. *I really can't give you any details,* he says. *HIPAA regulations. But I can tell you he's going to keep his arm.* He claps a hand on Faust's shoulder. *You probably saved his life with that tourniquet. He would have bled out otherwise. Good job.* Then the doctor turns and follows one of the lines painted on the floor toward his next emergency.

It was the same phrase Sergeant Berkholtz had used. *Each man we kill,* he'd say, *is ten of our own that get to live. Nothing wrong in that. We're saving lives, bro, saving lives.*

THE DRIVE HOME

All that had mattered to Faust at the start of the day had been his family and his suburban home in Westmont with the icicle-style Christmas lights still dangling from the gutters and a snowman in the yard wearing a red scarf and a Burger King crown. Now, he can't stop thinking of the desert. Even the salt chunks grinding under his tires and plunking off the Ford Taurus's undercarriage remind him of a Humvee crossing Iraq's rock-strewn plains. He turns up his Corinne Bailey Rae CD, but her silky voice fails to change his mood. Everything seems starker now, grayer. The sky, the grimy snow piled up on the side of the Tri-State Tollway, the drivers' faces behind their fogged-up windows.

Traffic is backed up due to four snowplows scraping the road and spreading salt behind them. On another day, Faust might admire the precision of their winged formation, the way each plow lags slightly behind the one in front, gathering up the snow its angled blade pushes sideways, then passing it on to the next plow in line. But today he's white-knuckling the wheel, the old anger itching behind his eyeballs. He looks around at drivers in luxury sedans and SUVs. They think they're safe but Faust knows better. He knows how easily a .50 cal could chew through their doors. He also knows if they charged at a guarded boom barrier, what grim pleasure a private would take in aerating their vehicle.

That's the thing civilians can't understand. Yes, war is horrific and devastating, but it is addictive, too. In the lull between battles, soldiers long for the next attack, for the next thrill of near-death. Once you're shot at, once the supersonic crack of bullets rips the sky above your head, once you stand amidst the maelstrom and survive, you feel more alive and vital than ever before. And when you do it over and over, firing back at those who want you dead, something changes in your mental programming. You lose the ability to view anything else with consequence. *That* was what he had buried. But maybe not deep enough. Miguel's blood had stirred something in his own veins, and the past is screaming from its pit.

He remembers when kudzu crept over a couple of ranges at Fort Bragg. Work details scythed it up one summer, completely clearing the ground of the leafy vine. But it popped up again three years later and spread its tentacles anew. The dormant pods buried underground were just waiting for the right conditions.

In one of the lanes beside him, a ranting man punches the wheel in the wake of the plows. *That's it,* Faust says to himself, laughing, *give it the old one-two.*

OSCAR NIGHT

Lounging on the black, faux-leather couch in the living room of Daniel and Olivia's split-level home are their friends, Jim, Rita, and Janet. Rita's husband, Barney, is on a stool by the bar. Olivia sits in a wing chair close to the women, Daniel in another wing chair beside Jim, who is sprawled over one corner of the couch, arms and legs spread wide, a tub of popcorn balanced on the mound of his belly. Mercy had been operating a makeshift candy counter—two sheets of poster board atop a low set of shelves and covered with a white tablecloth—but she'd petered out and gone up to bed. Magnus is still on duty dressed as a butler wearing a fake moustache and a dress shirt with pearl buttons. He is in charge of the mixed drinks. He only knows how to make two—a sweet Manhattan and a bitter one—but he delights in doing so.

Daniel keeps zoning out, blinking himself back from the desert to catch up with the Oscars ceremony playing on the plasma screen. At the second commercial break, Jim sets his empty tub on the coffee table and slaps Daniel's knee. *I really wolfed that down, huh?*

Daniel smiles.

Is this Orville Redenbacher's?

Not sure. I think so.

Janet never gets the microwave stuff. Says it causes cancer. But, this sure tastes better than the bland stuff she buys in a bag. Jim turns toward Janet. *Hey, honey, what's the name of that God-awful popcorn you buy?*

Shush, shush, Janet says, flapping a hand at him before turning back to her conversation with the women.

Jim turns back to Daniel. *She claims that stuff is healthier for you, but then, soon as she pours it in a bowl, she dumps this butter-flavored powder all over it. Pfftt. Give me the real stuff any day.*

Jim blathers on about his minor annoyances, and Daniel nods along, watching his friend's mouth flap in his moon of a face, dough of a double chin jiggling over his tight collar and paisley bow tie. He grunts monosyllabic responses when asked something, but otherwise is mum. Jim barely notices.

When the "In Memoriam" sequence comes on, and faces

of directors, screenwriters, and movie stars who died in the past year scroll across the screen, Faust feels something unspool within himself. His hand loosens and his cocktail glass falls onto the carpet, snapping into two pieces at the stem. Olivia rushes into the kitchen and comes back with a roll of paper towels, sopping up the mess as Daniel gathers shards into what remains of the glass. He follows her into the kitchen and dumps the broken pieces in the trash.

What has gotten into you? Olivia asks sotto voce. *I thought you were excited about this party, too.*

I am, honey. Sorry. Just a lousy day at work.

His phone rings in the living room, and he moves to get it. But Olivia grabs his sleeve.

A lousy day, huh? That all it is? 'Cause if something's bothering you, you know you can talk to me.

Like I said, it's nothing.

Okay, well, get it together then. 'Cause once we go back in there—she points to the living room—*I expect nothing but smiles and scintillating conversation.*

He gives her a big, showy smile.

Atta boy, she says and gives him a peck.

Magnus calls out, holding up Daniel's cell phone. *Daddy, some guy says he was in the Army with you.*

Daniel pulls free from Olivia and strides into the living room.

You were in the Army? Jim says. *I never knew.*

Daniel grabs the phone without responding, taking it down the hallway to the master bedroom. *Pearson,* he says into the receiver, *that you?*

Yeah, it's me.

Hey, we're kind of having an Oscar viewing party over here. Got people over and everything. So I can't talk long.

Ah. Sorry if I messed up your party.

No biggie, man.

The Oscars. Man, I'm watching it, too. How about this "In Memoriam" montage? It's like they're saying all these movie people's lives are more important than anyone else's, you know.

Yeah, yeah. I hear you.

Hell, can you imagine something like that for Berkholtz or Ramirez or Jackson?

No, I guess not.

Pearson sniffles and takes a deep breath. *Need to add another guy to that list,* he says. *Kid named Darrell Trawick. I pushed him to join up. It's all my fault, man.* His voice starts to crack. *All my fault.*

No, it's no one's fault. Shit happens.

That's it, huh? Shit just happens? That supposed to make me sleep better at night?

It's just the truth. He hears something like ice clinking in a glass, then a slurp and a loud swallow.

Anyway, man, I was just hoisting one for fallen comrades and thought this would be a good time to call you back.

No problem, Pearson. It's all good. I'll toast them myself soon as I get off here.

Yeah, maybe we can make this a tradition, huh? Me calling you up each Oscar night. Toasting.

Sure. That'd be fine.

But then, something happens to me, who you going to call about it? Huh?

The truth Faust knows—they both know—is nobody. But what he says is, *Anyone who'll listen.*

Pearson chuckles. *Yeah. You're all right, Sergeant Faust.* Then the line disconnects.

Faust stares at the phone. His hands are trembling. He exits the bedroom and walks down the hall. *Everything all right?* Olivia asks. The TV is muted and all their friends are staring at him.

He marches into the kitchen and through the door leading to the garage. He slaps the garage door button and bounds down the steps. As the doors rumble overhead, he grabs the axe from the wall and turns to see Olivia in the open doorway, a nimbus of light behind her head. He gives her a grim look and her eyes widen with fright. For the briefest moment, before coming to his senses, her shocked look gives him a feeling of pleasure. But it vanishes just as fast as it appeared. He forces a smile and makes an *okay* symbol with his thumb and forefinger. Then he waves her back inside.

When she retreats and closes the door, he shuffles through the foot-deep snow toward the woodpile. Pulling back the tarp, he knocks several logs off the stack. He sets the first one up on end and takes a ready stance, the axe handle gripped in both hands, its blade as hungry as his own pulsing need to break something solid into pieces.

All the Fractured Pieces

Between 2000–2018, US soldiers have
suffered 225,144 traumatic brain injuries.
—Armed Forces Health Surveillance Branch

2007

There was an explosion. Royce Tefertiller remembers that much. The *fact* of it, not the actual occurrence. Moments before the blast are clear as snapshots in his head—Staff Sergeant Muñoz giving the operations order, squad members checking equipment, the convoy racing down Route Hornet, dust pluming in its wake—but the blast itself is a brown spot. When his mind fast-forwards to what comes next, the mental picture skips. The Humvee is suddenly on its side, the air thick with gunfire and choking sand.

Under this microscope the remembered version of himself cannot move. He's weak and pinned in place by the Humvee's crumpled center column. All he can do is gaze at the shredded face of Corporal Rambali hanging over him like an accusation, blood leaking from his torn body like a dripping faucet. Tefertiller has no idea how long he lies there waiting for someone to cut him out and cart him to the combat support hospital.

Long enough for the red spatter on his uniform to harden into a black crust.

1993

Cub Scout Troop 113 forms up in a line. They've spent the past three days on archery, knot tying, and other badge-earning activities. Now here they are on the other side of Lake Osborn, where Brian Duffy's kayak is beached. It was against the rules to go to this side of the lake, out of bounds, so to speak. But Brian wanted to investigate the woods, curious about last night's ghost story, the one that had frightened Royce enough at one point to yelp and momentarily hug Brian seated next to him on a log. The story, ironically enough, was about a boy who disappears.

After scout leaders string the boys out at even intervals, everyone marches northward, calling Brian's name. The boy has only been missing a few hours, but daylight is giving way to dark. There's nothing to fear in the woods when the sun is out, but night is another story. That's when predators lurk in every dark hollow, in every rustle outside their flashlights' beams.

The boys chatter nervously as they tromp through the woods, some even joking that Brian will pop out at any moment and scare them. But *this* is a different kind of scary, different from the sudden jolts that leave you giggling afterwards. *This*, Royce thinks, is the kind of scary that his mother always warns about, the fanged mouth waiting to swallow children who wander too far from home.

The quest for Brian only lasts twenty minutes. His tiny voice responds to their calls, and the line of scouts breaks into a formless jumble trotting through forest. When they find him, he is scratched and dirt smudged but otherwise unharmed.

He's soon laughing, punching arms, falling in with the others as they march back to the lake, back to the long skiffs that had ferried them across from Camp Shands.

When Royce calls home that evening to tell his parents about the incident, he jokes about it like the other boys. But his mother sees no humor in the situation, only the near-miss warning that confirms her narrative of how things really are. She drives all night from the tip of Florida's Panhandle to the campsite northwest of Orlando to retrieve her only child. The scare is still fresh enough to Royce that he doesn't mind leaving the jamboree early. He doesn't yet realize that it's all over. No more scouts. No more camping. No more trips into the woods at all.

2007

It's Monoceros, Tefertiller says, his eyes half-lidded, his mumbling voice still conveying the professorial tone of one explaining something he loves to the ill-informed, *just above the bright Dog Star, Sirius. Monoceros is also called the Unicorn. See the way its body forms a horn on the left?* He raises his hand to outline the constellation, and the action brings him out of his daydream, back to the present, to a containerized ward at the 399th CSH. Instead of a night sky full of stars, he sees strings of Christmas lights fastened to reinforced walls. His bed has side rails and the back side is elevated, propping him into a sitting position. A sippy cup and a paper dish of half-eaten food sits atop a rolling table positioned over his lap.

He looks around for the soldiers who'd asked him about the night sky, which stars their loved ones could also view from home. Something taped to his face obscures the view from his left eye like a horse's blinder, so he turns his head in that direction and sees other patients in beds, some moaning, some bandaged so heavily you can barely tell they're human.

A nurse in an OD green T-shirt steps over to his bedside. *Well,* she says, *that sounds interesting.*

A sense of déjà vu knuckles Tefertiller's spine. She seems familiar, as does her voice and the platitude. *Has she offered it before? If so, how many times?* He shakes his head. Checking for his chronograph wristwatch with its calendar function, he finds in its place a plastic band imprinted with his name. He scans the walls for a paper calendar. *Has he been in here for days or years?* He's not sure, but he doesn't want to ask this woman with the pleasant, familiar face. Tefertiller is self-conscious about his wide face and overbite, so when he smiles, as he does now, it's all lips. *My serious boy* is what his father always says.

The nurse leans in to check the bandages on the left side of his face and neck. *Tell me again about that other constellation,* she says, *the one your soldier buddies liked so much. You know, the one that looks like a hunter.*

You mean Orion.

Yes, that's the one.

What else is there for Tefertiller to do but tell about Orion, to follow orders even when they aren't *really* orders. Besides, sharing his knowledge of stars that speckle the night's velveteen fabric is something he's always enjoyed. *Orion was once a great hunter on Earth,* he begins. And as the words spill out, he falls into the myth. And then he falls, once more, through time.

1991

Royce adores his father, an accountant who carries a hardshell briefcase and wears white dress shirts with thin black ties. Atop the desk in Royce's tidy bedroom, lined up evenly, each spaced an inch from the right edge, is an abacus, a slide rule, and a Rubik's Cube, which he can solve in a minute flat. The desk kneehole is on the left side, where Royce is updating baseball stats from yesterday's games. He logs the data on sheets of graph paper with player names written across the paper's long edge, updating one team at a time. After each one, he gathers the baseball cards for that team, wraps the stat sheet around them to form a tight package, secures it with two rubber bands, and then returns the team to its alphabetical spot in the orange Nike shoebox.

Whenever the Marlins game is televised, Royce and his father watch it together. His father sits on the brown-and-tan fabric couch, his son cross-legged on the floor in front of him, tracking the game on two sheets of graph paper spread across the coffee table's pale green glass. Royce has to move the wicker basket full of gold-trimmed *National Geographic* magazines from beneath the table so he can scoot in front of his father, wedged between his knees, close enough so he can tousle Royce's mop of rusty brown hair whenever the Marlins score.

They share a bowl of buttered Orville Redenbacher's and sip chocolate Yoo-hoo. Royce cheers along with his dad and listens attentively to his explanations of the game's nuances, but it's the stats Royce loves, not the players themselves. Numbers are his thing, as he believes they are for his father. He senses a forced enthusiasm behind his father's display, as if he's embracing America's pastime simply because he believes that is the example fathers should set for a boy his son's age. Royce's mother has read him O. Henry's "The Gift of the Magi" at bedtime, and he thinks he and his father are similar to the husband and wife from the story, each sacrificing something of his- or herself for the other.

2007

Tefertiller's eyes open slowly, the fog of sleep making the room hazy. He's in a room he doesn't recognize, a curtained wall hanging from the ceiling sectioning him off from the other side. On the wall facing him is a marker board with a procession of smiley and frowny faces indicating levels of pain. There are baskets of flowers and get-well-soon cards collected in a corner. And at his bedside, sitting in a rolling chair, is his father. At least he thinks it's his father. He looks so old. *Are we going to shoot rockets today?*

No, son, his father says, the tiredness of a much-repeated answer, *not today.*

Tefertiller can't seem to hold a thought. Whenever he tries, it slips away like string through splayed fingers, the once-held balloon of memory lifting into clouds, its shiny, red face shrinking to a dot. *Is it a school day?*

No, son. No school.

Talking hurts the left side of Tefertiller's face. He touches it and feels a swath of hard scabbing. Tefertiller squints and tries to make sense of it all. Where's Mr. Quint, his science teacher? Where's Rambali? Where's Mom? Where's his best friend, Brian? They're all calling out in his head, fragments of each one, voices jumping from one to the other like a skipping record. This must be a dream, he realizes. Or maybe that sliver of time between sleep and waking when reality and imagination merge together.

Don't think I'm quite awake yet, Dad. Okay if I nap a bit longer? Another five minutes?

That's fine. I'll be here when you wake up.

1998

He's a high school freshman now, age fourteen, sitting on the second floor of his house at the lip of the stairs, leaning down and straining to hear his parents as they argue about whether or not he can try out for the school soccer team. It's the same every time he shows interest in a team sport, his mother firmly opposed, his father saying they should let him at least try out, let him be a boy. *Chrissakes,* he says, *it's just kicking a ball around a field. How much harm can he get into?*

Sports arguments are the only ones his father regularly wins. The first round at least. After acquiescing, his mother runs off to the library and comes back with photocopied articles that condemn the chosen sport. *Look,* she says, *look at these statistics, the broken bones and concussions, the lasting harm to young bodies. How can I sleep knowing what might happen to you?*

With his slight build and shy demeanor, Royce had always been one of the last kids picked for teams throughout elementary and middle school. But high school gives him an opportunity to avenge that slight. Pensacola Catholic is a private high school and small enough that anyone who comes out for a team makes the roster. The sports themselves don't interest Royce as much as his desire to fit in. He reads manuals, boning up on rules and regulations, figuring the knowledge would make him a superior competitor. Once he gets out on the court or the field or the gym floor, rehearsing the things he'd read about, that is where his interest dwindles. He can't understand why he has to keep repeating the same simplistic movements if he already knows their purpose. His mind wanders in games and he gets benched, where everyone watching the game can tell he isn't good enough.

Each time he quits, he doesn't tell his parents why, and they never ask. He simply stops going to practices, trading the riotous realm of locker rooms for the quiet sanctuary of home.

2007

Tefertiller blinks awake, sees the older version of his father. *I was just at Mom's funeral. She really gone, or did I just dream it?*

Three years ago. Your first deployment. You got a pass to come home for the funeral.

But you're still alive, right?

Yes, son.

Good. I'm glad.

2001

The towers have just fallen. Hit by planes. The World Trade Center and the Pentagon and the scorched field in Pennsylvania. When it happens, everyone in school is called to the gymnasium and told by the principal. Then school is canceled and the kids file onto buses, some dazed and crying, some talking vengeance.

It's like Pearl Harbor, Brian says on the row seat beside Royce. *A sneak attack by cowards. We got to go over there and kick some ass, you know. Just like the Gulf War. Get some retribution from Saddam and all those towel heads. You with me on this?*

What do you mean?

I mean, I'm going to sign up. We're at war, Roy. Ain't been declared yet, but we're at war sure as shit. It's just like World War Two. Everyone who's able needs to drop what they're doing and join the Army. Get some payback.

Oh.

So how about it? You in? Brian's gaze is like a white-hot spot-light.

Yeah, Royce says, *I'm in.*

They shake hands and Brian claps Royce on the shoulder. *Atta boy,* he says.

Others on the bus talk about doing the same. For most, it's idle threats. But Brian follows through with his promise. He's only seventeen, but when he drops out of school, his retired Marine Corps father signs the papers that allow him to enlist.

When Royce broaches the subject, his father says, *Not a chance, son. Finish school and then we'll talk about it.*

Graduation is eight months away, long enough for his young mind to fixate on something else. But in early March, Brian calls. He just completed boot camp and is all jacked up about joining his unit, the 10th Mountain Division. *Don't forget your promise,* he says to Royce.

Back in September, Royce's father hadn't told his wife about the boys' pact. But he does now, and she's apoplectic. *Don't do it,* she pleads, kneeling on the kitchen floor and clawing at Royce's legs at the dinner table. *Don't do it. Think what it will do to me!*

2007

Tefertiller's hazy view hovers above the motor pool like an out-of-body experience. On the hard-packed sand below, alpha team gathers around a Humvee, a laminated map spread across its hood. Their route and target building are indicated with black grease marker. Red phase lines denote stages of advance and the availability of indirect fire support. It's nothing the team doesn't already know, but Rambali walks them through it anyway, his finger tracing the black line to the circled X, pausing at rally points along their axis of advance. Everyone nods, fidgets, spits tobacco into empty cans of Red Bull. They've done snatch and grabs like this a hundred times before.

After the walk-through, Rambali shows off a picture of his wife, Sabina, with their two daughters, Naina and Nishi, twins ages four. *Sure they're yours?* Miller asks. *Looks like they got my eyes.* Rambali orders Miller to get down and knock out fifty in full battle rattle, but he's smiling when he says it and so is everyone else. Everyone but Tefertiller. He feels the dread in his bones but is unable to say anything. It's like his mouth is full of molasses. Everyone's moving in slow motion, checking weapons, joking about home, unaware of the ambush that awaits them. Bergman makes a twirling motion with his finger, and everyone loads up into their vehicles. As the convoy snakes out of the FOB, Rambali turns to his crew. *Everything's five by five,* he says, clapping Tefertiller on his shoulder. *Nothing can get us with the professor at our side.*

Once they move onto Route Hornet, their faces blur together in Tefertiller's head, a jumbled kaleidoscope that won't stop spinning. His father appears in ACUs and sergeant stripes saying, *Better lock that shit down, soldier.* Rambali is sitting at his kitchen table begging him to stay home. His mother hangs limply in the Humvee asking, *Why?* Brian hoists an RPG launcher on his shoulder and says, *Yeah, boy, gonna get me some.*

He wakes and sees his father standing by the window, morning light streaming around him through the slatted blinds, as ethereal as the dream version of him but with gray-streaked hair instead of chestnut brown. Coming to the bed, he uses a towel to blot his son's cheeks. Until then, Tefertiller hadn't known he'd been crying.

I didn't see it, Dad. I didn't see it coming.

How could you? They said it was an ambush.

Doesn't matter. I should've recognized the signs before we rolled into it. They were counting on me.

I'm sure you did the best you could.

No, I should've seen it. I didn't and now they're dead. Oh, God, who's going to tell Sabina? Who's going to tell Miller's mom?

1995

On the wall above his desk is a poster of Albert Einstein, the great man wearing a beige cardigan and sitting with his hands folded in front of him. Bracketed above him is one of his quotes: *I live in that solitude which is painful in youth, but delicious in the years of maturity.* The words give Royce hope. While he'd classify his life as being more "cautious" than "painful," it is wonderful to dream of a future that a contemplative, bookish boy like him will find delicious.

A month ago, Royce's dad took him to Cape Canaveral to watch the launch of the space shuttle *Endeavour.* The technological marvel speared the sky atop a fountain of flame to rendezvous with the Russian space station *Mir.* Most of the squirming kids on bleachers talked of becoming astronauts, but Royce dreams of being one of the architects of space missions, a NASA physicist.

Royce's father buys him a four-inch metallic replica of the *Endeavour* from the NASA gift shop. It displaces the trio of mathematical memorabilia from their place of honor on the right side of his desk. Rockets are his new obsession. He draws them in the margins of his notebooks. He builds Lego models on the floor. He checks out library books detailing the history of rocket engineering, the evolution from Hermann Oberth's

V-2 to today's multistage vehicles with detachable boosters and
fuel tanks.

Tomorrow, he and his dad are going to Foley Field to launch
a three-finned Crossfire ISX model. All week, he's been imagining the Crossfire soaring into blue sky, then drifting back to
Earth under its parachute. They have three spare engines, so,
after repacking the recovery wadding, they can fire the rocket
two more times. But that won't be the end of it, he's certain. He
knows he and his dad will keep building and launching rockets, bigger and better each time.

2006

At the end of his four-year hitch, Tefertiller decides not to re-
enlist. He's fulfilled his contract and done his duty. But the
Army won't let him out. They "stop-loss" him. The war machine is gearing up for the Surge and it needs all its working
parts to operate at full capacity. Some soldiers are allowed to
leave; some are even forced out—the ones who beat their wives
and shoot holes in bedroom walls. *Got to lock that shit down,*
Rambali always says. *Leave that shit in the sandbox when you
go home.* Tefertiller has no problem compartmentalizing, focusing on one task at a time. It's what makes him a good soldier. It's also what gets him stop-lossed. The way his adherence
to orders is immediate and complete. The way his aim stays
true whenever the world around him erupts in gunfire.

Tefertiller is more frustrated than angry with the stop-loss.
Others yell and scream; some go AWOL. They can't *lock their
shit down.* But Tefertiller knows orders are orders. He steps in
line and carries on.

His squad is thrilled to have him back. He's the best in the platoon at identifying irregularities on the road, picking out the concealed bomb by the perfectly arranged litter in a sea of imperfection. His squadmates call him Professor. It's the first nickname he's ever had that hasn't stung.

2002

Spittle sprays Tefertiller's face as Drill Sergeant Aldridge screams at him. Shit rolls downhill in the Army, a lesson instilled in new recruits on day one. The first sergeant yells at platoon sergeants, who yell at staff sergeants, who yell at the teenaged privates, who have no other option than to suck it up. Shit flows down the chain of command and complaints go up. But Tefertiller's mom jumped all the way to the top of the chain, calling a senator to complain about how the recruits were being mistreated. The senator called some general, and ass chewings rolled down the line, ending here at the edge of Tefertiller's bunk, where his tight wool blanket is tucked into precision corners. *Get your ass to the CO's office on the double,* Aldridge says. *Get in there and call your momma. Calm her ass down.*

The platoon had recently finished the eight-week phase of Basic Combat Training and was preparing for Advanced Individual Training. This new status gave them use of a bank of pay phones. Tefertiller, too excited to censor himself as usual, told his mother how the whole platoon had been punished for one private stealing extra chow from the mess hall. *The DIs came in after lights out banging on trash cans,* Tefertiller said. *Everyone was asleep, but that woke us up fast. They made us low-crawl back and forth under barbed wire in our T-shirts and underwear for about an hour. Afterwards, they marched us back to the barracks and we climbed into our bunks all muddy. Then we got in trouble in the morning for dirty sheets, and they ran us under the wire again. At least the second time we were in BDUs.* When he's told her this, weeks after the low-crawling incident, he'd thought it a safe and funny story he could share. What else could he tell her? The way hand-to-hand combat instructors taught them to snap a neck? The way they worked through the concrete-walled MOUT city in teams, shooting at plastic torsos that collapsed when shot? The way they rehearsed hauling dead and wounded off the battlefield thrown over their shoulders like fifty-pound sacks of dog food?

I told you this was a mistake, his mother said. *If the insurgents don't kill you, your own sergeants will.* Then she started crying.

When he'd signed up for the Army, Tefertiller had done it knowing it was finally one thing he couldn't quit, no matter how much his mother insisted. Her fearful entreaties held no sway over Uncle Sam. Or so he'd thought. Now, standing at attention in the company commander's office, he wasn't so sure.

The first sergeant punches the speakerphone button on the desk phone and then the digits of Tefertiller's home number.

Mom, Tefertiller says, *you can't go saying lies like that.*

You said they were abusing you.

No, nothing like that. They're just training us to think of others before ourselves.

What do you think I'm doing? I'm thinking of you.

No, Mom, you're not. You're thinking of yourself.

She gasps.

He'd never said anything like that to her before. Tefertiller isn't sure if he would have said it if not for the other men in the room. But he's glad he did. In the past, when she'd harangued him about sports, after-school activities, or sleepovers at friends' houses, he'd never talked back. He'd submitted to her will and sequestered himself in the house. Occasionally his dad would argue on his behalf, and his mom would race to the mahogany hope chest at the end of their bed to retrieve the four-foot scroll with her family tree. *Look,* she'd say, pointing at Irish branches extinguished by famine, or her own Dust Bowl parents who'd died in their thirties, relegating their children to the care of an angry aunt. *Misfortune stalks our family. Our luck is bad enough without asking for trouble.* Tefertiller loved his mother and knew, in her convoluted way, that she loved him, too. What could he do but comply?

Now, after years of surrender, it feels good to finally stand up and say no. *I'm sorry, Mom, but it's true. You* are *thinking of yourself. You want me at home so you feel better, not me. But this is what I want. You need to respect that.*

The silence on her end of the line is deafening. He feels the urge to take it back. Instead, he says, *And don't worry so much. I can take care of myself.*

2007

Christmas lights are strung on the metallic ceiling and walls around Tefertiller. He vaguely remembers blood leaking from his ear, but can't remember why. He reaches up to touch his left ear and feels padding instead. People are moaning in the beds around him.

Unless he squints, everything he sees is sheathed in a shimmering outline. The word "aura" pops to mind, and that gets him thinking of the aurora borealis. And the northern lights gets him thinking of stars. And then he's drifting off into the inky black.

1995

On Santa Rosa Island halfway between Pensacola Beach's neon-lit Observation Wheel and the high-rise hotels at Fort Pickens, Royce's father pulls his silver Windstar minivan onto a patch of sand lit only by stars and a crescent moon. He helps his son set up his fat-bodied telescope facing the Gulf of Mexico. The 80mm refractor stands five feet tall with its tripod. It's an upgrade from the slender 50mm telescope he'd bought Royce last Christmas, and this is their first chance to use it.

Royce swivels the barrel through the heavens, bypassing the moon and its craters, locating Saturn and its mesmerizing rings. Stepping away from the side-mounted eyepiece, he invites his father to take a look.

Incredible, son. Simply incredible.

Stargazing is the latest in a string of intellectual endeavors the two have undertaken since shelving their charade of baseball fandom. They've played chess and backgammon and Trivial Pursuit. They've watched *Jeopardy!* together and kept a running tally of their individual scores. They've performed physics projects, like dropping Mentos into bottles of Dr Pepper to create jets of soda ten feet tall. But it was a trip to the planetarium that really dazzled Royce. He came back with a map of the moon and plotted every place man has set foot— from Neil Armstrong and Buzz Aldrin's Apollo 11 landing in the Sea of Tranquility to Gene Cernan and Jack Schmitt's Apollo 17 landing in the Taurus-Littrow valley. Royce printed a color picture of Earth seen from those early missions—a sliver of moon in the foreground, the Earth's *Blue Marble* floating in the black void beyond, half of its sphere eclipsed—and taped it on his bedroom door. After researching constellations, Royce's father stuck glow-in-the-dark stickers on the ceiling of Royce's bedroom in an accurate depiction of the night sky, every star in its proper place.

You think that's something, Royce says now, nudging his father away from the telescope. *Check this out.* Royce dials in a new set of coordinates and fixes his eye to the viewing aperture, zooming in until Jupiter appears as a bright orb with four objects in its orbit like electrons around a nucleus. They are the four largest of Jupiter's sixty-three moons, Ganymede, Europa, Io, and Callisto.

His father lets out a low whistle as he gazes into the eyepiece. When he pulls away, his face is pure joy. *No turtles there.*

Royce laughs. Whenever someone says something idiotic, the response that Royce and his father offer is, *You're right, turtles all the way down, I get it.* It's an inside joke from Stephen Hawking's *A Brief History of Time.* In the opening chapter, Hawking tells a story about a lecturer describing the solar system and a woman in the audience refuting him, saying the world is flat and rests on the back of a giant tortoise. The lecturer asks the woman what is holding up the tortoise, and she replies, *You're very clever, young man, very clever. But it's turtles all the way down.*

Exactly, Royce says, *no turtles there.*

Royce enjoys the scientific activities he and his father do together, but he knows it's best to keep them to himself. He once mentioned how they quizzed each other on the periodic table to one of his friends, and he razzed him for a week afterwards. Other boys brag about helping their dads with odd jobs—replacing storm-blown shingles, scooting beneath the family car to change the oil, huddling beneath the sink to replace a leaking pipe—each lesson laid out by fathers like a stepping-stone for sons on the path to manhood. But Royce's father teaches theory, not application. He can piece together a science project from a box if it comes with instructions; but he can't build one from scratch.

Not too long ago, Royce's parents called Handy Helpers to install a garage-door opener. Two men in gold overalls pulled their van up on a Saturday and spent an hour in the driveway. One of the neighborhood kids told everyone in school, and the taunts were endless. Royce just hung his head and took it, ashamed of his father, but more ashamed of himself for being embarrassed in the first place.

Lying in bed staring at his ceiling, he imagines the comeback he should have said. *Oh, yeah? Your dads may show you how engines and plumbing works; mine explains the mysteries of the universe.*

1999

In tenth grade, Royce takes physics. His teacher, Mr. Quint, provides practical examples of Newton's laws of motion and Einstein's theory of general relativity, but must rely on the chalkboard to explain atomic forces. *The strong nuclear force, which holds protons together in an atom's nucleus, is a million-trillion-trillion times stronger than gravity.*

When he asks the class if the macro- and micro-theories can be connected, almost everyone in the class says yes. *Einstein thought so, too,* Mr. Quint says. *He wasted the latter half of his scientific life chasing a unified theory of relativity. Just imagine what else he might have discovered if he'd devoted his great mind to one or the other.*

Royce disagrees, but keeps it to himself. He believes Einstein's quest for perfect symmetry was a noble cause, one that someone, someday, will prove. He hopes it's him. He'd love to be written about alongside Einstein, to be recognized as the person who fulfilled his dream, who pulled together all the fractured pieces of our universe into an orderly fashion that makes sense.

2007

Tefertiller is dreaming of rockets again. The Crossfire. The bigger and more powerful Estes Ventris. But mostly he pictures the rocket-propelled grenade that streaked down from sandstone parapets onto the driver's side of his Humvee.

Sometimes he sees the shooter, different every time—tall, short, black hooded, head wrapped in a red-and-white keffiyeh, bearded face snarling—but usually it's just the RPG itself, appearing at the top of the wall and scorching a perfect line segment through air from launcher to vehicle in slow motion, the circle of its nose widening from bottle cap to coaster to Frisbee to a disc that blots out the sun.

Eventually the loop of rockets raining down is replaced with components of the resultant ballet. The omnidirectional distribution of force from point of impact. The front axle's momentary launch off the ground. The metal interior's rippling like so much tinfoil. The ejection of Miller's torso from the gun-ring turret, his legs left behind. The remnants of Rambali's torn face hovering in the dust-choked air inches from his touch. Although the corporal's jaw is gone, his eyes are intact, boring down with accusation. The larynx is visible, its vocal cords wriggling, Rambali's voice hissing like a leaking tire, each word drawn out and tortured. *Supposed. To. Warn. Us.*

Tefertiller wakes and sees his father sitting beside him. He recognizes his father this time, knows where he is and what year. *We got hit*, he says.

I know, says his dad.

It was my fault.

It was nobody's fault.

You don't understand. It was my job. I should've seen it coming.

No one could've seen this, son.

Tefertiller can describe a hundred ways to detect a planted bomb or an ambush. The disappearance of civilians from a street. The closed shutters and doors. The raked sand in front of a pile of trash. Like pulled threads in a blanket, once you notice the aberrations, you can't see anything else. And he was good at it. It's as if he'd been built for this, the dissection of patterns granting purpose to his logical mind. Corporal Rambali said he'd never seen better. Tefertiller wants to brag to his father, to let him know that his son is *finally good at something.* But if he was that good, how did he miss it this last time? He hadn't noticed anything out of the ordinary at all.

You don't understand. They relied on me. It's all my fault.

Sure, sure, his dad says, *and it's turtles all the way down.*

The phrase is so unexpected that it makes Royce laugh. Then he's laughing so hard he's shaking and wheezing. When he regains control, he wipes tears and snot from his face with the back of his hand.

His father sets his briefcase on the rolling dinner tray and opens the clasp. He removes a tidy stack of clothes and lays them on the bed. A pair of Royce jeans, socks and underwear, a stone-patterned T-shirt with the words SCIENCE ROCKS! *Let me help you get dressed, son,* he says. *It's time to go home.*

The Dead Aren't Allowed to Walk

CAMOUFLAGE

The fall day is unseasonably warm as dusk settles across Virginia Beach. Traffic crawls past the thirty-four-foot statue of King Neptune as bikinied girls dart between cars and bronzed boys strut along the curb with surfboards under their arms. A band plays beach music on an outdoor stage for the throng of people fanning out from its center, some sitting on towels, some in lawn chairs, others shag-dancing in bare feet. No one notices Curtis Bradshaw in a mud-splattered Jeep Wrangler, his crew cut blending in with off-duty sailors from Norfolk. No reason to suspect that hidden under a blanket in his back seat are a .308 Winchester and a box of hollow points.

As Bradshaw threads south, the city's built-up bulk dwindles, strip malls giving way to residences, then to small farms with roadside fruit-and-vegetable stands. Where farmland surrenders to intermittent woods, he pulls off the road and wheels through swampy muck toward a stand of cedar. There he turns off his car and waits for the engine's ticking to silence, rubbing the stubble at his temples. The Black Hats in Ranger School had always preached patience. *Be slow. Be certain.*

Unstoppering both sides of a metal canister the size of a tube of lipstick, he presses his thumb into one end and pushes a hardened stick of grease paint out the other. Half of the stick is light green, the other half loam. He rubs the loam side on his face to darken the projecting areas—brow, cheekbones, chin— then flips it over and lightens the hollows—eye sockets, cheeks, neck. A check in the mirror shows the contours of his face are now no more than a blur.

Stepping out, he removes a duffel from the floorboards. It contains what looks like a pile of mulch. But when he dumps it on the hood, the amorphous mass resolves into clothes with grassy strips attached to the fabric. He inspects the ghillie suit's pants, shirt, and hood with a netted face opening. Then he slips into each piece, his mind focusing on the upcoming hunt.

NICKNAMES

Until his senior year of high school, Bradshaw's nickname on the football team had been Brainiac. Other players were called Flash, Ball Hawk, and Bam Bam. Teammates were more interested in talking smack, taunting receivers and running backs. Not Bradshaw. Between plays, he analyzed the other team's formations and tendencies. The only time he spoke was when he had something important to say. Each time the offense broke the huddle and came to the line, he'd call out shifts to fill gaps or tap linemen on their hips to let them know he'd be blitzing. Then he'd settle into his forward lean and wait for the snap of the ball. When the play unfolded as predicted, he'd launch himself at the ball carrier like a missile.

Off the field, girls cozied up to him, called him a great listener. Bradshaw had little interest in the idle blather that consumed so many of his classmates. It wasn't that he thought himself better than his friends. He just preferred actions over words.

Near the end of his junior year while sitting in the lunchroom commons, he'd caught a glimpse of his sister, Darla, ducking out a side door and felt a tickling at the back of his neck. He hadn't seen her at breakfast that morning nor dinner the night before. Exiting another door, he raced around the building and caught up with Darla. She shielded her face, but he pried away her tiny wrists and removed her Ray-Bans. A black mouse curled beneath her left eye. *He didn't mean it,* she said, eyes wide. *It was my fault.* Bradshaw didn't say a word. He turned and ran back the way he'd come, his sister yelling, *No, don't.* Bradshaw shot across the commons toward Darla's basketball boyfriend, Zeke, all momentum and forward lean. Zeke and his crew, standing in a semicircle, saw Bradshaw coming. The team's center stuck out a long arm, but Bradshaw knocked it aside and never slowed. He plowed into Zeke, drove him to the carpet, and pummeled his face into a bloody mask. It took four boys to pull him off.

Vice Principal Richter didn't expel Bradshaw. He also believed in the two-eyes-for-an-eye brand of justice. So Bradshaw only served a one-week suspension. About the same amount of time Zeke was out getting his jaw wired and his nose set.

Senior year, Bradshaw had a new nickname. Killer.

THE SLOW CREEP

Bradshaw eases through the soft matting of dry leaves and branches like a fox. He weaves around towering pines and tilting cypresses, steps over the mossy remains of moldering timber, and ducks the low-hanging branches of live oaks. A light breeze whispers through the forest, masking the slight crunch of twigs and pine needles underfoot. Even so, he heeds his training, stepping toe-heel, toe-heel, slow and certain.

His course parallels Horn Point Road at enough distance that he can hear occasional vehicles rumbling along the black-top without seeing their headlights. After a mile, he turns deeper into the woods, curling away from the home he's been casing all week, approaching from the rear. Soon, the two-story cabin comes into view, a patchwork of blue-tinged light from the television dancing across windows and the sliding glass door that leads to the back deck. Downwind, he smells hickory smoke. *Must have barbequed tonight,* he thinks, settling down with the Winchester beneath a tangle of honeysuckle.

He wriggles on the wet ground like a rutting pig until he's wormed into a comfortable firing position. Body slightly canted from the target line; left leg straight, right bent; left arm forward, with his weight on the elbow, hand clutching the fore-stock; right hand near his chin, finger resting on the trigger guard. All that's left to do is wait.

FIVE POUNDS OF PRESSURE

Drill instructors at Fort Benning wore brown felt hats with round, sturdy brims. If a recruit screwed up in the presence of Drill Sergeant Masterson, the blocky-headed sergeant would scream in the private's face and jab the edge of his hat into the private's forehead. This never happened to Bradshaw. It wasn't just that he paid attention and followed instructions; it was that everything here made sense to him.

When Masterson ringed the platoon around a sawdust pit,

it felt to Bradshaw like watching a movie he'd seen a hundred times before. It was as if he knew what the sergeant would say before the words rolled off his tongue. *We called grunts for a reason,* Masterson bellowed. *We ain't like them flyboys droppin' bombs, then goin' home to Mama. We in the street. We door-to-door. We special delivery. Our combat is personal, hand to hand. Rifles jam. Bullets run out. But bayonets don't. Your buttstock don't ever run out. When ammo's gone and some raghead get in your face, you gotta want to live more than Hajji. You gotta put that son of a bitch down. Can I get a hooah?*

The platoon screamed back the infantry battle cry. *Hooah!*

Two at a time, privates were called into the circle to fight gladiatorial bouts. They donned helmets and wore base-ball-style chest protectors. Each wielded a three-foot baton called a pugil stick. The pugil sticks simulated bayonet-tipped rifles, but with their padded ends they resembled giant Q-tips. Instead of stabbing and slashing as they'd practiced on life-sized rubber dummies, the men used the pugil sticks to club their opponents into submission. *Like middle drills during two-a-days,* Bradshaw thought, leaning forward like a chained dog waiting to be released. When Bradshaw knocked his man down and kept whaling on him, he half expected Masterson to pull him off. But the sergeant just laughed as the pummeling continued. *Damn, boy,* he said, *you a natural-born killer.*

First time Bradshaw held a rifle was at boot camp. He'd played *Halo* and *Call of Duty* and other first-person shooter games, but there was so much more to think about in real life. Recoil, for instance. And wind. Even gravity.

Gravity sucks like a ten-dollar whore, Masterson said. *On long shots, you need to shift your aim up to account for the down-ward pull. Every bullet fired hits something. You don't adjust properly, that bitch gonna suck your bullet down till it splashes in the dirt.*

The thing Masterson carped about most was breathing. *Way you breathe dictates the way you move. Breathe in and the barrel dips; breathe out and it rises. You need to take long, slow breaths. And in that natural pause between breaths, that's when you squeeze the trigger.*

Although line units had upgraded their weapons to M4s, trainees at Benning used Vietnam-era M16s. His first time on the range, Bradshaw fired forty for forty. Even when they removed the Aimpoint optics and everyone shot at targets with the old iron sights, he still fired expert.

Know why I love you? Masterson said. *You keep your ears open and your mouth shut. No bad habits to break like all these backwoods hicks think they know everything 'bout shooting.*

What stuck with Bradshaw most was how much power his index finger held, the consequences set in motion by its flexing. Only five pounds of pressure to depress the trigger. *Don't pull the trigger like you're jerking your meat,* Masterson said. *That'll just pull your aim wide. Squeeze it slow. When the rifle fires, it should surprise you.*

So little to kill a man. Just a pause between breaths. And five pounds of pressure.

RESOLVE

As his platoon's honor grad, Bradshaw earned a slot in Ranger School, a nine-week course that trained and tested elite soldiers in forest, swamp, desert, and mountain environments. In the pine forests of Benning, on the perilous cliffs of Dahlonega, in Eglin's bogs and Dugway's scrub-dotted desert, hard men in black berets tested the trainees with severe hardships. The men ran multiple patrols daily, ate one meal a day, and slept an average of three hours a night.

A few rare nights the trainees got to sleep for five hours nestled in a shallow grave—a body-length slot carved into earth as a hasty fighting position. Other times they'd go three days without any sleep, one patrol folding into the next, men loaded down with enough gear to curl their spines into question marks. Ranger candidates were so tired that they hallucinated half the time. Some talked to trees. Others saw vending machines in bushes and tried to purchase candy from them. Each night the weary soldiers snaked through woods in a long file toward objectives grease-markered on maps, each man following the reflective cat eyes sewn on the back of the cap of the man in front. Every fifteen minutes or so, a head count passed up the line so the patrol leader could tell if he'd lost someone. Occasionally the line broke when someone fell asleep standing up, half the patrol marching on, the remnants standing still and dreaming they were moving.

One gray morning at the end of a seventy-two-hour, sleepless marathon, a raiding patrol set up to attack a cabin at the base of a mountain. Bradshaw was part of the assault team that descended on it like berserkers. Behind them, the overwatch team lit up the target from an angle, marching their fire in front of the friendly troops as they advanced. The assault team tore into the cabin, double-tapped every man-shaped target inside, searched simulated bodies for intel, and hauled themselves back up the mountain to the rallying point. Adrenaline spent, their fatigued calves and thighs sparkled with needled pricks of pain.

The mission seemed a go until head count came up one short. So the assault team lumbered back down to where a Black

Hat had instructed one of the men to lie down as if shot. The dead aren't allowed to walk. Until found, they must lie mute, immobile, like stones at the bottom of a well. Bradshaw found the fallen man and heaved his dead weight over his shoulder in a fireman's carry, hauling him like a sack of dog food. The slope seemed to grow steeper with every step. Then, head count came up short again. The Black Hats were screwing with their heads, but what could the trainees do? *Leave no man behind. Hooah.* Next time, head count was short two men. Three trips down, three back up, the mountain growing tall as Kilimanjaro.

By the end of Ranger School, two-thirds of the original class had washed out. Those who remained were walking skeletons. Everyone came in lean on day one and lost about five pounds per week. Two and a half months later, the graduates stood in formation, prouder of the Ranger Tabs on their shoulders than anything before. Each man who graduated knew his mettle, what he was capable of once resolved to action.

THE KILL HOUSE

Bradshaw's first deployment to Iraq was no holds barred. In Samawah, Fallujah, and Baghdad, anyone with an AK was fair game. Put the floating red dot on their chest, then *Boom.* Same thing for anyone reaching for an AK. Or reaching for anything resembling an AK. Or running away. Or hiding and refusing to come out. *Dead Hajji's a compliant Hajji,* Sergeant Berkholtz always said.

Berkholtz was his squad leader, a blond, square-jawed body-builder from Minnesota. His piss was neon green from all the supplements he took. When Berkholtz wasn't on mission, he could be found in the Bedrock Gym, an outdoors concrete slab lined with hardwood benches fitted with lifting racks. The slab sat on the outskirts of the battalion's CHU city—the densely packed rows of converted shipping containers designated as "containerized housing units." Two tiers of sand-filled HESCO barriers encircled the makeshift gym as a shield against shrapnel from mortar shells that dropped into the compound on a nearly daily basis. The weights Berkholtz pumped were iron bars capped with concrete blocks on their ends. Not enough to max out, but that was fine with him. He was more about form—long, slow reps to maximize the burn.

That's how Berkholtz trained his squad as well. They crawled through rehearsals until every rifleman knew his and everyone else's task. Then they walked through the exercise. Then they ran, again and again. *Muscle memory,* Berkholtz said. *Keep doing it till it's second nature. When things go to shit on the battlefield, you'll still know what to do.*

The squad banged through the warehouse-sized kill house countless times. Inside its plywood exterior, the walls were made of stacked tires snugged against each other to eliminate any gaps. A column of concrete filled each stack to absorb bullets during live-fire exercises. Walk-throughs were "dry," but the run-throughs were "weapons free." The squad cleared rooms in buddy teams, one sweeping left, one right, shooting the chests and heads of torso-shaped targets that collapsed when hit.

When time came for the real thing and the squad stacked outside a courtyard wall or mud hut, soldiers would bang through the gate or front door without hesitation. Berkholtz's last words before every breach were always the same. *Speed and violence,* he'd say. And the squad would repeat it back like a mantra. Then it was go time and every action followed muscle memory. Just as promised.

There was only one thing Berkholtz couldn't prepare his men for. Captain Wonderful.

SALT IN OLD WOUNDS

Captain Nowicki—dubbed Wonderful by his men for the myriad ways he screwed things up—had tried to slink out of Camp Adder without anyone noticing. That had been during Bradshaw's second of five combat tours, back when he still thought they were making a difference. After the botched raid on the compound in Tikrit, the bumbling CO had been relieved of command and was being sent back to the States that very night. The brass wanted him out of there before someone fragged his ass. When the squad found out, they gathered along the chain-link fence surrounding the motor pool waiting for Nowicki to appear. They stood there, fists balled, ready to climb the fence and risk the razor wire on top if Nowicki said or did the wrong thing. In their mood, that could've been just about anything. Bradshaw can still recall the shameful flush of red on Captain Wonderful's face before he dropped his head and slid into the up-armored Humvee.

Six years was time enough for Captain Wonderful to pass entirely out of mind. But then a week ago Bradshaw pulled into the parking lot at the Navy PX and saw Nowicki leaving the building with an armful of groceries. He was wearing a contractor's polo shirt, his hair was out of regs, and he'd put on fifteen pounds. But otherwise he looked the same. Contentedly oblivious. So the rumors were wrong. If he'd gotten a dishonorable discharge, he couldn't work for Uncle Sam, not even as a civilian contractor.

The few times Bradshaw imagined bumping into Nowicki, he'd pictured the disgraced man slump-shouldered in some dim bar downing shots of Jack to forget what a piece of shit he was. But there he was, happy, healthy, gainfully employed.

Bradshaw told himself to forget about it, that Nowicki

wasn't worth his time. But then Captain Wonderful got into his shiny new Escalade, and Bradshaw saw the c.i.b. sticker on the rear window and the license plate with the bronze star. He squeezed the steering wheel and clenched his jaw until cords in his neck stuck out like guy wires. He was breathing heavy through his nose like a bull about to charge. Then something clicked in his head like a subconscious on-off switch, the same way it had just before going out on combat missions. Nowicki would pay his due. Bradshaw would make sure of it.

Bradshaw's muscles relaxed as a hyperalert clarity washed over him. He followed the SUV out of the parking lot and trailed him to Pungo, where Nowicki pulled into a driveway on Horn Point Road. The home was a two-floor cabin set back from the road on an acre of property. A basketball pole stood in the driveway and a row of purple azalea bushes fronted the porch. By all evidence, he was living the American dream.

That night, Bradshaw lay in bed imagining a giant scale with all the dead and wounded in one dish, all the brass-hatted pencil pushers in the other. He thought about ceremonies for Ramirez and Berkholtz, their rifles stabbed into the sandbags like headstones, their desert boots set in front as if they were still standing at attention. He thought about Nowicki, pink faced, sailing along as if choices had no consequences. He tried to remember Berkholtz in his prime, pumping concrete in the Bedrock Gym, running the squad through the kill house, preaching, *Speed and violence, speed and violence.* But his mind kept coming back to the last time he'd seen his squad leader in one piece: the night Nowicki accompanied them on their raid.

TIKRIT

Everyone knew Captain Wonderful was a fuckup. Generally he stayed in the rear, so NCOs on the ground were able to counter his ineptitude. The CO would denote mission-critical buildings, and then sergeants and privates would kick down the doors. In homes filled with innocent civilians, sergeants had the fire discipline to stay their trigger fingers. But occasionally Captain Wonderful would come along, desperate to earn ribbons for his chest. More than anything, he wanted a medal with a bronze V for valorous conduct. And so he came along on the raid of a three-story building in Tikrit.

In high school, Bradshaw's only image of the desert had come from movies like *Lawrence of Arabia, Mad Max,* and *The Mummy.* When he deployed, he'd expected endless sand-scapes of shifting dunes. But Iraq's deserts were expanses of rock-scrabbled hardpan fissured with deep wadis. There were fig groves and lush stands of wild oak, hawthorn, and willows. And in Tikrit, a city of blocky sandstone buildings pressed shoulder to shoulder, acres of scrub brush climbing up out of the Tigris River to fill the surrounding slopes.

At 3 a.m., first and second squads packed into a four-vehicle convoy that rolled through streets lined with palm trees. The convoy halted one intersection from the target compound, which was surrounded by an eight-foot wall. Tefertiller and Rambali stayed with the vehicles on overwatch. The rest of the squad made up the breach team.

Tefertiller and Rambali each manned a .50 cal pointed at the second story of the building inside the wall. The .50 was a thunderously loud weapon whose barrel spat a six-foot tongue of flame as if Zeus himself were hurling lightning bolts. Today's load was aluminum-tipped rounds with steel cores, the type of bullets used to punch through light armor and aerate anything within.

Sergeant Berkholtz gathered the breaching team outside the front gate as Corporal Faust taped a demo charge to the locking plate and wedged a three-foot stick against it to hold it in place. Faust spooled wire back from the block of C-4 and ducked behind a reinforced blast blanket. The rest of the team stacked behind him, careful to keep their asses pulled in tight. *Speed and violence,* Berkholtz said. *Speed and violence,* everyone parroted. As soon as the gate blew inward with a loud boom, the stacked men curled around Faust and raced through the billowing smoke. They tore across the courtyard for the front door. Lights came on in the house, followed by muffled yelling. Berkholtz swung the ram at the front door and the team ran inside, everyone calling out doors and hallways as they appeared, lead man aiming into the opening, two followers peeling around him to clear the space. The team had only made it into the first room when an insurgent blindly fired down a stairwell. Berkholtz grabbed a grenade to toss around the stairwell's corner when bullets ripped through the walls accompanied by a jackhammering *boom-boom-boom.*

The overwatch guns were supposed to fire upon the second floor, then shift to the third when the breach team called over the radio that they were headed up the stairs. But Captain Wonderful had ridden in with a second convoy tasked with transporting any prisoners captured in the raid. His men were surprised to find the compound's rear gate open, so Nowicki had his gunners take aim at the first-floor doors and windows. When shooting began inside the house, he ordered the gunners to *Light that bitch up.*

The .50 cal punched through the building like paper. One

round hit Berkholtz at an angle on his left pec, shearing off a chunk of his chest and taking his left arm with it. He lay on the ground, aware for just a moment, gazing at the frying pan–sized hole where his shoulder had been. Inertia had pulled his innards along and they protruded through snapped ribs, so the last thing Berkholtz saw was his own heart, which beat two more times before settling like a stewed tomato.

Faust was now in charge of the breach team. He pulled the pin on the dropped grenade, let it cook off a couple of seconds, and tossed it toward the stairwell. Then he signaled the team back to the front door. Grabbing Berkholtz's collar, Bradshaw dragged the body along the floor and Ramirez took the severed arm. As they scrabbled backwards, Faust radioed over the company net that the breach team was taking fire from heavy guns. Captain Wonderful finally realized his error but sat frozen in his Humvee with the handset clutched to his ear, a blanched look on his face as his vehicle's gun continued to hammer the building. And that's when Ramirez took a round in the head.

TARGET ACQUIRED

Lying in his rut beneath the honeysuckle, Bradshaw stills his breathing and listens to the forest. On the creep up, he'd been an intruder, and the forest's denizens had silenced in response. But now, as he lies in wait, the environment comes back to life, the chirp of birds filling the air, the buzz of insects, the murmur of rustling leaves announcing the passage of small creatures.

With a practiced finger, he flips off the front and rear sight covers of his optics, then peers through the telescopic lens, roving the crosshatched reticle from one end of the cabin to the other. Then he settles the crosshairs on the sliding glass door and waits.

He's ready to lie there for hours if needed. He was always good at waiting. But in just a few minutes, his target steps through the sliding door with a bag of birdseed. Joining him on the deck is his Wonderful wife in a polka-dotted sundress. And his Wonderful daughter in a purple jumper. Giving his blond daughter a scoop of seed, Nowicki lifts her up so she can pour it into a bird feeder.

Bradshaw peers through the lens, lines the crosshairs center mass, his finger poised outside the trigger guard. In his mind's eye, he sees Captain Wonderful's chest exploding, the smile on his face becoming a shocked O, his spouse and child splattered with red.

Bradshaw's finger slips off the trigger and rests against the guard. He'd been alert a moment ago but now feels a weight settling on his shoulders, pressing him into the cold earth. It's as if the sleepless nights have suddenly come to demand their due. *How could the stink of war not stick to this asshole?* he wonders.

He wants retribution so badly, but he just can't do it with the wife and kid there. He wishes he hadn't seen them, wishes he could do the job and go home knowing Nowicki was no longer a man but a lump of meat. He pulls his hand away from the trigger guard, knowing what lies ahead. Another sleepless night.

But he imagines another possibility, and it fills him with a sense of peace.

He'll slip back through the woods to his Jeep and no one will know he'd ever been here. He'll drive home to his Spartan apartment. Even if he can't forget about Nowicki and Iraq. Even if he can't erase the image of Berkholtz gazing into his own chest. He can still crawl into his bathroom tub, put the barrel in his mouth, and apply five pounds of pressure.

Her Brother's Apartment

FRONT DOOR

Darla arrives at her brother's apartment as dawning sun limns the tops of pines and cottonwoods. The police had said the crime scene tape *should* be gone, but if it wasn't to just rip it down and go inside. So she isn't surprised to find two yellow Xs crisscrossing Curt's front door. Even so, her gut clenches and a spout of bile fills her mouth.

Coming from hardy German stock, Darla's mother is normally stoic as a marble bust. But when the police made their next-of-kin notification and she called Darla to pass on the news, she only got out, *It's your brother,* before dropping the phone and howling.

Darla had raced over, traditional roles reversing, daughter consoling mother, promising everything would be all right. It also fell upon Darla to call the extended family; to inform them of Curt's death; to say, *Gunshot wound;* to avoid the words "self-inflicted" and "suicide."

The only time Darla had been to Curt's apartment previously was the day he'd moved in, newly discharged from the

Army. She'd helped him unpack his U-Haul, grabbing one end of furniture and toting armloads of cardboard boxes, their contents scribbled on the side in black Magic Marker. He'd provided pizza and beer, and she'd given him a housewarming gift—a glass ball called a suncatcher that she'd created herself at a nearby glass studio. *I don't get it,* Curt had said. *What's its purpose?* He always needed a reason for everything. *Can't something just be pretty?* she'd said. To which he'd popped his skull-head T-shirt and replied, *Hey, I'm all about the pretty.*

Now she stands outside her brother's door worrying the dog tags on his key chain. She rubs her fingers along the raised letters of the tag's silver surface. BRADSHAW, CURTIS J. 228-73-1286. O POS. CHRISTIAN.

The beaded chain also holds a door key and a mailbox key. He'd given her this spare set for emergency purposes, meaning, she'd always supposed, in case he got locked out. But not this. Never this.

ENTRYWAY

Darla enters the front door to a swell of musty air. At least it's not the stench of decomposition she'd imagined on the drive over. Stupid to think that, she knows. It's only been two days. The coroner removed the body right away and the cleaning service came in yesterday. Still, the mind goes where it wants.

Closing the front door, she turns and slides open the closet's accordion door. A row of footwear forms a line with their toes touching the back wall—a scuffed pair of desert Army boots, a set of Corcorans with spit-shined toes, a pair of boat shoes, and two pairs of Nikes with well-worn soles. Also on the floor are two neat stacks of board games.

When they played games as kids, Curt almost always won.

Like ESP, the way he knew what she would do before she did it, sitting there stone-faced, watching, waiting for her to step into his trap. He always ribbed her when he won, lifting his arms and shouting, *All hail the undisputed champion of the world.* But it was just a playful show. The only times she remembers him truly gleeful were those rare occasions when she won. *Damn, girl,* he'd say, smiling his lopsided grin, *you got me on that one.*

Hanging on the closet rod are a few coats and jackets, a yellow rain slicker, an umbrella, a reflective vest, and two uniforms—a starched set of desert camouflage and a set of dress greens sheathed in a dry cleaner's poly bag. She lifts the gossamer wrapper and inspects the staff sergeant stripes on the arm, the 82nd Airborne patch and Ranger Tab on the left sleeve, the additional 82nd combat patch on the right. Fastened to the left breast are a blue pin of a rifle within a wreath—the Combat Infantryman Badge—and a silver pin of a winged parachute topped with a star—the Senior Parachutist Badge.

Sandwiched between the two pins is the colorful rack of ribbons that Curt called his "salad bar." He always deflected questions about his awards, so she'd had to look them up online. The four full rows of ribbons are arranged in descending order of importance. A fifth row on top has a purple ribbon enclosed by two vertical, white bars—the Purple Heart—and a red ribbon with white trim and a vertical, blue bar in the center—the Bronze Star. Pinned to the center of this topmost ribbon is a bronze V for valor.

KITCHEN

The kitchen is Spartan, the counters bare but for a microwave, a Keurig single-cup coffee maker, and a rack of K-Cup pods. In the fridge is a smattering of delivery containers with half-eaten meals. She opens cabinets, finding stacks of plastic cups, rows of mugs, mismatched plates and bowls. Under the sink is the typical collection of cleaning supplies, but there is also an unopened box of dishware with a red bow affixed to its top. Darla takes it out and sets it on top of the gas stove, thinking of the dinner that had prompted this replacement gift.

In the first ten months after getting out of the Army, Curt kept his hair short while growing a beard. *My George Clooney look,* he'd said. At first, he came over to Mom's for meals once or twice a week, but those visits tapered off after the first couple of months. His demeanor became fractious, his eyes ringed and tired, searching every corner. But asking what was wrong would just set him off. The last visit had been a disaster. Mom kept after him until he snapped. *I don't want to fucking talk about it,* he screamed, throwing his plate of spaghetti across the dining room where it shattered against the wall. That was three months ago. Last time Darla saw him alive.

Now Darla removes the bow from the box and looks at the glossy picture underneath. It shows the sixteen-piece Pfaltzgraff Venice dinnerware set in teal with a pattern of starfish and seashells. A set of dishes just like Mom's.

DINETTE

Just off the kitchen is a nook set aside to be a dinette. But the five-foot wooden table and four ladder-back chairs are not set for eating. They are loaded down with the same Magic-Markered boxes from the day Curt moved in. Is that even the right term? Had Curt ever really *moved in*? Had he ever *moved on*?

She lifts the top off a box labeled *Odds and Ends.* Inside are football trophies, a Rubik's Cube, a roll of papers, and a piggy bank that looks like a British phone booth. She removes the rubber band holding the papers together, unrolls them, and discovers they are shooting targets. In the center of each one is a cluster of small holes. Until the police notification, she hadn't even known Curt owned a gun, let alone that he went to a range to practice with it.

She re-bands the papers and picks up the red phone booth. The piggy bank rattles when she shakes it. Popping the top, she finds several coins the size of silver dollars. Curt had told her the tradition behind military coins, how each unit minted specialized coins to proclaim their pedigree or to signify particular accomplishments. One of the coins is stamped with an airborne insignia and etched with Curt's name and rank. The other side bears the 505th Parachute Infantry Regiment crest, a leaping panther with wings and a scroll with the words H-MINUS, referring to the regiment's airborne drop into France five hours before the beachhead landing on D-Day.

The other five coins denote his "hardship tour" deployments. Coins for the peacekeeping mission in Albania (Operation Allied Force), the War in Afghanistan (Operation Enduring Freedom), and three for the war in Iraq (Operation Iraqi Freedom I, "The Surge," and Operation New Dawn). So much war in such a short time.

She remembers her big brother on the football field in high school colliding with running backs at full speed. She'd never doubted Curt would be the one to stand up first and saunter away triumphantly. He was her man of stone, impervious to anything the world could throw at him. But even rock erodes, succumbing to the tiniest drip of water and the ceaseless way it cuts.

LIVING ROOM

The living room contains the usual items: couch, end table, lamp, coffee table, telephone, entertainment center, wide-screen television, DVR, Xbox, a BarcaLounger with cigarette burns in the arm, and a dartboard surrounded by a scattering of tiny holes. The room also has something unexpected—two caved-in spots in the walls about shoulder height. Each about the size of a fist.

Hanging on the same wall are two pictures. The first is a framed poster of Muhammad Ali standing over an inert Sonny Liston after knocking him to the canvas. Ali is glaring down at the flattened man as if the knockdown wasn't enough; as if he actually wants to kill him.

The second picture is a print of Edvard Munch's *The Scream*. Darla studies its harrowed, otherworldly look of anguish and imagines Curt's face squeezed onto the howling skull atop the wavering, wraithlike figure. She wonders if Curt had seen the same thing, too, and if so, how long he'd stood transfixed.

Moving to the cream-colored couch, she sits and notices a series of deep grooves carved into the edge of the cherrywood coffee table. She's seen Curt's Rambo-style knife and wonders if that is what he'd used to saw the wood.

A blinking red light on the telephone tells her there are seven unanswered messages queued up. The last time she'd spoken with Curt, he'd apologized for his outbursts and promised things would be different soon. *If I don't do something drastic,* he'd said, *I'm going to hurt someone I love.* He'd seemed so at peace, like his old self.

She presses the Play button and hears her own voice on the first message. She sounds bubbly, going on about a half-off sale at Men's Wearhouse and asking if Curt would like to go there with her. *About time you added another suit to your collection,* she'd said with a laugh, knowing he only owned one suit, purchased in high school for a formal dance. The next two are robocalls from telemarketers, and then it's her again. Her second message begins upbeat, but even now she can hear the worry fringing her false front as she begs her brother to *Please call back.*

The next message is from Mom; it starts out as an invitation to dinner but quickly devolves into crying jags before hanging up. Then there are two calls from friends. Darla assumes they are soldiers by their terse manner and the way they refer to Curt by his last name. The first one says, *Yo, Bradshaw, call me back.* The second one says, *Bradshaw, what the fuck, man? You ain't got nothing to apologize for. Shit, man, I can't count the lives you saved. So don't go getting all mopey on me, you hear?*

The silence after the last beep was deafening. How many other "apology" calls had he made? As if getting his affairs in order. How could she have been so blind?

Beside the telephone sits a scrapbook, and next to that the glass ball she'd given him resting on a folded towel. Seeing that he'd never hung the housewarming gift hurts her almost as much as the phone messages. She remembers once making a woven dreamcatcher at summer camp and giving it to Curt when she'd come home. He strung it between his bedposts and never took it down, even when his friends came over and razzed him. She'd loved that whimsical side to him and hoped he'd do the same with this ball, stringing it up in a place of honor because it was a gift from his little sister.

With a sigh, she turns to the scrapbook and flips it open, Curt's life progressing through a series of still frames. The gurgling baby. The rambunctious toddler. The wild-haired boy always digging forts in the woods. The preteen showing off new muscles. The confident teenager in football pads. The shave-headed soldier at boot camp graduation.

The next pictures show Curt at Fort Bragg, he and his buddies posing with girls, cutting up in the barracks, or drinking in various bars. Then come photos of his first deployment, a peacekeeping mission along the Albania-Kosovo border. It was wintertime in Europe, the landscape harsh and bleak, the trees stripped and the earth hardscrabble. The streets in ancient villages were narrow with cracked shoulders, the buildings old and weather beaten, many with minor damage, a bullet-pocked wall here and a patched section of roof there. But all the residents were smiling, the straight-backed men in threadbare blazers, the wide-cheeked women in babushkas, and the wiry kids in oversized clothes and muddy boots. Even the soldiers seemed happy, both the AK-wielding Albanians and the flak-jacketed Americans. Curt had told her afterwards how proud he'd been of this mission, how rewarding it had been to make a positive difference in such a troubled area.

The next page shows a squad of soldiers on a rock-strewn plain in Afghanistan. They all look so young and cocky, smirking as if someone had just told a joke and they're trying not to laugh. Curt is on one end with his arm draped over the shoulder of another sergeant. It's the last picture in the book. As if everything that followed wasn't worth memorializing.

One of the few times he'd opened up to her about the Middle Eastern wars, he'd confessed his own puzzlement. They'd gone over to aid the citizens, to assist the building of democracy. But the same people who would smile and call you friend one day might shoot you the next. *This one time,* he said, *we went in to a village overrun with typhoid. We cleaned up their well, brought in a team of docs, and gave them a load of antibiotics. But the village leader said we were trying to poison them*

*and they buried the drugs in the desert. A dozen villagers ended
up dying. We were supposed to be "winning hearts and minds."
I mean, how can you understand minds that think like that, let
alone win them over?*

Darla flips the scrapbook pages back to a picture of Curt
when he was ten, seated on an orange banana-seat bike and
getting ready to jump a homemade ramp in the middle of their
street. He was paused and smiling, both fists pumping the air
as if celebrating a jump he'd already completed. *This* is how she
wanted to remember him. So certain of the future. Ready for
anything.

BATHROOM

A short hallway elbows off the living room and leads to doors
to the bathroom and bedroom. She'd intended to save the bathroom for last, but now that she was within reach, she couldn't
avoid it any longer, the doorknob calling to her like the handle
of a pot on a hot stove to a curious child. Darla reaches out,
twists, and pushes the door open.

The police had said the few things they'd taken had come
from the bathroom. Darla had wondered what that cryptic
message meant, but was afraid to ask. Now she sees the shower
curtain missing and her mind races. The police might not pry
up tiles spattered with blood, but the curtain? Yes; that could
be bagged and taken into evidence.

A foot above the tub's rim is a thick hole in the wall with fis-
sures radiating out from it. It looks like someone swung a pick-
axe into the tiles. This, she knows, is where the bullet passed
through her brother's brain and lodged in the wall. She's so
thankful that the police suggested the biohazard cleaning service. She hates to think how she'd react to a wall dripping with

blood and brain matter. The thought alone makes her shiver. The gravitational tug she'd felt moments ago is gone. Now she feels repulsed.

Turning to the medicine cabinet, she swings open its mirrored door to reveal toiletries of all sorts on the top and bottom shelves. On the nearly empty middle shelf are bottles of Tylenol and cough syrup. Gone is the medicine she knew Curt had been prescribed, the Klonopin for panic disorder, the Lexapro for depression. The police took them or the cleaning service. Either way, she doesn't care. All she would've done is flushed them down the toilet.

BEDROOM

When Darla swings the bedroom door open, she gasps and her legs nearly buckle. What she sees is as surreal as a Salvador Dalí landscape. Eventually she will go through the dresser and the clothes neatly folded and stacked within. She'll open the closet and rifle through everything on hangers, his high school letterman jacket, his one suit, his parade of solid-colored polos and long-sleeved flannels. She'll open the athletic bag stuffed with racquetball gear. She'll even look under the queen-sized bed and root through the half dozen shoeboxes filled with baseball cards and knickknacks. But for now, she is too stunned to think about any of that.

Dangling from thin wires, filling the width and breadth of the ceiling, is a profusion of glass suncatchers. Each globe is unique, streaked with different dyes and striated with patterns created when it was a molten ball spinning at the end of a blowpipe. She stretches out her arm and touches the bottom of the nearest one, setting it swaying on its string. It clinks against a couple of the other balls. She wonders how long it had taken

Curt to craft all these at the glass studio. And why hadn't he told her? She understands keeping what he did in the war a secret, but not this.

She nudges more of the balls, creating a tinkling like that of wind chimes, then moves to the bed with its tightly tucked sheets and blanket, the corners creased at forty-five-degree angles. Lying down, she removes one of the two pillows from under the blanket and holds it up to her nose. Her brother's scent fills her head. Hickory and soap and sweat.

The headboard is butted against the window. Reaching behind her, she pulls the string on the shade and it retracts, flapping upward and wrapping around the roller. Morning sun streams through, refracting and reflecting, sparking through what now resembles an ocean of alien worlds. As she sniffs the pillow, she remembers Curt's joking response to her gift—*I'm all about the pretty*—and for a moment she smiles, as light twinkles through the room and the sun creeps higher in the sky.

Falling Backwards

Looking around to make sure nobody's watching, the dirt-smeared man rolls his shopping cart into the woods behind Hattie B's Hot Chicken. He infiltrates far enough to lose sight of the road, then searches for a memorable spot. Kneeling beside a hawthorn bush threaded through with honeysuckle, he retrieves a collapsible entrenching tool from his layers of grungy clothes. He unsnaps its green case and expands the E-tool to its full size. The digging is rough this time but gets easier once the shovel's sharp edges cut away the bush's fanning roots. His excavation is as wide as a two-man foxhole, but not as deep. After he drops in this week's collections, he backfills the hole and evens out the mound the best he can. He's buried similar caches throughout Atlanta. All his little treasures gathered up from all his patrols.

Once done, he treks back to his underpass in the Old Fourth Ward. Crawling beneath cardboard sheets, he listens to the boom and roll of tires across the segmented concrete slabs overhead. It reminds him of bowling balls hitting a buffed lane and spinning across the slats. At night, when traffic becomes intermittent, when cold turns his sweat to frost, he sometimes twirls like a pig on a spit just so the newspaper stuffed inside his clothes will make its crumpling music. Anything to drown out the voices in his head.

As the sun rolls into the horizon and night unfolds, he scoots to the edge of the underpass to gaze up at the sky. It's hard to make out much of the stars with all the ambient light, but he squints and tries to identify the constellations that once fascinated him so much. He'd memorized them all as a child, but their names are now fuzzy, hard to view through the fogged glass of intervening years. He feels the weight of personal history buried inside him like the treasures he hides around the city, waiting to be uncovered one day once he remembers their purpose.

There was a time when his mind could focus, when he could hold a thought and turn it over to explore every facet. Now, the harder he reaches for a memory, the more it recedes. He's learned a trick though, a way to unjumble the past. If he just focuses on his surroundings and tries to remember how he got here, he can rewind his life like a home movie in reverse. It's like falling backwards through time.

He starts with the overpass, focusing on what came before its shadowed corners became his huddled home.

Before his expeditions through residential neighborhoods to sift through trash and gather up useful discards.

Before the sight of him made pedestrians cross to the other side of the street.

Before the tics and trembles, the angry, explosive rants, the tightened fists cutting half-moons into his palms.

Before the flame of his purple Bic lighter tongued the curved belly of a spoon.

Before doctors at the VA discontinued his meds.

Before the eviction notice.

Before unplugging the phone and boarding up the windows of his apartment.

Before fallen comrades rose from graves to whisper recriminations in the hazy gloom.

Before slamming doors became the enemy.

Before America's plenitude became asphyxiating.

Before the war. And the one before that.

Before the RPG blast scrambled his brain.

Before shielding himself in thirty pounds of protective Kevlar.

Before his new brotherhood changed his concept of family.

Before he signed the papers.

Before his crying mother begged, *Don't go. Please don't go.*

Before his stoic father said, *Be safe, son.*

Before high school bullies beat him up for spoiling the curve.

Back to the time his father bought him his first telescope, standing in Foley Field peering into its eyepiece, certain of his place in the universe, certain, if he thought long and hard enough, he could solve its myriad mysteries.

And finally, the sought-after memory tugs loose and starts to take form. Holding a hand up, he traces an outline across the sky. *Orion,* he says. *Your name is Orion. You are the great hunter.*

Penultimate Dad

HOME FRONT

At the end of his shift on the kill floor, Brendan Mueller exits the Smithfield processing plant and enters the swelter of a summer afternoon. He pries open the creaking door of his Honda Prelude and settles into its cracked vinyl seat. His home is fourteen miles away, but there are times, when the breeze is right, that the smell of pig shit and death wafts from the plant to blanket all of Bladen County. Fortunately, the wind is calm today, and as he drives beneath the boughs of hickories and pines overhanging his narrow, dead-end street, all he can smell is cut grass and a hint of honeysuckle from the valley beyond his property.

Pulling into his yard, Brendan plows through scrubby grass, following twin stripes of packed earth to the front of his blue-and-white bungalow. He parks beside another vehicle covered by a camouflage tarp, a classic '77 Chevy Chevelle, red with a fat white stripe bisecting its hood. One of these days he's going to hammer out the dents, paint the body, tune up the engine. Then he can cruise the Wilmington strip and turn all the honeys' heads. For now, it remains one of those daydreams that occupy his mind after work, something to make hot and sticky evenings more bearable.

Earlier this week, he'd set up an accordion-style screen on his front porch, angling it toward his Chinese neighbors, a family with three generations packed into one house. Standing behind the screen, he strips off his uniform and dumps the foul garments in a plastic tub beside his boots. He even sheds his socks and underwear, doing all he can to keep the stink out of his home. His teenage daughter, Chrissie, will be living with him for a week starting tomorrow, and he wants her stay to be as pleasant as possible. He's been burning incense the past three days and leaving windows open, a white flutter of curtains licking over their sills like cat tongues as summer wind scrubs through the house. He just hopes it works. His nose is deadened to the pervasive stench of swine, which clings to his clothes and plugs up the pores of his skin and slowly drips out like rain from a gutter.

Stepping through his unlocked front door, the first things Brendan sees are crayon drawings strewn across the floor. He scoops them up and sets them on the coffee table, anchoring the drawings with his wallet and keys. When his ex phoned earlier in the week to ask him to take their daughter for a week, he'd retrieved the cigar box from his bedroom closet and displayed its contents around the house—Chrissie's crayon drawings, her framed school photos, the ceramic handprint from when she was one year old. All those reminders of how things used to be that he usually keeps hidden.

After showering and dressing in a comfortable pair of jeans, he decides to go shopping to get Chrissie a present. The quick scrub and fresh change of clothes is not enough to spur him toward the mall in Lumberton, where uppity clerks wrinkle their noses at workers like him despite making three hundred dollars a week less. So he stays in Elizabethtown, crossing Broad Street to Leinwand's. The warehouse-style department store is used to serving men from the plant, its interior as rugged as its customers' exteriors, worn pile carpeting hard as Astroturf and exposed HVAC pipes running along the wall.

Women's clothing fills the middle of the store, centered on a display of half-torso mannequins sheathed in cocktail dresses. Brendan heads that way but stops at a jewelry counter. As he studies the cubic zirconium ring settings and faux pearl necklaces, he fingers the small scar curling through his eyebrow, a reflexive habit. Acquaintances who know his history as a paratrooper, his four tours of duty in Iraq and Afghanistan, assume it's a remnant of those forever wars. He lets them think it, too, even though he earned the gouge at fifteen, brawling with football players from another school, some linebacker dinging him with a class ring. Fighting and fucking are the only two things he was ever good at. The first ushered him into the Army, the second—after getting caught screwing an officer's wife—forced him out.

Beside the glass case is a stand-up rack full of necklaces. He spins the rack in a slow circle until one catches his eye, a mermaid pendant on a silver chain. He pulls it off its hook and drapes it on his hand, imagining it around Chrissie's neck. He has no idea what her tastes are, and the realization makes his ears burn.

Two years—that's how long it's been since he's seen Chrissie. On her last visit, he'd bought her a McDonald's Happy Meal for dinner, thinking she'd get a kick out of the toy inside. She went nuclear on him. *Dad, I'm thirteen! I'm not a kid anymore!*

Brendan knows he's been a shitty father and, before the divorce, a shitty husband. He feels the truth of it in his bones like a cancer. But there were some good days, and that's what he wants Chrissie to remember. Days when she thought of him as a god, back when she was five and just learning to ride a bike, him holding the seat and running behind, afraid to let go.

Thumbing the mermaid necklace, he imagines handing it to Chrissie and having her jump up and down in glee. He's given jewelry to women plenty of times before, usually as a form of apology. The gifts work about half the time. Some women throw earrings back in his face; others accept necklaces and say, *You know me so well.*

Brendan returns the mermaid to the rack and looks around for assistance. A twentysomething woman with blond high-lights is folding clothes into neat squares in the girl's section. He sidles over and studies the prim stacks—purple tank tops with pink flowers, white half shirts with cartoon faces, T-shirts with pop-culture slogans. He picks up a yellow shirt with DADDY's LITTLE GIRL scrawled in blue cursive across the chest. Smiling at the woman, he asks, *Think a fifteen-year-old girl would like this?*

The attendant scrunches up her face and shakes her head.

Brendan folds it in a sloppy square and tosses it back on the pile. *Okay, darling. Any suggestions?*

Well, you can't go wrong with casual wear. She leads him to a circular rack of jeans with precut rips down the front. *These are all the rage. I've got several pair myself.*

You're a lifesaver. He gives her shoulder a quick squeeze. *What size is she?*

Brendan looks from the rack to the woman, his gaze taking her in from head to toe. *About your size. Maybe not so shapely.*

She laughs and slaps his forearm. *Aren't you nice.*

Chatting up strange women has never been a problem for Brendan. It's the ones in his family he can't seem to get.

DISINFORMATION

Chrissie came from an accidental pregnancy. At the time, Sophia had been a freshman at Duke and Brendan had been a private fresh out of boot camp. They met at a frat party where Brendan was sitting on one of the kegs. He poured Sophia a beer and she asked him about the scar above his eye. *Shrapnel from Iraq,* he said, even though he had yet to see combat, and she had to touch it, had to run her finger across the smooth line.

They rushed to her dorm, barely keeping their clothes on long enough to make it into her room. Their one-night stand stretched into a weekend. Then two. Then a month. They were still getting to know each other when she missed her period and a plus sign materialized on the pee stick.

They eloped to Myrtle Beach before their parents even knew about the pregnancy. Young fools that they were, the newlyweds thought their romance would endure. They didn't ponder the hardships that lingered after the flush of infatuation paled: rent, utilities, food, health care.

When Sophia dropped out of college and moved to Fort Bragg, Brendan felt more adult than ever. Married, a kid on the way, a secure career ahead of him. The future brimmed with possibilities. But he just couldn't stop his hound-dog ways. One night, he came home with a hickey on his neck and everything changed.

Sophia cried and smashed dishes. She beat him with one of his boots as he sat there and took it, shielding his face with a forearm. *Cheat on me again,* she screamed, *and we're through.*

Brendan crossed his heart with an index finger, *Never again, baby. Never again.*

In the early days, making promises to Sophia had been fun,

almost like a game. *A two-story house with a white picket fence? I'll get you one someday, just wait and see.* He thought of them as pure fantasy, like Jimmy Stewart in *It's a Wonderful Life* telling his girl he'd lasso the moon, pull it down, and give it to her. But Sophia scrawled his promises in a mental notebook and flipped through its pages each time he failed to deliver.

Sophia's questions wore Brendan down. *When are you going to do this? Remember you promised me that?* She missed the country-club lifestyle they once mocked together, the one she gave up to be with him. The constraints of an enlisted soldier's budget, the spendthrift ways of stretching a dollar, were too much for her. *Things'll get better soon as I make sergeant,* he promised. But she was tired of his promises, and he of making them. So his honeyed tongue dripped acid. *Right away, your majesty. Let me fetch your tiara, princess.*

The first weekend after Brendan got his third stripe, he celebrated with buddies and got arrested for public intoxication. He was caught pissing on the glass front of a restaurant and shooting the bird to the well-dressed folk inside. The memory of their shocked expressions still made him smile. Worth being busted back down to corporal.

Sophia seemed willing to stick it out, obeying the "or worse" clause in their vows. But five months later, Brendan was caught in bed with a captain's wife. The captain started beating on his back, so Brendan jumped out of bed and kicked his ass. When a pencil-neck in a suit served him with papers, Brendan figured it must be for a court-martial. But it was a divorce summons. No surprise there. Sophia had always been good to her word.

RANK HAS ITS PRIVILEGES

Approaching the Fort Bragg gate, Mueller girds himself for the humiliation of being treated like a terrorist threat. Only retirees and severely wounded soldiers are given military IDs after separating from the service, so Mueller, a veteran with two Bronze Stars, has to queue up in the civilian traffic lanes and pull beneath a long carport for inspection. Once there, a security team instructs him to shut off the engine, open the doors, trunk, and hood, and step away from the vehicle. Brendan leans against the wall by the carport exit and stares at the dazzling blue sky, ignoring the armed men as they sweep a long-handled mirror beneath the vehicle's chassis to check for bombs.

Brendan's mood doesn't improve as he drives into the officer's quad, his grip tight on the wheel, the rattling muffler trailing clouds of exhaust. The radio is tuned to a pop station, its upbeat, synthesized schlock like glass in Brendan's ears. He's more of a classic rock guy—Pink Floyd, Skynyrd, AC/DC—but earlier this week he changed the presets to stations he thought his daughter would like, and he's been acclimating ever since.

The grand homes on this street are set back behind lush, manicured lawns. Square footage of military housing is commensurate with rank. Compared to these mini-mansions, the last on-post quarters he'd been assigned was a garden shed. Cruising at fifteen miles per hour down the wide boulevard, he takes in the trellises with climbing ivies, the perfectly shaped hedges, the trampolines in backyards. A gaggle of kids play croquet in one yard; two others hopscotch on a sidewalk. This is the type of bliss advertisers wet themselves over. He should be thankful that his ex-wife and daughter live in such splendor, but something about it rankles.

Brendan parks in Sophia's driveway next to a gleaming Lexus SUV. A sticker on the bumper reads, FLYING IS THE GREATEST THRILL KNOWN TO MAN. LANDING, THE SECOND. Sophia's new husband, Derek, is an Air Force major, and the two of them are headed to Paris for a weeklong honeymoon. Brendan and Sophia only took two vacations during their marriage, one to Nags Head when Chrissie was in diapers, and the other a long weekend at Big Meadows when Chrissie was four. They camped out in a tent and Sophia complained the whole time, saying he should loosen his purse strings and move the family into one of the nearby cabins. *Stop being so cheap*, she said. Judging by the Lexus and the stately home, she finally got what she wanted.

Carrying the Leinwand's gift bag with Chrissie's ripped jeans, he strides up the walkway to the gabled front door. He feels more nervous reaching for the lion-head knocker than he had kicking down doors in enemy compounds, ready to empty his magazine at the first instigation. He dreads the look of contempt she's certain to give him, the one that says, *Where the hell have you been all these years?*

The divorce agreement grants him custody every other weekend, but Elizabethtown is over an hour from Bragg and each mile of the drive feels like a form of shameful torture. Painful minutes stretch long as he reflects on the path his life has taken. After the first year of their divorce, Brendan started canceling some of his weekends with Chrissie. After the second, he only saw his daughter on every other holiday. The past three years, not at all. He deserves Sophia's and Chrissie's venom. He'll just have to suck it up.

Behave, Brendan tells himself. *Be a good father for once.* He raps the knocker twice and plasters on a smile. When the door swings open, there stands his daughter with her arms crossed.

The girl who once wore taffeta dresses to beauty pageants is wearing short shorts with fishnet stockings and a too-tight T-shirt, its neck cut to her sternum and the bottom knotted to expose her midriff. On her hip is a tattoo of a red apple with a green serpent encircling it and slithering across her abdomen. Gold rings pierce an eyebrow and a nostril, and a jeweled chain dangles from her belly button. Her makeup is troweled on, dark eyes and cheeks, crimson lips.

Brendan's face goes slack, the word "stripper" flashing in his mind. He's dreamed of this moment, of saying something meaningful to repair the damage he's done. But nothing he's rehearsed fits in his mouth. Instead, the words that tumble out are, *What the fuck?*

AMBUSH

Intel officers often describe combat situations as "fluid." During Mueller's second deployment, the battalion S2 explained how insurgent forces were shifting efforts from head-on conflicts to roadside bombings. American forces employed jammers to block cell phone signals from activating bombs. So the enemy switched to laser triggers. Americans then changed convoy tactics, speeding down trash-littered streets so that triggered bombs would explode after vehicles passed. So the enemy configured timing mechanisms to detonate earlier. Measures, countermeasures, counter-countermeasures, and so on, an endless progression of tactics with no endgame in mind. In the rapidly changing battlefield, soldiers were trained to expect attacks at any time from any quadrant. Mueller thought that experience had prepared him for anything. Until now.

What the hell happened to our little girl? he asks Sophia.

It's been three years, she says from a white linen couch, her

demeanor frosty. She's wearing pearl earrings and a gauzy plat-
inum top that complements the gray in her eyes. Derek sits
beside her, unflinching, rigid as a smooth-skinned mannequin.
Brendan is across from them in an ochre armchair, sitting on a
towel Sophia laid out to keep him off the fabric.

Yeah, it's been three years, but—

But nothing. People change. Sophia slits her eyes. *Most people anyway.*

*She's gone from cheerleader to whore. How could you let that
happen?*

I didn't let *anything happen. She doesn't listen to anything
anyone says. You'll see soon enough.*

Brendan drops his head into his hands and rubs his brow.
Beside him, the interminable ticking of the grandfather clock
jabs like a dagger in his brain. Same with the lemony scent of
Pine-Sol slicked across its burled walnut case; it brings back
too many memories of Sophia scrubbing down the meager
furniture from their past life. This clock is the only thing from
their marriage she deemed good enough to keep; the rest of
their once-shared possessions were either sold off or donated
to Goodwill.

I was going to paint her room pink before she came, Brendan
says. *Glad I didn't do that.*

"I was going to"—they'll put that on your tombstone.

And what'll they put on yours? Mother of the Year?

Hey, says Derek, pulling his hand free from Sophia's and
holding up his palm like a traffic cop. *No need for that.*

Brendan shoots to his feet and steps toward the couch.
Derek starts to rise to meet him, but Sophia grabs hold of his
sleeve and pulls him back down.

Look, Sophia says, *this was obviously a big mistake. Chrissie can stay with my mother. I just thought you'd want to see her one last time before we left.*

One last *time? What's that supposed to mean?*

She dips her chin and twirls a ringlet around an index finger, a nervous tic Brendan knows well. It means she's got bad news.

Derek's got his orders, she says. *We're moving to California next month.*

ON FOREIGN SOIL

Brendan stands in the upstairs hallway, his knees a little shaky. On Chrissie's locked door is a sign reading DANGER: HIGH VOLTAGE with a lightning bolt in a triangle. Loud rap music blares on the other side, the thrum of bass vibrating his bones like a plucked string. He knocks but there's no answer. He knocks louder. *Come on, Chrissie, open up.* After a pause, he yells, *Unlock this door right now or I'll knock it off its goddamn hinges.*

The music snaps off, the bolt clacks, and the door swings open. *No need to get huffy,* Chrissie says, smirking.

Brendan steps inside and lets out a low whistle. His own childhood room had been messy, but nothing like this. Scattered about the floor are shoes, clothes, and, in the vicinity of an overflowing trash can shaped like Kermit the Frog, balled-up food wrappers and Diet Dr Pepper bottles. More clothes are piled on the bed and the bench seat at its foot. The bed itself is a four-poster with tangled sheets spilling over the side and Christmas lights strung around its posts. Beside it is a wicker rocking chair with a line of bras draped across its arms and crest rail. On the far wall is an elegant diamond-shaped window with a built-in window seat and shelves on each side teeming with knickknacks and stuffed toys. The wall to Brendan's left has a cluttered desk, an oak dresser with clothes spilling out of half-open drawers, and a vanity strewn with makeup and photos stuck into the mirror's frame. The wall to his right is filled with posters of wild-haired bands and celebrities Brendan doesn't recognize, all of them posed to look tough or slutty. In the center of this swirl of posters is a quote painted on the wall: *It's fucked up how people get judged for being real and how people get loved for being fake.—Tupac.*

What springs to his mind is: *How can you live in such a pigsty?* It's the type of reproach his mother would spit at him. *That* shocks him almost as much as everything else this morning, to see himself as he once saw *her,* old and shuffling, worn down by circumstances, all the spirit gone from her sallow face.

Chrissie leans against the vanity, hands on hips, chin jutting as if she's eager to battle. But Brendan doesn't mention the mess. He points to the saying on the wall. *Hadn't heard that one before. I like it.*

Chrissie's eyes flick toward the wall and her posture softens.

We had plenty of fakes in the Army, Brendan says. *Especially the officers. Had this one we called Captain Wonderful. Dude could get lost walking to the latrine. But he had it in his mind that he was a tactical genius. Kept sticking his nose in on active operations, screwing things up. Sometimes we ended up shooting hostiles we could have captured; other times they got away. This one time though, he ordered men to shoot at a building that my squad already occupied. Killed two of our own guys. Friendly fire. Now there's a screwed-up phrase.*

Chrissie's brow wrinkles. *What's any of that got to do with me?*

I don't know. Guess I just don't want to be like Captain Wonderful, you know. I don't want to stick my nose in and make

*things worse. But that's all bullshit. You're not a soldier. You're my
daughter. You're my responsibility and I should have never turned
my back on you.*

No, you shouldn't.

*And I apologize for that. I'm sorry, kiddo, sorry about all my
screwups. I can't change the past. All I can do is show up today.
Today I'm here. This week I'm here. I don't have a lot of experience as a good father, but I'm going to try. You can hate me all
you want—I deserve it—but you're coming home with me.*

He puts his arms out, hoping to hug her, but Chrissie turns
her shoulder to him. *Okay,* he says, *okay. So, where're your bags?*

BATTLE PLAN

Beneath his stoic visage, Brendan's mind is racing. He drives by
rote, not really seeing the road, the stop signs, the other cars.
He's focused on the coming week, the likely fiasco, wondering
how to avert catastrophe. Yesterday, he'd jotted activities on a
legal pad—a day at the beach, a shopping spree in Lumberton,
a trip to one of the local nail salons. Now he can't think of a
single thing his daughter would enjoy. If he'd had a son, they
could shoot cans off a log or go zip-lining at TreeRunner Adventure Park. Hell, they could take a canoe out on White Lake
and fish all day.

Staff Sergeant Berkholtz had always said that a good battle
plan can flex to accommodate any situation. But Brendan can't
find any wiggle room in this situation. Acting like a hard-ass
won't win over his daughter, and letting her do whatever she
wants will hurry her headlong rush toward self-destruction.

He glances at Chrissie, who's sulking in the passenger seat,
staring fixedly out the side window. At least she's changed from
short shorts into the ripped jeans he bought her. When they

reach Fayetteville's scruffy fringe of strip malls lined with pawn-shops, nail salons, and tattoo parlors, Chrissie tugs out her ear-buds and turns sideways. Over the radio, Katy Perry is singing, "Wide Awake." *Change that if you want,* Brendan says.

Nah, it's cool, she says, smiling weakly.

Brendan sees Chrissie twirling strands of hair around her index finger and feels a bristling sense of apprehension.

Listen, she says, *sorry I was such a bitch before. This whole moving across the country thing has me freaked out.*

Chrissie pulls her finger out from the curl of hair and puts on a sad expression. *So, anyway, I get what you were saying before, you know, about this being a second chance for us and all. And I'm looking forward to this week. I really am. But I was wondering if you could do me a favor first.*

What sort of favor?

Some friends want me to come for a sleepover tonight. To kind of say goodbye, you know. You've met them before. Alyssa and Janet.

Brendan vaguely remembers them. A couple of Chrissie's cheerleader friends, or something like that. *I don't know.*

We'd be staying at Janet's house, just watching TV and stuff. Her parents are going to some work party tonight. They'll be back by eleven so we can't do anything too outrageous. Please. They're my best friends and this is one of the last times I'll get to see them.

Brendan considers her request, and though he knows it makes him an even worse father, his first emotion is relief. The extra time might allow him to get his bearings and figure out how to be a proper dad. Plus, by granting this favor, she'll owe him one in return. Maybe this week doesn't have to be a shit-show after all.

Please, she says again. *Janet's got her license. She can drop me at your place in the morning.*

You even remember where it is?

She rolls her eyes. *End of Marvin Street, the shitty blue house with the rusty car out front. It's still there, right? Still under the same hideous tarp?*

Brendan forgot that she'd been the one, three years ago, to insist on covering up the car. Her nonstop begging to buy a car cover frazzled his nerves and he finally acquiesced. He chose the camouflage pattern because it seemed to piss her off the most. At the time, he'd hummed, "Anything you can do, I can do better," thinking it hilarious. Now the memory embarrasses him. Antagonism has been the touchstone of their relationship far too long. Time to find a new way. *Okay,* he says, *where's this Janet girl live?*

RECON BY FIRE

Brendan is filled with a feeling of good cheer as he drives south on Highway 87. When Chrissie's friends had met him on the porch, they didn't seem skanky at all. Like Chrissie, they'd grown over the past three years, but their faces were the same. Alyssa with her dimpled chin and Janet with her curtain of dark bangs. They greeted him politely and promised to get Chrissie to Elizabethtown before noon tomorrow. Chrissie even kissed him on the cheek.

Still, some niggling thought tugs like a fishhook in his brain. Berkholtz had drilled into the squad to heed intuition. *Your senses can register irregularities that your thinking mind doesn't realize,* he'd said. *A stretch of city road with no civilians. A pile of litter too neatly arranged. Even if you don't know what it is that bothers you, call out the warning. After the blast, it's too late to do anything but pick up body parts.*

Obeying his deceased squad leader's command, Brendan

turns his Prelude around and heads back to Fayetteville. He parks two doors down from Janet's house and reclines his seat, intending to wait until the parents return.

Spying feels creepy, but the stakeout gives him time to plan. Seven days was all it took for God to make the Heavens and Earth. Why couldn't he win back his daughter's affection in the same amount of time? He's always believed that life could be sectioned by critical events, the person after each event changed so greatly by it that an entirely different entity emerges on the other side. The segments of Brendan's life could be titled "Soldier," "Civilian," "Husband," and "Divorcé." The one role he sidestepped was "Father." But this week could be his next critical event. If things go well, Brendan could step up as a full-time dad. Sophia and Derek could fly away and leave Chrissie with him. Elizabethtown's slow pace might be exactly what Chrissie needs to straighten out. Brendan could actually save his daughter. And she, in turn, him.

The fantasy barely has time to gel when a black Mustang pulls up in front of Janet's house. The long-haired driver honks the horn, then slouches in his seat. Chrissie bolts from the house and jumps in the passenger side, leaning over for a smooch. Then the car fishtails away, tires squealing as they lay down black stripes.

Dazed, it takes Brendan a moment to start his car. He chases after the Mustang, but it's already out of sight. It could have turned down any of the intersecting streets in this subdivision. He continues a little farther, then punches the wheel before turning around and driving back.

At Janet's house, the knob turns in his hand, and he enters the front door without knocking. The two girls laze on a red sectional sofa in the living room, one of the *Real Housewives* shows playing on TV. A half-full bottle of Jose Cuervo sits on the coffee table next to a couple of shot glasses, a saltshaker, and a bowl of lemon wedges. Both of the girls are leaning into their phones, tapping away. When Janet sees him, she lets out a startled yip. Putting a hand on her chest, she says, *God, you scared me.*

The girls stand up, close to each other, looking both guilty and frightened. Brendan invades their space and asks about Chrissie. The girls play dumb, but Alyssa caves when Brendan threatens to call their parents. *They went to Horne's Motor Lodge.*

You mean Horney's, Janet adds, and they both titter.

Brendan points at the phones in the girls' hands. *You're going to warn her soon as I take off, aren't you?*

Uh-uh, says Janet. *I swear.*

Brendan snatches Alyssa's phone and reaches for Janet's. He has to pry her hands open before yanking it away. *Hey!* she yelps.

I'll return them after I get my daughter back. You warn her, I toss them in a dumpster. Got it?

The cowed girls nod in unison.

TARGET ACQUIRED

Brendan rockets toward the motel, his senses amped. His speed creeps up to fifty, sixty, sixty-five miles per hour, until he notices and, not wanting to get pulled over, slows to the posted forty-five. Then it creeps up again. He reaches Horne's in a daze, entering the lot that circles the U-shaped motel, searching for the Mustang. The building has two stories, so Brendan prays he doesn't find the car parked near one of the stairwells. That could lead to any of the rooms upstairs. But as Brendan drives around to the back side, he sees it in a slot between two doors.

Brendan puts his ear against the first door. Nothing. Behind the second door he hears rap music and laughter. He eyes the flimsy knob. Stepping back to arm's length, he kicks as hard as he can and the door smashes inward.

Both Chrissie and Long Hair have their tops off, stripped down to their underwear, locked in a kiss. The boy tosses Chrissie aside and jumps to his feet, crouching as if to grapple.

Oh my fucking God! Chrissie shrieks, covering her breasts with an arm. *What are* you *doing here?* She grabs the waistband of the boy's underwear and tries to tug him back. He swats her hand away, the continuation of his swing slapping the side of her head. Brendan knows mistakes like this can happen in conflict. But he also sees, in his daughter's casual reaction, that the slap is nothing unusual.

Brendan launches himself at the kid, and when the boy tries to wrap him up, Brendan grabs his long hair and yanks hard enough to induce whiplash. He slams the boy against the wall, one hand on his throat, squeezing.

Get off him, Dad, Chrissie screams, clawing at his arm. *Get off!*

He releases the boy's neck and flattens his hand on his chest, pressing him against the duck-patterned wallpaper. *Stay right there.*

He scoops up the boy's jeans and fishes out his wallet, removing the driver's license. *So, Troy, is it?*

Yes, the boy croaks.

According to this, you're twenty-one. Know how old she is? Fifteen. That's statutory, my friend.

But, like, we're in love, man.

Brendan glances around the shabby room. *Yeah, grade A romance.* He switches off the boom box on the nightstand and tells Chrissie, who's clutching a bedsheet to her chest, *Get dressed.*

I'm not going anywhere with you.

Get dressed or it's five to ten for Romeo.

She drops the sheet and stands half naked and defiant. Then she grabs her clothes and stomps into the bathroom.

Troy tries to move away from the wall, but Brendan waggles a finger, freezing him. The boy leans back and clutches himself. Remembering the girls' phones, Brendan pulls them from his back pocket and tosses them on the bed. *Give these to Janet, okay?* The boy doesn't reply so Brendan says again, louder, *Okay?*

Yeah, man, whatever.

The bathroom door swings open and Chrissie marches out. *You can't do this, Dad. I don't see you for three years, and now you're kicking down doors. Who does that?*

Me and every soldier I served with.

You're a total dick, you know.

Yeah, he says, *I know.*

RULES OF ENGAGEMENT

The long drive to Elizabethtown is filled with cursing and yelling, followed by bouts of dead silence. Chrissie argues that she's old enough to be with whatever guy she wants, and Brendan counters that doesn't apply when the guy is a pile of shit stacked six feet tall.

If you don't leave when someone hits you, Brendan says, *he's going to do it again.*

It was an accident. He was only trying to knock my hand away. I mean, God, a strange man just busted through the door.

Okay, so tell me he's never done it before. Never smacked you in some fit that you explained away. Tell me that's never happened. When she doesn't answer, Brendan blows air out through his teeth and hits the wheel. *I've met too many guys like that. And the girls who put up with them. The battered woman who stands by her man until he puts her in the hospital or runs off with someone else. And once he's gone, she hooks up with another creep who smacks her around the same way. One after another. I don't want that for you, princess. You deserve better. You deserve a prince, not some loser who doesn't know that a real man* never *hits a woman.*

Troy's not like that. We're in love.

And so the argument circles back to the beginning and starts up again, round and round until they finally arrive home. Inside, Brendan had optimistically stacked a couple of board games on the chestnut coffee table, Life, once Chrissie's favorite, and Stratego, his. Now, he shoves those onto the floor, grabs Chrissie's purse, and dumps its contents on the table.

Hey, you can't do that, she says.

Watch me. Brendan roots through the jumbled mess, investigating each item. A cell phone in a bright pink case, a brown leatherette wallet, a pack of Wrigley's, a hairbrush, a Lady Speed Stick, a tube of cherry ChapStick, sunglasses, tissues, a blister pack of birth control pills, wadded-up receipts, and several hard-shell makeup containers. Snapping open each of the cases, he finds three joints stashed inside a compact. He stuffs them in his shirt pocket, relieved there hadn't been any needles or pills.

My house, he says, tapping his chest, *my rules. First off*—he holds up her phone—this *is a privilege. You want it back, you've got to earn it.*

What does that even mean?

Means you're going to have some jobs while you're here. Do them to my satisfaction, you earn privileges. Do them poorly or not at all— He shrugs.

Let me at least call Troy and see how he's doing. I mean, you nearly strangled him to death.

Uh-uh. Not tonight.

There's probably like a thousand texts from Mom checking up on me. You don't want her freaking out, do you?

Brendan sets the phone on the table and turns it on. *We'll check it together. What's your password?*

She crosses her arms and pouts.

Okay. Brendan starts to slide the phone off the table.

Wait, wait.

She tells him the code and he punches it in. When the phone comes to life, she reaches for it and he blocks her hand. *Anything you want to say, tell me and I'll type it in.*

Why couldn't you have just died in the war?

Brendan chuckles. *Hey, you sound just like your mother.*

She drops into a chair next to him and reads the texts as he scrolls. Nothing from Sophia, but several messages from Troy.

Want me to answer him? Brendan asks, amusement in his voice.

Go to hell, Chrissie says, standing up and sweeping the clutter back into her purse.

Already there, sweetie.

NEVER SURRENDER

Sitting in a white wicker armchair on his porch, Brendan sips a bottle of Budweiser as the gray gloom of evening fades and the chirr of crickets grows to a pervasive chorus. Next door, one of the Chinese grandmothers comes outside with her two youngest granddaughters, ages six and eight. The two girls giggle and chatter away in Chinese as they run about with mason jars trying to catch fireflies. The glowing bugs sputter through the night's glassy sheen, eluding the girl's leaping attempts. When they notice Brendan on his porch, the girls freeze. He waves and says hello, and the two girls run back into their house, followed by their grandmother.

Brendan shakes his head. He seems to be having the same effect on everyone lately. He'd been a fool to think one week could undo years of wasted time. These next few days might be his last with Chrissie. He's destined to become a footnote in her story, something she'll trot out whenever people ask about her biological father, the penultimate dad before Sophia shacked up with Flyboy.

Setting his beer down, he fishes Chrissie's phone from his pocket and stares at it a moment. *What the hell,* he thinks. *I'm already hip-deep in the shit. Might as well wade in deeper.*

He opens the texting app and checks for new messages. There's one from Janet asking if Chrissie's all right. Troy must've gone straight over to give the phones back. He also sees several shorthand texts from Troy. They read like a foreign language he can't make out. The final message, though, is easy enough to follow: *Yr dad gonna call cops?*

He starts to reply, *Yes, you dumb motherfucker,* but doesn't send it. He scrolls through Chrissie's text history to get a sense of her lingo. He erases his original message and retypes a new one to Troy. *U let an ol man own u like that? Eat shit loser.* He changes "shit" to the emoji of a swirling turd. Then he hits Send.

HAND-TO-HAND COMBAT

We got off on the wrong foot, he says to Chrissie the next morning in the kitchen, both of them seated at a round oak table with mugs of coffee. *No chores this week. I'm going to teach you something instead. And if you pay attention and learn, you get your phone back.*

Chrissie squints at him and takes a long, slurping sip, looking for the trap in her father's words. *Learn what?* she says.

Brendan wants so badly to be the guy Chrissie looks back on as having taught her how to live her life properly. He'd stayed up most of the night bent over a legal pad listing the various things he could teach her, jotting items down, then scratching them off, tearing off pages and starting again. Every idea he came up with was either too superficial—changing a flat tire, checking a fuse box, snaking a clogged drain—or hypocritical—becoming your best person, following your dreams, forgiving others. As the balled-up lists piled on the floor, he realized how ridiculous it was to think *he* had something of value to teach. His life was an example of what *not* to do.

Brendan slumped onto the sofa and fingered the notch in his eyebrow. As his mind drifted back to the brawl that gave him that scar, a new idea struck him. There was *one thing* he knew well enough to teach, a skill his daughter could use considering her taste in men.

I'm going to teach you to defend yourself, he says now. *You might even like it.*

Chrissie laughs. *That's how you want to spend this week? In a cage match?*

If you'd rather, you can mow the lawn and clean the attic and—

No, no. Fighting's good.

Brendan agrees. Fighting *is* good. All through school, his quick temper had gotten him into scuffles. He'd learned through trial and error how to throw and take a punch, paying for knowledge with split lips and bloodied knuckles. The Army took his unrefined talent as a scrapper and taught him the science of hand-to-hand combat. Drill instructors at Fort Benning showed him how to aim for soft spots and vital organs, how to dislocate a knee and snap a neck. Lessons he could now pass along to his daughter.

Brendan takes her to a dojo in town owned by one of his friends. Inside, the wide rectangular space is mostly covered with mats. One of the two long walls has mirrors running the length of it, and the other is plastered with posters of Bruce Lee, *The Karate Kid,* and various motivational sayings. Ninety percent of the dojo's business is karate classes for elementary kids, but a section of floor is set aside for boxing as well.

Before they glove up, Brendan explains the importance of keeping a straight wrist. He bends his wrist slightly and jabs toward her chin in slow motion. *See how it turns inward on contact?*

Chrissie nods, her eyes intent, for once actually listening to him.

You can damage your wrist like that, take yourself right out of a fight. But, if you keep your wrist straight, all the power of your arm hammers right into your target. Brendan turns sideways to her and extends another slow-motion punch to form a line from his shoulder to his knuckles. *And if you step into it, transferring all your weight to your front foot, you add all the power of your body as well.* He repeats the motion a few times, rocking back and forth like a piston, standing with his weight distributed evenly, then leaning forward as he punches.

They shadowbox in front of a mirror for fifteen minutes, with Brendan making minor corrections to her form. Afterwards, he tapes Chrissie's wrists and slips bag gloves over her hands. Standing behind a heavy bag and gripping it to his chest, he tells her to try a few punches. *Slow at first. Work on your form.* Her strikes are too light, losing power before making contact. *You've got to strike through the bag,* he says. *Aim beyond your target. I should feel it on the other side. Don't be such a wussy.*

That does the trick. Pissed off now, she logs some solid punches, rocking the bag back into Brendan's chest, his pride growing with every muffled thump. Finally, he steps back. *Real good, kiddo. But, no one's going to stand still and let you keep on pounding the same spot, so let's work on some combos.*

They move to the mats and change gloves, sparring gloves for her and focus mitts for him. He holds one padded oval high and one low, absorbing her strikes and telling her, *Atta girl. Way to go.* When she extends too far, he pushes her over onto the mat. *Keeping your balance is just as important as landing a punch.*

He explains the mechanics behind the jab, the cross, and the hook. How to recognize a brawler's haymaker and swivel out of the way, popping the attacker in the side of his head when his whiff leaves him off-balance. He shows her the explosive power of an uppercut, how to propel a fist under someone's chin while powering up with your legs. *You should do that right out of the gate,* he says, *before the guy realizes you've got skills. Hit him squarely, the lights will go out long enough for you to get out of there. No such thing as a sucker punch in a street fight.*

She takes to it well, this violent business of inflicting harm. Just like her father. After working through a mix of punches, she's eager to spar. Nowhere near ready, but that doesn't matter. Overconfidence is another trait passed on from her father. She stands with a cocked hip, arms crossed. *I didn't agree to this just to slap mitts all day. I want to knock your head off and not get in trouble for it.*

Brendan tells her to put on padded headgear but goes without himself. *Give you some incentive,* he says.

They circle around at first, Brendan explaining footwork, the way every shuffle forward or back by one foot should be followed with a similar step by the other. *Keep your stance a little wider than your shoulders and your hips bladed at an angle. If you square up, you're too big a target; and if you turn sideways to make yourself smaller, you're too easy to tip over.*

They shuffle about a bit, then Brendan starts jabbing, quick strikes with little force, poking her gut, her side, her forehead, which, even without padding, is a great shock absorber. She punches back, thinking too much about what she's doing, telegraphing her shots. He parries with ease, sometimes swiveling and pushing her sideways. Then Brendan decides to let her get in one good lick. He stands flat-footed as she throws a right cross to his left cheek. His daughter is only five feet five and 110 pounds, but she puts her entire mass into the blow and it rocks his head back. She seems more dazed by it than him, dropping her gloves to her waist. Brendan teeters but doesn't fall. Seeing her open position, he pops her right in the mouth, a solid right cross that turns her legs to jelly, and she crumples to the mat.

Never drop your guard, he says, helping her up. *Long as you're in the fight, you're in it completely. Got it?*

Yeah, she says, an edge to her voice. *Won't happen again.*

PSYOPS

Chrissie is amped up when they get home, talking so fast Brendan can barely follow what she's saying. He just nods along, riding the wake of his daughter's bliss. Until she asks about her phone. As he recalls the text he sent last night, a cold fist clenches in his gut.

Maybe tomorrow, Brendan says.

I don't get it. Do you hate me or something? Is it your job to make me miserable?

No, kiddo, listen—

I don't want to hear it, she screams. *You're a shitty father. A shitty father that smells like pig shit in a whole town of pig shit. I hate you!*

After she storms off, Brendan thinks how right she is. He *is* a shitty father. He should give the phone back to her now and take his licks. In the dojo today, Chrissie had looked at him with actual respect, something he didn't think he'd ever see again. Soon as he returns the phone, she'll freeze him out again. He can't allow that.

Kicked back on the sofa, he sips a Bud and rolls the cool bottle over the divot in his brow, studying the problem from every angle. No solution comes to mind. Chrissie's phone stares up at him like an accusation. He tells himself not to turn it on and fall deeper into that pit, but it's too great a temptation to resist.

He scrolls through unread texts and opens them up. A couple are from Sophia, one saying how wonderful Paris is, with an attached selfie of her and Flyboy with the Eiffel Tower in the background. The other text asks if she's surviving the week with her dad. He replies to that one: *Luv it here. All good with Dad. Enjoy Paris. XO.* He hits Send, not questioning what he's doing until the phone makes its blooping sent-message sound. Nothing he can do about it now.

Opening Troy's text history, he scrolls back and deletes the message he sent and all the angry responses from Troy. He pauses on Troy's last message, which is apologetic. *Sorry I was so cray Bae. Wanna hang? XX.* Brendan should leave it alone, but he can't help himself. He types into the return field, *Never again. FU pencil dick.* Then he hits Send and shuts the phone off.

BOOT CAMP

Brendan wakes early the next morning and heads out into his backyard just as birdsong is giving way to the high-pitched whine of mosquitos. The only flat ground free from the knuckling roots of loblolly pines is covered by the stack of plywood he keeps on hand to board up the house whenever a hurricane barrels up the coast. Gathering up the boards, he leans them against the oil tank at the side of the house and rakes pine needles and gumballs from the cleared patch. Then he spreads out a ten-foot square of overlapping blankets.

When Chrissie wakes a few hours later, he takes her out back to where the bedding is spread. *We having a picnic?* she asks, hugging herself, looking anywhere but at her father.

No, he says. *This is where we'll practice. There's an old saying that preparation is half the battle. But my squad leader told us preparation is the* entire *battle. We're going to start with the types of ways a guy might grab you and how to break free from each one.*

Brendan explains that a smart woman should break away and run from a bigger man instead of trading punches. The backyard training progresses better than Brendan had hoped. At first, when he grabs Chrissie and asks her to break free, she wrestles, elbows, and claws, but can't escape his grip. *Don't compete with me strength for strength,* he says. *Find the weakest point of my hold and escape from there.* He shows her the weak points for each hold and walks her through the proper steps. She breaks his grip every time, the two of them separating like uncoupling train cars.

If an attacker comes from the front, Brendan says, putting his hands around her throat in a stranglehold, *your natural reaction will be to pull his arms away from your neck. But the weakest point is his thumbs. Understand?*

Yeah.

Okay, so what you want to do is step backwards with one of your feet to give you leverage, and then duck your head forward and down, breaking the grip of his thumbs. While his hands are wide open behind your head, duck underneath and spin away. Easy as that. Now, try it with me.

Chrissie follows his instructions and pops out of his choke, spinning away before turning back with a satisfied look on her face.

Okay, ready for the fun stuff?

Hitting?

Uh-huh. Once you break free, you need to land a quick, debilitating strike. Most guys will underestimate a woman. They'll be sloppy. But once you slip his hold, he might start to worry. You've got to knock his dick in the dirt before he gets his guard up. Then get the hell out of there. Got it?

She nods.

He walks her through the attacks, striking the soft spots, gouging his eyes, chopping his windpipe, kicking his balls, wrapping a hand around the back of his neck and kneeing his face. *You only need to know a handful of strikes,* Brendan says, *but if you master them, you can knock anyone senseless.*

SHIFTING FIRE

The morning sessions go great, but each afternoon Chrissie asks for her phone back. *Maybe tomorrow,* he says, all the goodwill fostered from their workouts smothered in an instant. On day five, he decides to return her phone and pay the consequences.

But first he checks the text history one more time. Troy's messages are angry, some on the verge of being threats. But he stopped texting two days ago. Brendan erases them all.

He also sees a few texts from Sophia, who is both surprised and thrilled that things are going well. He closes Sophia's thread and opens one by Alyssa. There's one new text from a few hours ago. *Troy & Janet hanging since u gone. OMG. Thought u shld kno.*

Brendan stares at the message wondering how pissed it will make Chrissie. One more thing to blame him for. But then he turns the situation over in his mind, searching for the proper angle of attack, a way to break the news where someone else can be the bad guy. An idea comes to him and he closes the phone. Smiling.

DISOBEYING ORDERS

Chrissie threw a fit when Brendan told her he'd accidentally run her phone through the washer. *I forgot it was in my jeans,* he said. *I'm real sorry. But listen, today we can head into Fayetteville and I'll get you a new phone. Top of the line. I'll even bring you by to see your friends.*

Now, they were on the road, Lady Gaga's "Born This Way" on the radio, Chrissie singing along with the music and looking excited. *Can't wait to show Alyssa and Janet what I've learned. Might even throw them around the yard a bit.*

That'll be something, Brendan says.

Wish I could call Janet, let her know I'm coming. But I don't know anyone's number. They were all in my phone, you know.

Sorry again about that.

No problem, Pops. Joy radiates from his daughter and stirs the same feeling in Brendan. When he bobs his head to the music and sings the chorus, Chrissie actually laughs.

Brendan can't remember the last time he felt this good. But when they pass the first sign for Fayetteville, worry creeps back into his brain. The closer they get to Janet's house, the worse he feels about his plan. He'd been hoping Troy's betrayal would overshadow his own. But that seems ridiculous now. Troy will just bring up the texts and Chrissie will explode. The realization hits Brendan like scalding water. Each parking lot they pass, he thinks, *I should turn in here and stop the car, admit what I've done. I should sit quietly as she calls me all the horrible things I deserve.* But he keeps driving, feeling as helpless as the stunned pigs at the slaughterhouse before they're eviscerated and bled dry. As he pulls onto Janet's street and sees Troy's car in the driveway, dread finally overcomes his momentum. He takes his foot off the gas and the car slows to a crawl. *I got to tell you something, sweetie.*

That's all he gets out. Chrissie's eyes widen when she sees the Mustang. She throws her door open and leaps out, bounding toward Janet's and pushing her way into the house. Brendan closes her door, then pulls into the driveway, unsure what to do. He's just about to step out of the car when Chrissie storms from the house. She's followed by a shirtless Troy who is buttoning up his pants.

Troy grabs Chrissie's wrist and spins her around on the front porch, and Chrissie's reaction is immediate. Her other hand reaches around Troy's neck and pulls down. At the same time, she smashes a knee up into his face. He staggers sideways and topples over the porch railing into an azalea bush.

Now would be the time for Chrissie to escape, to run to the car and let her father whisk her away to safety. But she ignores the "hit-and-run" lesson he'd stressed in their sessions. She runs around the railing and reaches Troy as he's rolling out of the bush, blood already speckling a trail of scratches across his chest. He tries to shove Chrissie away, but she grabs the meaty portion of his hand and twists his arm back, punching his jaw below the ear as he's forced forward. She punches again and again, doing the exact opposite of Brendan's instructions, ignoring the *smart thing* to do. Same as he's done a hundred times himself.

Brendan witnesses Chrissie's fury as she lashes out, her wrist straight, her strike true. All week, he's longed to make an impact on her life, and now, unfolding before him, here it is—the contract of his genes, the legacy of DNA, the savage seed passed from father to daughter finally come to fruition.

Words Outlive the Tongue

BRADSHAW

Bradshaw still hears his squad leader's voice, his words emphatic as a burst of .50 cal. No matter that Berkholtz died years ago from friendly fire. No matter his ghost is missing half his chest and jagged skin flaps from his neck to reveal his larynx vibrating in its chasm like chicken bones. Berkholtz's voice is still firm and true. *Anything worth doing,* he says, *is worth doing well.*

And so Bradshaw punches his rifle's detent pin with a knuckle, and the receiver assembly opens like a hungry mouth. He pulls the charging handle to free the bolt and feeds it oil. Then he threads a cotton swab into the slot of a cleaning rod and rams it down the barrel's throat. He's done this a thousand times before, could do it blindfolded if need be. *Practice every task until it's second nature,* Berkholtz says. *Until you can do it without thinking. Just like breathing.*

Bradshaw barks a quick laugh. This next task is the one thing *nobody* can practice. Reassembling his weapon, he thinks of the gift he left for his sister on the coffee table. He hopes she understands. If not, he can visit just like Berkholtz and whisper in her ear. Taking a deep breath, he lowers himself into the tub and puts the barrel in his mouth.

PEARSON

You want them to fear you but not hate you. That's the trick. If they hate you, they'll do anything to take you down. Even if they have to die to do it.

Sergeant Berkholtz had been referring to Afghans, both the insurgents and the general population. His own brand of "winning hearts and minds" did not include lowering your weapon. And though his old squad leader's philosophy was meant for the desert, Pearson applies it years later to the poker room. Many players talk smack and embarrass their opponents whenever possible. But Pearson would rather players fold to his bluffs than stubbornly chase him down.

So, as he rakes in yet another big pot, he doesn't point out the foolhardiness of the other player in going for an inside straight. Instead, he nods and says, *Smart call with pot odds like that. Just hard to beat someone on a lucky streak.*

TEFERTILLER

Tefertiller is having a good day. The jackhammer in his traumatically injured brain is a minor throb right now. His memory is still as foggy around the edges as a pane of cloudy glass, but it's clear enough that he can picture the face of his old squad leader Berkholtz, that musclebound, Midwestern giant.

In Iraq, Berkholtz had walked each squad member through a trash-littered alley and asked them to investigate the detritus. He'd planted simulated bombs made out of ordinary things.

Artillery shells aren't the only IEDs, he'd said. *A child's toy with the stuffing ripped out can be packed with C-4 and ball bearings. Never let appearances fool you. Anything can be repurposed.*

That last line is what still resonates with Tefertiller today. *Anything can be repurposed.* It's his mantra on reclamation missions to the junkyard. Amidst pestering flies and pecking gulls, he roots through mounds and rescues broken discards that a bit of care might mend, finding value in almost every item that greets his touch. A broken toaster. A mutilated Barbie. A bag of old VHS tapes. Packing them all in his cart, he retreats through the hole he'd clipped in the wire fence, certain that he and his treasures will somehow save each other.

ZAHN

Zahn is handcrafting a Windsor chair in a rustic shack on the Eastern Shore. The weeklong class is one of those therapy programs for service members with PTSD. The instructor reminds him of Sergeant Berkholtz, even though he stands a foot shorter and speaks with a Southern drawl. But his manner is the same, the patient way he walks students through every step of the process. Using shave knives to trim down arms, bows, and spindles. Steaming and bending the arms and bows. Drilling holes in the seat with a hand-cranked drill. For each phase, the instructor demonstrates the proper method, then guides the students as they try to copy him, making minor suggestions on technique. And each time, Berkholtz's advice echoes in Zahn's mind. *You've got to crawl before you can walk. You've got to walk before you can run.*

Whenever he's heard Berkholtz before, it's been tinged by the circumstances of his death. His parents—never informed of specifics, merely told a friendly-fire investigation was ongoing—could never properly grieve their son's death. This, Zahn figured, was why Berkholtz's ghost haunted him, his tone full of resentment. But now he hears something else threaded into the words of his squad leader's message, his care for men whose lives depended on whatever spilled from his mouth. A frisson courses down Zahn's spine. The same tingle one gets when a magician's sawn-in-half assistant comes back to life.

MUELLER

Mueller isn't shocked when his daughter, Chrissie, asks her stepdad instead of him to give her away at the altar. He *is* surprised, after all the shitty things he's done, that he got a wedding invite at all. He mulls over what to give her as a wedding gift while out on his porch drinking Budweisers. He'd like it to double as an apology. So it needs to be something he dearly values so she'll know that she is even more precious to him.

When Mueller finally takes the camouflage tarp off the '77 Chevy Chevelle in his front yard, the rusted hulk seems an impossible restoration challenge. But his old squad leader's voice goads him into action. *When something seems too big to conquer, focus on the smaller components. Laying out a defensive position, the whole front can seem impossible to cover. But if you cover your sector of fire, and the soldiers next to you cover theirs, then all of them will interlock to form an impenetrable shield.*

Mueller starts with the battered body, pulling fenders, hammering dents, and power-sanding rust-bit edges so that sparks flash like the tail of a comet streaking through heaven. It takes weeks, a little bit each day after his shift at the slaughterhouse, before he's ready to move on to the engine. And when he climbs under the hood, he focuses on one piston at a time, one rod, one gasket, surrendering his every atom to the individual task. Forearms and biceps straining, brow dripping, pain blossoming in the small of his back—none of that matters as he works. Just the grace of giving hands a chore. Just the wrench's mouth cupping a lug nut like a babe discovering its mother's breast. Just the strain of joints as he pulls and pulls, as if ripping free every hangman's knot he's ever tied.

FAUST

On a cool autumn day, Faust flies in from Chicago and Mueller picks him up at Norfolk International in his restored Chevelle. *All the times you bragged about what you were going to do with this car,* Faust says, *I can't believe you're giving it away.*

Yep, says Mueller. *Things rarely turn out the way you plan.*

Hell of a gift though. When's the wedding?

Next month.

As they bullshit about old times—the time Mueller and Bradshaw jousted on camels; the time Berkholtz fought through an attack on their outpost in his BVDs; the time Zahn tore a path of destruction through Fayetteville on a stolen bulldozer—the roadway dips through the Hampton Roads Bridge Tunnel, spools past Hampton and Newport News, and dumps them off in Yorktown. Mueller takes the scenic route to Williamsburg, slowing down as they pass by the memorial at Surrender Field where four hundred years ago General Cornwallis knelt before the first American Army.

Between two hills topped with ancient cannons, Mueller turns the Chevelle onto the Colonial Parkway. Composed of river gravel and concrete aggregate, the roadway's unpainted, undulating surface rolls along like a path meandering through the woods. Surrounding it, the branches of the live oaks, ma-ples, and sycamores are dappled with a patchwork of auburn, red, and gold.

As Faust stares at this view fit for an impressionistic paint-ing, he recalls Berkholtz's advice, the words that brought about this trip. When Mueller had thrown away Captain Nowicki's potted ficus tree during a police call, Berkholtz had taken the blame, saying his orders to the squad had been to dispose of anything that didn't belong. *Specialist Mueller was just follow-ing orders,* he'd said, standing at attention in the commanding officer's office as the first sergeant chewed his ass. Later, when Faust had asked why he did it, Berkholtz said, *You guys are my family. And you always stand up for family.*

Now, Mueller pulls off the Parkway, follows Henry Street, and turns onto Roycroft. The residential neighborhood is filled with brick Colonials and wide lawns. He stops on the road be-side a mailbox with stenciled letters reading, BERKHOLTZ.

They walk up the flagstone path to the home where Berk's parents now live, relocating here from the Heartland after burying their son and selling off the farm. Faust presses the buzzer. The face of the man who comes to the front door is loose skinned and weathered with crags and valleys, but it still resembles their old squad leader in all the ways that matter. *Yes,* he says, *can I help you?*

I'm hoping it's the other way around, Faust says. *We served with your son. We've come to tell you the truth about how he died.*

ACKNOWLEDGMENTS

My writing mentor, Billy Walsh, pushed me to write about my war experiences. This book might never have been written without his insistence that I had something valuable to say. Once the soldiers in these stories came to life, I met with Terry Cox-Joseph for weekly editing sessions, where she carefully examined and offered advice on these stories as they evolved over several years to their current form.

I feel incredibly fortunate that Henry Hart put me in touch with my exceptional agent, Jacques de Spoelberch, who helped sand off some of the last burrs before sending my manuscript out into the world and landing it with St. Martin's. I am deeply indebted to George Witte and his team of tireless editors for their keen observations and scrupulous attention to detail. Working with them has been a joy.

Grateful acknowledgments are due to the editors of the following publications where these stories first appeared, sometimes in slightly different form:

Cottonwood: "Dirge"

The Deadly Writers Patrol: "Words Outlive the Tongue"

Doubly Mad: "Falling Backwards"

The Florida Review: "First Drunk Night Back" (originally published as part of "The Desert Came Home")

Iconoclast: "River Crossing"

The Northern Virginia Review: "Her Brother's Apartment"

Proud to Be: Writing by American Warriors: "Exodus" (originally published in volume 6 as "Doors") and "What Won't Stay Buried" (volume 9)

Several stories in this collection began as narrative poems. Grateful acknowledgments are due to the editors of the following publications where they first appeared:

Artemis Journal: "The Beatitude of Touch" (incorporated in "Dirge")

Barely South Review: "Night Jumps" (incorporated in "Red Legs")

Boston Literary Magazine: "Challenge Coin" (incorporated in "Dirge")

Common Ground Review: "The Dead Aren't Allowed to Walk"

The Missouri Review: "Theories of Flight and Forbearance" (incorporated in "Red Legs") and "Unstitching" (incorporated in "In the Early, Cocksure Days")

The William & Mary Review: "All This Useless Knowledge" (incorporated in "Bright, Inconsequential Things")

Thanks are also due to the judges and committees responsible for the following awards:

Missouri Humanities Council: "What Won't Stay Buried," winner of the 2020 Veterans Fiction Award

The Northern Virginia Review: "Her Brother's Apartment," winner of the 2019 Robert Bausch Fiction Prize

GLOSSARY

.50 cal: A .50-caliber machine gun that is operated from a mount. The M2 Browning machine gun is the heaviest small-arms weapon in the U.S. arsenal.

Aimpoint optics: A battery-operated targeting device used with the M4 that places a red dot where the rifle is aiming.

airborne: A mission where troops and/or equipment enter the battlefield by parachute drop. The term can also be used to refer to a paratrooper.

AK: An acronym for Avtomat Kalashnikova. The Russian-developed AK-47 is the most commonly used automatic assault rifle in the world.

ALC: Advanced Leaders Course. A course to train NCOs in the responsibilities and duties of a squad leader.

Article 15: A company-level disciplinary action.

ACU: Army Combat Uniform. A camouflage uniform with a pixelated pattern of tan, gray, and green, allowing it to blend into multiple environments. It replaced the DCU (Desert Camouflage Uniform) from the Gulf War era.

Black Hats: Refers to Army Rangers, who wear black berets.

BLC: Basic Leaders Course. A course to train NCOs in the responsibilities and duties of a team leader. Earlier versions were called the Warrior Leader Course (WLC) and Primary Leadership Development Course (PLDC).

boot camp: The facilities and period of time where new recruits are trained in military custom and basic tactical concepts.

brass: Refers to officers due to their shiny rank emblems.

breach team: A combat team that forces an entry into an enemy installation.

Bronze V device: A symbol affixed to the center of a uniform ribbon to denote that the award had been earned with valorous action.

brown round: Nickname for a drill sergeant; drill sergeants are the only military members who wear the iconic campaign hat, which is brown with a large, round brim.

C-4: A plastic explosive formerly known as Composition C.

CamelBak: A back-mounted, three-liter bladder with a long tube for drinking. Soldiers strap them on like backpacks and drape the tubes over their shoulders to their mouths.

CHU: Containerized housing units, typically the size and shape of a tractor trailer container.

CIB: Combat Infantryman Badge. An award given to infantry soldiers who have served in combat.

CO: Commanding officer.

court-martial: A military court proceeding.

DFAC: Dining facility.

double-tap: The practice of firing a second shot into a body to ensure it is dead.

DZ: Drop zone. The designated spot for paratroopers to land on an airdrop.

ETS: Expiration term of service. Refers to the end date of a soldier's enlistment.

fam-fire: Familiarization fire. This refers to someone firing a weapon he normally doesn't operate so that he'll know how to use it should he ever have to do so later.

flyboy: Derogatory term for a pilot.

FM: Field manual. The official how-to book for military operations.

FOB: Forward operating base.

frag: A fragmentary grenade or the use of one.

ghillie suit: An outfit with attached strips of fabric patterned to resemble the environment. Mostly used by snipers.

grunt: A soldier.

HESCO: HESCO bastions are flexible cages with fabric liners that link together to form walls; these walls are then filled with sand to serve as a blast barrier. The name HESCO (not an acronym) is derived from the British company that manufactures them.

HHC: Headquarters and Headquarters Company.

high and tight: A military haircut that leaves hair only on the crown of the head, giving the shaved sides a shiny appearance.

hooah: A catchall word in Army parlance that can be used as a general battle cry or to mean "Understand me?", "I understand," "Are you ready?", or "Let's go."

Humvee: Phonetic for HMMWV (High Mobility Multipurpose Wheeled Vehicle). An all-terrain, four-wheel-drive military vehicle. A Hummer.

hundred-mile-an-hour tape: The military version of duct tape.

IED: Improvised explosive device. A bomb culled from whatever is readily available.

intel: Intelligence. Refers to information about target locations and enemy units gained through captured documents, digital intercepts, and word of mouth.

iron sights: Refers to the front sight post on other weapons such as an M16 rifle.

keffiyeh: A Middle Eastern scarf.

KIA: Killed in action.

kill house: A training space used to practice live-fire exercises within a building.

klick: A shorthand term for kilometer.

M4: Standard-issue automatic rifle for U.S. military. A shorter version of the M16, it can strap to the shoulder to allow quicker and more accurate firing in fluid situations.

M16: Formerly the standard-issue automatic rifle for U.S. military. Part of the U.S. arsenal since Vietnam.

M240: A heavy platoon-level machine gun. It fires a heavier round (7.62mm) than the M4 (5.56mm), is belt fed, and uses a three-man team for firing: the gunner, the assistant gunner (the man who feeds the belt into the gun), and the ammo bearer.

MRE: Meals ready to eat. Field rations that come in dark brown pouches, which are labeled by the main meal contained within.

Also included are crackers, peanut butter, cocoa powder, coffee, creamer, salt, pepper, and a dessert.

NCO: Noncommissioned officer.

OPFOR: Opposing force. This term usually refers to friendly soldiers who pretend, during field exercises, that they are enemy soldiers.

overwatch: A position from which an individual or team provides supporting or covering fire for another individual or team that is moving.

PFC: Private first class. An enlisted rank, E-3, attained after about a year of service.

POW: Prisoner of war.

PRC: Pronounced "prick," PRC is a shortening of AN/PRC, which stands for Army/Navy, Portable, Radio, Communication (basically, a military radio). AN/PRC is followed by a numeric designation to specify one particular radio from another.

pugil stick: A three-foot baton padded on both ends. It is used to stand in for a rifle by soldiers practicing hand-to-hand combat against other soldiers.

PX: Post exchange. This is the military version of a department store.

QRF: Quick reaction force. A well-armed, mobile unit that is ready at a moment's notice to assist other units in danger.

QuikClot: A powder poured directly on a wound to activate coagulation and stem bleeding.

Ranger Tab: The arched, black-and-gold patch that soldiers who have graduated Ranger School wear on their uniform shoulders.

RPG: Rocket-propelled grenade. It launches from a tube that a soldier can hold on his shoulder.

S2: The staff section that deals with "intelligence."

SAW: Squad automatic weapon. The M249 Squad Automatic Weapon is a belt-fed, light machine gun that fires the same caliber round as an M4.

Section 8: A category of discharge from the military signifying that the individual is mentally unfit for service.

shallow grave: A body-length slot carved into earth as a hasty fighting position.

SOP: Standard operating procedures.

thawb: An ankle-length garment commonly worn in the Middle East. It usually has long sleeves.

TOW missile: Tube-launched, Optically tracked, Wire-guided missile. The operator controls the flight pattern from a tracking unit that sends messages via 3,750 meters of tiny wire that spools out from the rear of the missile.

AUTHOR'S NOTE

I am not only a combat veteran, I am the son of a combat veteran. I grew up on Air Force bases overseas. First Japan, then Okinawa when it was an American protectorate, then England. My father flew an F-4 Phantom, a fighter-bomber with a muscular fuselage and a shark's mouth painted on its nose. In the dining rooms of our various homes, a squawk box mounted on the wall would occasionally sound an alert and Dad would leap to his feet, grab his kit bag, and run out the door. We never knew where he was going, when he'd come back, or even *if* he'd come back. Usually it was a drill, but in those Cold War days, it was the real thing often enough.

Of necessity, the children on base formed tight bonds with one another. We'd scrabble over the bomb shelters in long-running games of tag. We'd pay a quarter to watch movies on Saturday at the base theater, then stand with our hands over our hearts when the national anthem played. And we'd race bikes beside the runway, chasing Phantoms as they streaked through the sky and scored the blue with white contrails. When it was time to go home, I'd root through my father's closet, put on his g-suit with compression leggings, and strut in front of the mirror.

When a military member deploys, it affects the whole family. Every knock on the door carries the dread that a notification detail may be on the other side. The year my father spent in Iran was the same year that Ayatollah Khomeini rose to power and overthrew the shah. That same year, my mother barely slept and took up smoking, a Virginia Slim smoldering between her fingers as she watched the riots and revolution on TV. My sisters and I did all we could to distract Mom, but her mind was seven thousand miles away. In my stories, I tried to show not only what it feels like for soldiers to deploy, but what those who are left behind have to deal with as well.

I wanted to be a pilot like my father, but my eyes were not good enough. I became a paratrooper instead. If I couldn't fly a plane, at least I could jump out of one. I fought with the 82nd Airborne Division in the Gulf War, part of the forces that stormed into Iraq in 1991. Nearly twenty years later, I met up with my old college roommate, Brad Lawing, who had also been commissioned as an officer. His once-brown flattop contained more salt than pepper, but otherwise he resembled the same athletic, bullet-headed poster boy for the Army that he'd always been. I'd gotten out after five years of active duty, but Brad had made a career of it. Earlier that year, I attended his promotion ceremony and watched a general pin the silver oak leaf clusters of a lieutenant colonel on his collar.

Brad's wife was a Southern belle from South Carolina with perfect teeth and long brown hair. They had been married for eleven years and during that time Brad had left Rebekah six times to serve a hardship tour—a military posting where family is not allowed because the assignment is in a war zone or another seriously threatened area. One assignment in Haiti, one in Bosnia, and four combat tours in the Middle East. And he'd just received news that he would be leaving again for his second tour in Afghanistan.

"Rebekah handles it well," Brad had said. "But I hope this is the last one. She's put up with a lot."

During my father's twenty-three years of service, he had deployed on two hardship tours (Vietnam and Iran) and I had deployed on one. But Brad was about to ship out on his *seventh*. And that was no anomaly. Multiple extended deployments had become the norm in America's "forever wars." Imagining the toll it demanded from each individual soldier was mind boggling. The only way I could come to grips with the cumulative cost was to create youthful, exuberant characters who become scarred by battle and follow them home as they struggle to regain some sense of normalcy. I placed them in a single squad in the 82nd and then dispersed them across diverse hometowns as civilians, a cross section of working-class Americana.

My father is a quiet man. But get him talking about flying, and he lights up. He'll tell you how the plane used to shudder when he toggled the stick between his knees; he'll describe the sight of the world on end when he banked, the dive through clouds, and the blur when he fired the afterburners and the twin engines' thirty-five thousand pounds of thrust pressed him back into his seat. He'll gladly talk about any of that, but he won't talk about his war. The one story he told me about Vietnam was what it was like to dodge surface-to-air missiles the size of telephone poles. The rest of the war remains locked behind mute lips. The same is true with so many soldiers today. They bury all they've seen and done deep inside and hope to forget.

For those of you with loved ones who are veterans, my

hope is that this book will shed some light on what's going on beneath their stoic exteriors. And for those of you who have served in war, my hope is that you will see some commonality and know you're not alone.